Noreen—
Thank you.

Somewhere
in the Middle of
Eternity

Edited by Phil Giunta

Phil Giunta (signature)

Firebringer Press
Baltimore, Maryland

Published by:
Firebringer Press
6101 Hunt Club Road
Elkridge, MD 21085

ISBN: 978-0-9773851-6-4

August, 2014

Printed in the United States of America

Cover & Interior Art by Michael Riehl

Cover Design by Chris Winner

INTRODUCTION

There is so much to be said for science fiction fandom, more so than can be expounded upon in a brief introduction. One thing is certain, its cup runneth over with talent. Nearly all of the stories and art in this book came together as a result of my nearly quarter-century involvement in SF fandom and conventions.

In the mid-90s, I met Stuart Roth and Susanna Reilly as fellow members of a Philadelphia-based chapter of STARFLEET, the international *Star Trek* fan club. We wrote fan fiction for the chapter's 'zine (that's short for fanzine, folks). Since then, Stuart and Susanna have gone on to write some of the most imaginative original fiction I've ever read.

At about that same time, I began attending Farpoint and Shore Leave, two long-running SF conventions in Maryland. It was at one of the first Farpoint cons where I met Steven H. Wilson. Steve is the co-founder of Farpoint and by that time, had already written for DC Comics. He's also won both the Mark Time and Parsec awards for his podcast audio drama series, *The Arbiter Chronicles*. Steve had started in fan fiction, so we shared common ground. As soon as I met him, I knew I wanted to be that guy! Who would have thought that 15 years later, *that guy* would become my publisher, my mentor, my brother?

It was through Steve and the Maryland convention scene that I was later introduced to three more tremendously talented chaps—Lance Woods, Daniel Patrick Corcoran, and Michael Critzer, further expanding my fandom family (go ahead, smush those two words together. Let me know what you come up with).

In recent years, Amanda Headlee and I met as co-workers. After learning that I was about to publish my first paranormal mystery novel, she let me read her first short story in the same genre. I loved it! Over time, Amanda developed it further, and I am proud to include it in this collection.

This book is not only a culmination of my decades-long friendships with fantastic writers, it also exemplifies the sheer joy of collaboration with a group of wordslingers I deeply admire.

When I proposed this project to Steve, I knew I wanted to include Mike Riehl as our cover artist and illustrator. My close friendship with Mike goes back over 15 years. From the *eye*-popping cover to the interior illustrations, Mike's mastery of the canvas, as well as the sketchpad, is undeniable.

For some of the aforementioned writers, this anthology is their first professional publication. It is for them—and through them—that I found myself perpetually inspired and excited during the two years it took to bring this dream to fruition, to put this book in front of your eyes…and to invite you to join us *Somewhere in the Middle of Eternity.*

Phil Giunta
April 2014

Table of Contents

The Obligation of Kitsune by Stuart S. Roth   6

Don't Go In the Barn, Johnny! by Steven H. Wilson   34

Evelyn by Michael Critzer   43

Form & Substance by Susanna Reilly   51

Apartment Hunting by Daniel Patrick Corcoran   73

Photos from the Attic by Phil Giunta   84

Parallax by Amanda Headlee   108

Dead Air by Lance Woods   132

Thorn by Michael Critzer   169

Water to Share by Phil Giunta   177

Deluge by Stuart S. Roth   211

Perchance to Dream by Susanna Reilly   227

Don't Go Fussin' Over Me by Phil Giunta   241

THE OBLIGATION OF KITSUNE
by Stuart S. Roth

The hills surrounding Kyodo were lined with bamboo forests in the lower reaches, and oaks and other good woods further up. The city resided in the central Japanese island of Honshu and was one of the country's most ancient places. It was dotted with Buddhist monasteries and Shinto shrines that provided a framework for its row upon row of worker housing, with their tiny chimneys and charcoal cookeries. Very rarely was it cursed with snow, but in the year that the War in China became the Pacific War with the United States, a white blanket covered the ground.

This is when the young people of the town left school early to go as a group into the high hills to gather firewood. Boys and girls alike participated; most of the men were off in the service of the Emperor.

The war had forced everything to change. Heating oil was scarce, so wood was needed, but as the season went on they had to travel farther and farther to gather it, and they were but one ward of five in Kyodo. There was always a flutter of bravado and chatter from the two groups when they first met up. They sang patriotic songs and the boys would sword fight with sticks as they slogged on to the good wood. Daily radio

broadcasts told tales of the victorious Imperial Army and Navy. Every boy wanted to go and fight, and every girl wanted to hear their stories of bravery–all, except for Daisoku and Mari.

He was fifteen and she was fourteen. Each afternoon they would meet in the cobbled street that led up to the Kiyomizu-dera Shrine, near where the incense sellers and produce merchants set up shop. He would arrive with the boys from the primary school dressed in their navy style uniforms under black wool jackets. She would be waiting with her friends from the formal school, already having changed into baggy work trousers and overcoats.

For five days in a row they all walked up the same steep trail to the same richly wooded place. Despite the rigors, it was the easiest of the paths. Yet with each trip they had to stay out longer and longer.

One day, Mari finally spoke up about an idea that had been in her head for the past couple of days. Just beyond the tall stilt supports that held Kiyomizu-dera above its precipitous gorge was a ten-foot rock ledge that led up to a steeply sloping hillside. She stopped to contemplate the icy wall, reaching out with her mitten-covered hands to see what kind of hold she could gain.

"What if we were to try up there?" she asked.

One of the boys, Shimanazu, their leader–for boys always had a leader–studied it with more attention than his intellect really allowed. Then he looked at the girl as though she was stupid. "No. There's no good way." He trudged on and the others followed.

"Wait." Mari startled herself with her own voice. "I… I think we can climb it."

A hush fell over the boys–some were eager to try–but Shimanazu glared them down, for he wasn't so sure about climbing up there. He also didn't like being countermanded when it was cold and going to be dark soon. He pounded the rock. "Ice, nothing but ice."

"See, here, like this." She reached over her head and scraped the rock with a stick until her fingers could grip it.

"Don't be an idiot," he said, as she lost her grip and tumbled backward into the snow. Everyone laughed, except for Daisoku, who hung near the back of the group. He felt sorry for the girl, but wasn't bold enough to step forward. There was little to understand about Shimanazu's bullying. He was from a prestigious family. Something had to be said for one's place in life. The angry-faced girl looking back at him should have known that.

He turned and pulled the closest boy along with him. "Leave her."

"*Wakarimasuka?*" she yelled. "I don't understand." She got up to confront him.

Shimanazu didn't have to explain. He shoved her backward and she landed hard onto the path. This time Daisoku stepped forward, but held his tongue.

Mari stood up again, but could not face the bully. Her face was red with the "heart's glow" and she felt ashamed. She returned to the rock wall, found her handhold again and pulled herself up. Her shoes were old worn out things, wrapped in cloth to help keep her warm. This made it difficult to find a foothold. She slipped and fell. Her face grew redder as her tears welled up and her breath came out in short, cloudy puffs in the cold air.

Daisoku stood awkwardly between her and Shimanazu.

The girl refused to give up. Her next ascent drew the others to cluster around. She not only maintained her foothold, but she pulled herself up to the point where her right hand could feel the upper edge of the wall. In what Daisoku considered an act of pure malice, Shimanazu reached out, seized her leg and yanked her down.

Daisoku jumped forward, half-catching her and breaking her fall, but landing them both in the snow.

"There is nothing up there," the bully shouted down at them. "Go on, be an idiot. You can go with her too, Dai." Shimanazu waved the others to follow him. No one else disobeyed. Even Daisoku got up and took a few hesitant steps up the trail. He looked back at the girl huddled in the snow.

———

Mari refused to look at him. She barely knew him and didn't expect him to stay behind and consequently was not surprised to hear his footsteps receding up the trail.

All that was left for her now was the wall. She turned to it again. This time she was too angry and hurt to think straight. Her handholds slipped, she scraped her leg and gave in more and more to frustration.

By the time her hands grasped the top again only sheer blind rage drove her. As with life, that was no solid base with which to make progress. Exhausted and bruised, she felt her grip slipping, slipping, gone…

Suddenly, a pair of hands was there, holding her from falling. The boy who had caught her before was standing awkwardly below her, steadying her. "Quickly, take hold."

Mari regained her place on the wall and took firm grip on a root at the top. The boy allowed her to use his shoulder to boost herself up. Finally, she was safely atop the challenging summit. She waited on all fours for her breath to return.

"Here, take my hand," she called down. As he climbed up, their friendship was secured. They didn't talk much. He was shy and she was told never to speak directly with a boy, which gave her a convenient excuse to hide her own shyness. Fortunately for them, the trip had been successful. The hill was lined with wood just waiting to be picked up. Soon their wire back-carriers were brimming with wood and they made the dangerous journey back down the wall and were on their way to town well ahead of the others.

They reached the pagoda where their paths parted. Daisoku spent most of the time looking at the ground as though the weight of his load was bowing his head. "Well, I… I go this way."

Mari was truly arched over by the weight of her load but still managed an awkward bow. "Thank you for your help."

He returned the bow. "Tomorrow." That was all he could manage.

She nodded and backed toward the alley that would lead her home. "My name is Suzuki Mariko."

He flashed a quick smile. "Terachi Daisoku."

"I'll see you tomorrow then?"

"*Hai*, tomorrow."

This was enough. Boy and girl each went their separate way, pleased by the encounter and eager for tomorrow.

Daisoku waited in the alley that he knew Mari would take to reach the point where the girls and boys met at the pagoda. As the gaggle of girls approached, he motioned for her to come over. His presence went unnoticed by the others, and Mari only had to slow her pace for them to go on out of earshot.

"Mariko," he bowed nervously a couple of times. "I, I think that maybe we could wait until the others are gone and try the wall again."

She nodded enthusiastically. They waited for Shimanazu to lead the others up the long, tired trail. Then they crept out of the alley and returned to the climbing spot.

Each day that winter he would help her up the slope and she would turn and offer her hand for him to follow. At first they concentrated on gathering their wood and returning home as early as possible. It was cold and there were other chores waiting to be done. But soon they became comfortable enough with their ritual that they began to linger and talk.

First it was simple gossip and daily news. She enjoyed origami; he liked to fly kites. This boy had done something or other at school, while some girl was a terrible nag and everyone hated her. They both agreed that the baker's wife was mean and that Shimanazu's father, the tax collector, was probably stealing from the till.

She would hide her face behind her hands when she laughed, while he had a boy's boisterous laugh that he didn't mind letting out.

They also took to noticing each other. She had long black hair and deep brown eyes. Daisoku had grayish eyes, that, she was embarrassed to say, made her blush when she thought of them.

They systematized their gathering process, collecting large piles beyond what they could carry that day in order for them to be ready to pick up the next day. This gave them more free time and their conversations began to happen freely. They didn't need to talk about idle things or other people. They were growing to know each other.

Mari learned that the boy's father was at some place called Kota Bharu. Dai was worried because they hadn't heard from him in some time. "I don't even know where that place is. He's in the army and sent me photographs from Singapore after they freed the city from the British."

"Where's that?" Girls weren't taught geography.

Daisoku shrugged again, not sure how to describe the place. Finally, he drew a map. "We're here, China is over here and way down below are the French and the British colonies. Singapore is down there."

"My brother is dead," she blurted out. "We don't know where he was. His ship sank and... and I miss him."

He didn't hesitate to reach out to her. "He died in the service of the Emperor. Even if you have no ashes to remember him by, they keep a shrine in Tokyo for all the men who died in all the wars. The shrine is tended and venerated. He will be there. Maybe someday you can go and burn incense for him."

Mari nodded. "Maybe, some day. If the war ever ends."

"It will. We're right and strong. We defeated the Russians at Tsushima. They were a modern Western power and we beat them."

"I don't care about that. I just want my brother back."

"I know. I would give anything to hear about my father."

The winter went on this way. There were only a few times that they dwelled on the war. Each knew the other's heart regarding that bigger thing. It was much better to talk about all sorts of other matters. That lightened the load of life, and they were still children after all. Life wasn't that dark or gloomy, even in winter.

Spring was coming and they knew that their paths would soon separate for good. The boys and girls would no longer gather to collect wood. They would return to their separate lives.

The weather was warm on the day the boy turned sixteen. Only the tiniest patches of snow held up against the onslaught of rising temperatures.

"Why didn't you tell me it was going to be your birthday?" Mari said. "I could have brought you something special."

"That's why. Just didn't want to have you go to any trouble." They sat side by side on a rock overlooking the valley.

Kiyomizu-dera was a complex of shrines built on raised platforms held above the valley floor by tall stilts. With its angular eaves, thick wood posts and dark brown and green colors, it blended in with its surroundings, yet held majestic vigil over the city below. They had grown up in its shadow and had attended ceremonies there. She had been dressed out in a fine kimono for girl's day in that shrine. Despite its beauty, they had never really paid it much attention, until now.

"There is a lover's shrine there," Daisoku said boldly. She knew the story but let him tell it to her anyway. "There is a stone on the ground in the courtyard up near the top. It is said that if you stand at the far end of the courtyard, face the rock, close your eyes and say a name out loud, you can find out if the gods approve. With your eyes closed, you must walk to the rock and place your hands on it. If you fall, or trip, or miss and go tumbling down the stairs or something, then you know it was not meant to be."

She looked into his face and saw wistfulness there. The sun glowed on his cheeks and sparkled in his eyes. He must have felt the weight of her gaze and did what most boys did when the moment was just right, he broke the spell. "The keepers disapprove of such things of course. I imagine if they caught me or you stumbling across the courtyard with our eyes closed they would cane us good."

Their parents would tell them whom they would marry. That's the way it had to be, and she decided that it was time to tell him firmly that they shouldn't talk about such things. Before she could form the words, a terrible yelp came from the woods behind them.

They dropped their carriers of wood and ran back to see what was the matter. There, caught in a trap, was a brown fox. It squirmed and called out pitifully, for its back paw was caught in the nasty teeth of a steel trap.

Superstition and pity made the children hesitate. Legend held that a fox was clever and shrewd. It could bring great good or great misfortune. Tales to spook small children, but neither of them wanted to tempt fate.

The fox looked up at them with frightened, feral eyes before turning to gnaw at its leg. Back and forth its attention went, one second on the humans, the next on its trapped paw.

"We have to help it," Mari said.

"But how," he answered. Daisoku had enough experience with wild animals to know that the thing would bite them if they tried to get near it. What could they do for it even if they managed to free it? The paw was clearly broken. "Go down and get one of the carriers," he said. She nodded and was just about to leave when she realized the wire carrier would do no good. Daisoku had hunted up a large rock.

"No, you can't."

"Go," he ordered, but his voice lacked conviction and she returned to his side. The fox continued its struggle.

"There has to be another way," Mari pleaded.

"I don't see what else we can do."

She had to agree. It tore at her heart to see the thing suffering. "Wait." Unwrapping her headscarf, she draped it over the creature and then turned away. Daisoku lifted the rock. He thought it would be easier to bring it down on the struggling bolt of cloth, but it wasn't.

Mari cringed when she heard the heavy thud of the rock. "Is it..."

"I couldn't do it," the boy said miserably. "Sixteen and I can't even put a wounded animal out of its misery."

"Compassion is a good thing," she answered with a whisper. Mari learned more about the boy from this one gesture than from all of their conversations together. "We'll let it go; leave it up to the gods to decide."

Daisoku felt weak and useless, but agreed to throw his coat over the fox and hold it down while Mari pulled the steel trap open. To their great surprise, the creature leaped out of the coat as soon as its paw was liberated. All they saw was the flicking of its tail and a red-brown streak. It ran as if it hadn't been injured. The children were left to gape after it.

A week had gone by since the day of the fox. This was their last day together. No more wood was needed. The other children no longer came up the trail. Neither of them needed heavy coats, and they could sit on the ledge of the wall and allow the sun to warm them. It was April, and the cherry blossoms were beginning to bud.

A flock of geese flew low over the Shinto shrine. Normally the birds would be honking and calling to each other as they returned to the north, but today they were silent except for the woosh, woosh, woosh of their wings as they flew almost at eye level across the valley.

The boy and girl held each other. Their perch over the trail leading into the woods was dangerous. Subconsciously, Daisoku guessed they wanted to be caught. It seemed better that they be forced to part instead of weakly saying goodbye.

A new sound could be heard in the sky. It was distant and high above them. Planes. They weren't the usual trainers out of Doko Matsura. They were much too high up for that. They were American bombers! He didn't know how he knew that. In fact, down below he could hear townspeople cheering "banzai" over and over. Obviously, they thought the aircraft were from the Imperial Air Corps.

Mari sensed something was wrong. He explained, but said that they weren't about to attack. The planes continued on as a surreal reminder that the war was going on somewhere out there.

Later, Mari discovered from an uncle that the planes were truly American. How could they be? Why wasn't the navy protecting us? They must have come from aircraft carriers. Much later, the truth came out. The bombers were flying a one-way mission to bomb Tokyo and fly on to China. It had been designed to scare the population. It had worked. Air raid drills and civilian militia exercises were taken much more seriously from that day onward.

The flight of the American planes, and not the silent geese, was what Mari feared would be her lasting memory of that day. But then the boy turned to her and kissed her. It was a shock, inappropriate, a mark that her emotions would not be able to hide. He saw her look and felt certain he had gone too far. She trembled and cried silent tears before reaching around to hug him and return the kiss. "This is how we have to say goodbye." She broke their embrace, gathered her carrier and waited for Daisoku to help her down from the wall.

———————

Two weeks passed. The glow of Mari's first kiss had lightened her heart, but day after day the shadow of lost opportunity grew longer. Mama and her sisters would hear her sob late at night, but she refused to tell them what the matter was. She spent long hours lying awake. Younger Sister, who shared the same sleeping mat would nudge her and nag her for information. Older Sister, who was already married and who came to help with the market stand, had guessed that Mari had found some romance. She and mother gossiped about it, but still they could not crack her silence.

One night Mari felt someone tug her hair. She was about to admonish her sister, but when she turned over she found the boy looking at her.

"Ssshhh." He called her out into the common room. A lantern hung from the low rafter and cast a reddish glow on his face. "I know you are unhappy."

"I am. Thank you for coming. It is so good to see you again." She moved to embrace him, but he pulled away.

"What's the matter?"

"We can't touch, not tonight anyway. I need you to answer two questions."

"*Hai!* Yes, what are they?"

His eyes twinkled and glowed in the flame light. "First, is your heart sincere? Don't answer now. Go to the shrine tomorrow and answer the question for yourself. Young love is a flighty thing. You must be sure, very sure that you are in love."

She wanted to answer him now, but his manner and words were so strange that she felt compelled to remain silent. Again she reached her hands toward his and he pulled away.

"What is your second question?"

He dropped to all fours and seemed ready to leap away if she moved any closer.

"Will you be brave?"

Mari waited for him to explain.

"You must be brave and resolute, no matter what may happen."

"I will, of course I will."

He smiled a sly grin that was warm and good, but not quite like the normal smile she had fallen in love with. Daisoku stood up. "You must go back to bed now. Good night. I can't explain. Go to the shrine tomorrow and seek your answers."

He escorted her back to the sleeping room and slid the door closed after she had climbed beneath the covers of her bed.

She laid her head down and watched the shadow of the boy through the thin rice paper. His silhouette turned away, and then crouched down, morphed into something else. When the change was done she recognized the body and tail of a small creature... a fox! It bounded out of the house and she heard the rattle of a shutter as it sped over the windowsill.

Mari approached the bell pull of the main shrine. It was early morning, and dawn's mist still swirled between and around the *torii* and supports of the temple. She clapped her hands three times, in order to seek the notice of the gods, and then pulled the bell cord. A deep-toned throng echoed down from the rafters and eaves, dislodging a pigeon from its nest. Mari closed her eyes and prayed. It was a well-thought-out prayer, in which she asked to know whether her heart's desire was truly wise. It wasn't simply a plea to see Daisoku again, for the fox was right, her desire today may only be like the flight of the geese—here today and somewhere else tomorrow.

She found the rock that legend told would help lovers find their desired ones. She placed a hand upon it and whispered Daisoku's name. Then she walked to the far end of the courtyard.

Her heart raced. If the monks caught her... all the temples were urged to focus their attention on veneration of the Emperor and his direct lineage to the Sun Goddess who begot Japan. There was no longer a place for frivolous things. Mari faced the rock, closed her eyes, and then walked blindly across the space as quickly as she dared. The distance was only eighteen meters, but that was enough for one to become disoriented. She could miss the stone, fall over it or trip before ever reaching it, a sure sign that the gods did not favor her wish.

She neither cheated nor counted her steps. This was a journey of faith. Then, on impulse, she stopped. With eyes still closed, she reached out her arms. They were shaking and her heart beat hard against her chest. Mari brought her hands together and bent at the hips. Her palms felt the cool surface of the rock. It was there, exactly where it should be! Opening her eyes, she looked down on the gray lovers' rock.

The happiness she felt was overwhelming. Looking about, she found the fox sitting on the railing watching her with intense eyes. It flicked its tail and scurried off. The mystical visitor had seemed like a dream last night, yet she had come here on the power of that dream. Seeing it manifest in the daylight turned her joy to awe. The shrine was so peaceful. The large *torii* gate was half-cloaked in mist, and, as she walked toward it, she felt as though she were passing from the land of the gods back to her own world.

After passing beyond the grounds of the shrine her giddiness returned, for she was only fifteen and this is the way a fifteen-year-old girl was.

————

"Ahh!" Mama screamed. Mari and her sisters ran to the common room to see what was wrong. A gaping hole in the roof shined light onto the spot where their mother was standing. A large piece of the wood planking had collapsed from the winter snow and the work of squirrels. They had heard the creatures scurrying about at night. Sometimes one was brazen enough to run across the rafters over their sleeping mats.

Mari's father had died of consumption two years ago and money was tight. Mother had always been resourceful and now operated the market shop that father had started. But its profits would hardly be enough to cover something like this.

Uncle came over to review the damage. "I hear that old lame Kenjiro can repair this. He is retired, but has a nephew, a boy who is just apprenticing, so they'll work cheap."

"Who is 'Old Lame Kenjiro', Mama?" Mari asked.

"Of the Terachi, down on the south side," Uncle explained.

The girl's face brightened. "And his nephew?"

"How should I know," Uncle answered testily as he poked at the hole with a stick. "Daisoku. I think that's his given name."

———————

"Old Lame Kenjiro" was aptly named. He had been wounded in Korea during an uprising there and carried a scar that he liked to show off, particularly now that Japan was at war. It wasn't the wound, but rather *saké*, that had turned the craftsman into a pauper scraping up cheap jobs in his twilight years. Now, he contented himself with bossing around journeymen and his nephew.

Mari waited for the day when Kenjiro arrived with his men to begin work. Until she saw the boy with him she dared not hope that it was the same Daisoku. Etiquette demanded that she remain discreetly away from the workers, but her furtive glances at the nephew did not go unnoticed. She would bring him water or pass up tools and the pitch basket as he worked on the ladder. Eventually, she dropped all pretenses and would stand beneath the ladder and talk with him while he tuned out Kenjiro's harping.

Finally, the old man noticed their preoccupation and assessed the status of the two families. There was money to be made in a good match. He presented the idea to the girl's mother one night. "For all of my nephew's apparent idiocy, he works well with his hands, and I am sure that he will carry on the tradition of becoming a master roofer."

Mari's mother evaluated the old drunk. Such tendencies often were passed down in the family. However, her daughter did seem to know the boy, and there was affection there.

Kenjiro pressed on. "Your daughter, if I may say, is quite beautiful and looks well suited to bear children."

"I will consider it," she answered vaguely.

"Favorably?"

"*Hai*, with favor." It wasn't wise to irritate a contractor who was working on one's roof.

Mari's sister was sent to consult the matchmaker in Gion. There, in the midst of the geisha quarter, was an old woman with a steel-trap memory. Once said to be a former geisha herself, she had turned to the art of arranging marriages. She would consult the stars and the vagaries of how the season's weather turned, and then she would study the family registries. Every family maintained a registry of their ancestry. The Suzuki's of the north quarter were of equivalent status to the Terachi's —excluding the destruction on their harmony wrought by Kenjiro's behavior. Yes, it could be sold. Kenjiro would be marginalized; the boy's father was of farmer stock and was now in the army. The mother was from a poor family, but one that had produced a number of Buddhist monks. Devotion to Emperor on one side and devotion to the divine on the other, certainly a rogue uncle couldn't cheapen that. As for the girl's side, there was a strong will in the women, not bad will, simply strong and very resourceful. They were poor, though. Poor did not fill dowry chests. Hmm.

Mother and Older Sister waited nervously, along with the mother of the boy and Kenjiro as the matchmaker summed her conclusions. "An equal matching, and very good for both sides if one is talking harmony, which I always say is the paramount issue. You need harmony to have a stable house and family. Many children are what is needed for these two."

"Yes," Kenjiro said, "But certainly the material must be considered." He tried to sound casual, but wasn't very good at it. "One can't live on harmony."

"You will get no dowry other than *giri*—obligation—from this match, Kenjiro-san." There, it was out for all to digest. "Maybe if there was no war," she looked at the mother of Daisoku who remained silent, allowing her brother to do all the talking.

"No!" the man growled. "That just isn't acceptable. I have the makings of a craftsman in that boy. I won't give him away."

"They knew each other since winter," Madame Terachi interrupted. "I feel they have been inappropriately fond of each other for some time."

Madame Suzuki bowed her head with a bit of shame.

"You misunderstand," Terachi added. "Daisoku's father is not coming back." She closed her eyes and let herself press on. "I want my son to have a family before the war comes for him." She held out a firm hand to prevent her brother from stopping her. "I will accept your obligation as dowry."

"Good, then it is agreed," the matchmaker said, clapping her hands together. "There is always a way to bind a harmonious match."

Mari and Daisoku were told the news. She, of course, showed her heart on her face. He tried to act surprised, but his mother-in-law explained that she knew all about their friendship and that they were dense if they didn't think it wasn't clear for the entire world to see. She laid down strict guidelines for their courtship.

Over the next year, Mari's older sister acted as chaperone. Modern tradition called for a period of familiarity, where the young couple was allowed to meet and talk. Mari's sister could see that this had already happened and chose to walk discreetly behind them as they enjoyed the Philosopher's Path that ran beside the canal. Two years had passed since Daisoku and Mariko had first begun to notice each other.

Among the cherry-blossomed branches that shielded the stone walk were the watchful eyes of a fox. Such things naturally didn't concern a fox, however she was pleased to see that the Suzukis' roof was properly sealed, for that gave one less place for squirrels to hide, and that was of great interest to her.

The siren sounded just after dusk. Mari and her sisters quickly extinguished the lights and huddled together in the common room. The roar of aircraft overhead rattled the pots and pans that hung from the rafters over the cook stove. A week ago the Americans had bombed the factory in the next valley. Messengers carried news that steel mills in Yawata had all been bombed. The Americans were barbarians, and Mari wondered what they would do if bombs were dropped here in Kyodo.

The fox huddled in its burrow. It could see many things that it didn't understand, such as the birds with men inside them, but only a few of these things really mattered in the end. There was family—she had pups now—and *giri*, obligation, there was still that.

An Army Air Corps unit drew large crowds as it paraded down the street. Daisoku and the other recruits filed in behind the band and the Rising Sun banner leading it. Mari waved goodbye to her new husband. She tried to leave him with a lasting image of confidence, but she knew things weren't going well. The officer leading the Air Corps unit had a wooden leg. More and more men and boys were leaving the city and very few were returning.

Daisoku and Mari had married the week before, and they had spent their first night together in a *ryokan* in the eastern hills. A creek had flowed just outside their room, reflecting moonlight that made their bodies glow as they shared each other and became lost in the peaceful sound. As they lay together afterward, she told him the dream about the fox. He'd laughed, but she shushed him. It wasn't nice to belittle the fates that had brought them together. Daisoku had agreed and they talked and caressed each other into sleep. The entire world seemed created just for them that night.

Compassion is not a weakness. The words she had said to the boy the day they had released the fox from its trap came back to her now as she rested her cheek on her husband's chest. He had fallen asleep, but reached an arm around to embrace her.

Now, as Daisoku waved and disappeared down the street with the new recruits, she wondered if she would ever see him again.

———————

The next winter was cold and wet. Mari received two letters from her husband but no more. Each evening their families would gather at the Kurazamas' to listen to the latest news on the radio. For so long the radio had broadcast nothing but victory tales, but lately the tone had changed and they realized that all the earlier stories had been lies. Now, they were told how Saipan had fallen to an overwhelming force and that American soldiers were slaughtering men, women and children.

"They will be coming to our shores next," Kenjiro said. "They will do the same thing here. Westerners have always intended to wipe us out. Russians, Englanders, Americans, all of them—"

"Stop it, just stop it, Kenjiro-san," Mari finally couldn't take it any more.

"All I am saying, Mariko, is that we must be vigilant and prepared to give up our own lives to save the nation."

Madame Terachi tried to silence her brother, but without success. "And another thing you should remember, Niece, is that your own husband is fighting for his Emperor. He is out there now, maybe even dead."

Mari's mother clapped her hand on the floor mat for silence. Then she placed a reassuring hand on her daughter's lap. "Kenjiro-san, you drink too much. Perhaps it would be better if we retire for the evening."

Mari avoided the radio gatherings after that. Instead, she spent the evening walking Philosopher's Path, contemplating life much as the Zen monks had done along this very trail. She also made frequent journeys to Kinkaku-ji, the Golden Temple. The shrine cast a perfect reflection in the water of the pond that fronted it and was meant to symbolize harmony— something the rest of the world had lost.

As she climbed the steps leading to the gold-gilded Kinkaku-ji she noticed the strong wind blowing down from the hills. The pine trees that once shielded the valley had been felled recently. Their sap was being used to produce some sort of fuel to power trucks. Oil was no longer available and the pine-sap burning trucks that were seen in the streets left behind a noxious odor.

The wind whipped her hair out from under her kerchief.

"Ignore the wind."

Mari turned to see who had spoken to her. The evening was lit by moonlight and she couldn't see anyone. "Hello?"

There was no response. She decided to run home. Superstitious thoughts of *Yamanba*, mountain witches, raced through her mind as her *geta* clogs sounded off of the stone flagging.

She didn't want to be alone after that and made her way to the radio gathering. As she removed her shoes and bowed to the Kurazamas, the radio announcer began a jingoistic diatribe. "Our brave men have formed a new air corps–the *kamikaze* corps–who will use the ultimate weapon, their own lives, to destroy the enemy ships. Divine wind, the same spirit that protected our lands from the Mongols, will again protect our shores from invasion."

———————

Mari returned home from closing the shop. Little money had been made because there was little to sell. Today, an old woman had yelled at her, calling her a thief for charging so much for eggs. It hurt her deeply that neighbor was turning on neighbor.

As soon as she walked through the door to her home, she knew something was wrong. Mama and Older Sister were there talking with Madame Terachi. An official brown envelope with typewriter printing waited on the table. It was addressed to her.

The indentations from the typewriter felt like tiny pinpricks as she opened the envelope and unfolded the letter within. "Madame Terachi," the letter began, "it is with great sorrow that I must inform you of the honorable death of your husband, Airman Terachi Daisoku..."

"No! No!" She threw the letter away and pushed past her mother and sister. They caught up with her on the stoop and forced her inside and made her sit down until she sobbed and let her emotions loose.

"He died as a *kamikaze*." Sister somehow thought this would help. She often voiced romantic views of the wind that carried the planes to their targets.

"It wasn't divine wind!" Mari shouted. "It was just death. The wind took my Daisoku and killed him. I wish I was dead, too."

They sat around the radio with bowed heads and heard, for the first time, the voice of his majesty, the Emperor. His voice was not like they had expected. Privately they knew he was just a man and not a god, but still, he was the Emperor, and certainly that alone created some expectations. His voice sounded tired and old. He announced that the country was surrendering. A strange new bomb had been developed and he was assuming personal responsibility for the protection of his people by suffering the ultimate dishonor for them.

"We must arm ourselves," Kenjiro said. "They will come for us. We must do something."

"But the Emperor has commanded us to obey."

"He was tricked and betrayed by disloyal advisors."

Time passed and information trickled in. Army units in Tokyo had clashed with each other shortly after the announcement. Some soldiers were like Kenjiro and wanted to fight on. Then they heard of the new bomb. It was powerful enough to destroy an entire city in one explosion. Some said it was the end of the world.

Very little of this mattered to Mari. She was sleepwalking her days. Even the horribly frank preparations of her mother didn't faze her. Mama explained to her and her sisters how the Americans might treat young women and she taught them how to commit suicide if it came to that. This was a stark reality. Mama never talked of such things. It only affirmed in Mari's mind that there was nothing left to live for.

Summer arrived and the trees that remained uncut around Kiyomizu-dera were in full splendor. They framed the elegant form of the shrine and its precipitous stilt support legs overlooking the gorge.

Do you have the faith to leap from Kiyomizu-dera? It was a local expression that Mari contemplated as she stood at the railing. It asked *do you have the conviction to step forward and act?* She vowed that there would never be another husband in her future. If that was to be so, then what future did she have?

It was easier than she had thought to climb up onto the railing. She told herself that this was a spontaneous act, but it wasn't. She had replaced her blue *obi* sash with a red one even though it did not match the kimono that it was meant to tie. She also removed her clogs so that she could feel the edge with her toes.

Now, she looked down into the deep gorge. She had always been afraid of heights. Even when she was passing water to Daisoku on the ladder to their roof, she would only go up halfway. But somehow this didn't seem difficult.

There was no note left behind for Mama. At least when they found her body, the red *obi* would provide assurance that it was suicide and not something else. Red was the color of suicides. She had to compose herself, though. Suicides would return as "Hungry Ghosts" if their souls were not reconciled before death.

All that was left to do now was to let it happen. Hardly any effort at all. Given enough time, simply standing in place would cause her to become disoriented and— "A long jump, I would say." The voice was spoken in a low female tone so as not to startle her.

"I have committed to this." Mari tried to turn around but the female voice warned her not to unless she was prepared to climb down. "You cannot talk me out of this."

"No one has the right to do that."

"Then please allow me a moment of peace."

"Obligation is a difficult thing," the woman soothed. "I am under an obligation to advise you, and I think it would be unwise to jump from such a height."

"What obligation do you have to me?" Mari brushed a tear from her cheek. "All I want is to be alone."

"Once I told you to be brave. I asked you to be sure that you could be brave."

Mari perked up. "W-who..."

"Don't turn around! I don't want you to fall off while doing so." She waited until the girl settled herself and nodded. "I also told you to ignore the wind."

"That was you? Are you the Fox Spirit?"

"Did you know what the mascot of your mate's squadron was?"

She shook her head.

"Kitsune. It was a fox. Consider that. I will leave you to your decision."

"Tell me more."

"Why should I? You are your own spirit and must decide for yourself. There are other ways to show conviction."

Instead of footsteps, Mari heard the patter of small paws. Her fear of heights returned, and she had to lower herself from the railing with great care. The shrine and the porches surrounding it were empty.

Crowds gathered at the central train platform as a list of names was posted. The American authority had released a register of prisoners who would be repatriated from the Philippines, Okinawa, Australia and China.

"He's alive, Mari, he's alive!" Older Sister pulled her through the crowd and pointed to one of the names on the list.

She felt the characters with her finger. "Terachi is a common name," she cautioned.

"He is listed as an airman?" her older sister asked. "We can ask Kenjiro or Mother Terachi-san, they would know if there is another Daisoku."

———

There was no welcoming parade to greet the train. Family and close friends were there to witness the arrival of the bedraggled veterans. Wounded and haunted figures walked from the train. Most had young faces, but old eyes. Red Cross workers had to help some.

An airman stepped down from one of the carriages, hobbling on a crutch. "Dai! Daisoku!" Mari called out excitedly. "Oh, my husband." She ran over and hugged him tightly. Few showed such open emotions and he seemed embarrassed by it. He returned the embrace but only with a light, trembling touch.

She took his hand and led him on through the crowd of numb ex-soldiers.

———

The Daisoku who had left for war was kind and thoughtful; the man who returned was morose and withdrawn. He snapped at her quite frequently and then would turn to brooding instead of apologizing. He went to the cemetery and visited his own gravestone. The marker bore both the names of himself and his father. Papa had died in Malaysia. When word arrived that his son had also died and that his body would never be found his name was added to the marker.

Mari found a white headband in her husband's things. On the front was the Rising Sun emblem of the Empire. On the sides were written the characters for Kitsune Squadron–Fox Squadron. She held it to her chest and thought about how the gods had worked to bring him back.

Daisoku entered the room. When he saw what she was holding he became angry.

"Can't you see, husband, see how fortunate you were?"

He snatched it away and stuffed it back into his army bag. "Leave this stuff."

"But I—"

"Leave it! Throw it in the closet. I don't want to look at it."

Days passed with no change in Daisoku's mood. He began working as a roofer again. Times were hard and most could only pay him with promises or with barter goods. Everything was still rationed. People were starving in some parts of the country; at least in that regard they were fortunate. Kyodo had been spared attack, they learned, because of its unique cultural heritage and lack of direct military infrastructure.

Mari returned to running the shop with her mother and tending to her mother-in-law, who had developed influenza. Mother Terachi explained that Kenjiro had returned home from Korea like this. It was a humiliation to be injured.

Daisoku would talk in his sleep and would occasionally scream out until she was able to calm him and put her arms around him. Other than when he was asleep, he gave no sign that he wanted intimate contact. She grew sadder as he drew further and further away from her.

Finally, one day, she waited for him to come home from work. He entered and found her sitting on one of the floor mats, her palms extended and flat against the floor. There was a look of determination on her face. "We will go for a walk tonight."

"What about dinner? I'm hungry."

"You need this walk more than food."

"I need my dinner after working all day!"

She got up and extended her hands to his chest and held her eyes firmly on his. Would he strike her? It wasn't unknown for men to beat their wives. His face looked angry enough. But he weakened and turned away. She took his hands. "Come along." It wasn't an invitation, it was a command. "I shall help you. We have a short distance to go." Mari let him lean against her and use his crutch to propel him. They hobbled through the streets. People that looked out at them bore stern looks. Daisoku knew he wore a stigma.

"Where are we going?"

"I think you know where we must go."

She led him beyond the Kiyomizu-dera temple and up the trail to the rock wall. "We must climb to our perch."

"I can't." He pushed away, but she grabbed him.

"You will. I will help. I know your leg is not fully healed. If you don't come then I will go to our place by myself. It will no longer be our place if you don't even try to come."

She began ascending the rock face. To be truthful, she had anticipated Daisoku's difficulty and had come the day before to harvest out several good handholds. It wasn't winter, so there was no ice or snow to contend with.

Daisoku watched her climb to the top with relative ease. He remembered their visits as children. He had always had to help her, but now she was independent and he was the one who needed help.

"Come along," she reached down her arm. "Take it, Dai."

Reluctantly, he obeyed. His crutch had to be abandoned and he had to grit his teeth from the pain as he climbed the rock and took her hand. At last, he was there. This was the ledge where they had once watched the geese fly past in the valley below. She took a seat behind him, embracing his waist with her arms.

"Now you will tell me," she whispered.

"There is nothing to tell."

"I will not have you become like Old Lame Kenjiro. He gave up, you won't do that. I won't let you."

For a long time he remained silent. Then his voice began in a halting, gravelly manner. "We received our flight training in Kyushu, but I was too young and they were going to transfer me to the army. Then a general arrived. He asked for volunteers for a new squadron. He explained that most of their planes were gone and that they were low on fuel. He... he said that it would be very dangerous. I wanted to fly, so naturally I joined. I wanted to prove myself."

"They were the *kamikaze*?"

"Not at first. At first we were being trained to fly lighter, poor quality craft. I thought it was a way of using washouts and saving the better Zeroes for the best pilots, but when we arrived at the base, he explained who we were to become."

"You volunteered. Couldn't you change your mind? You had a family."

His jaw quivered, but he kept it locked and stared off into the air for a time. "How could I, Mariko? It was too late. We were there. The others... everyone... They told us that the enemy navy was just off our shores. We were to accompany the battleship *Yamato* to save Okinawa."

She remained silent and laid her cheek on his back.

"My father was dead. They told us about what the Americans would do if they came to Japan."

"How would your death have helped?"

"I failed to do my duty. I shouldn't be here at all."

"You didn't fly that day?"

He pounded the ground with his fist and let out all of his bottled emotions. "No. I flew. The plane's nose was loaded with explosives. We were given a cup of *saké* and they cheered us as we left the airfield. I didn't even know how to land the plane properly. It wasn't necessary.

"There was gunfire all around us. Hundreds of ships were laid out across the water. I saw one of my squadron get hit. The plane exploded in a ball of fire. It was just gone. It didn't crash, it just fell apart."

She waited until he had controlled his sobbing. "Go on. You must tell me all of it." She stroked the side of his head.

"I saw my target. We were told to hit their carriers. I saw one before me. The escorts opened fire with anti-aircraft guns. They make a popping sound all around you as they whistle past. Occasionally one explodes with a loud boom. I angled toward the carrier. All I had to do was fly down. The fire was still all around me. Even if they hit me I would still strike the flight deck and do some good."

"But you didn't?"

"No. I swerved at the last minute. I was going to crash myself into the water. It sounds cowardly, I know. You must be so ashamed. But I was there, in the fire. It was too late. I was going to die."

"Ssshhh. I know your heart. I know that you are not a coward. Don't ever call yourself that."

"There were people on that ship. I could see them running and trying to fight back at us. They didn't look like soldiers, like the enemy, they looked afraid."

He began to sob again. She could feel the tension in his muscles as his shoulders heaved with the effort of releasing the terrible pain. "Compassion is not a weakness," she whispered. "Remember the fox spirit. It has always been with us. You can't deny it and even if you can, then you can't deny who you are. You couldn't crush that poor animal with a rock and you couldn't kill those soldiers on that boat."

"The plane didn't explode." He laughed. "It wouldn't have exploded even if I had hit the carrier. Some idiot forgot to set the charges properly. I woke up on a hospital ship."

"You must accept that you are not a killer."

"But our homeland… the Emperor…"

"You are not a killer. Just as I cannot repair a roof, you cannot kill a living creature. It isn't the mark of a coward." She told him of her own effort to die. He was horrified. She allowed him to comfort her. He had never thought about how his death would affect her. Suicide seemed like such a noble gesture at the time, but now he realized that it wasn't.

That night they returned to the *ryokan* where they had spent their honeymoon night. There, next to the small creek, which had not changed at all during his time away, they made love as though this had been his first day back—for in a sense, it was.

———————

A fox could hardly influence things she didn't understand. War was something the two-legged creatures did. They were always doing such things. These didn't concern her. What mattered was a den of young ones and making sure there was enough food for them. She could sense that family mattered to the boy and girl, too. Therefore, she was inclined to indulge her obligation to help them. *Giri* was fulfilled.

DON'T GO IN THE BARN, JOHNNY!
by Steven H. Wilson

There's a barn--or there used to be--in the cornfield next to the house where I grew up in Clarksville, MD. I don't know how old it is, or was. It stood until sometime in the 1980s. I know I have pictures of it somewhere.

Here's the thing... I loved that barn. It stood, from my vantage point in the back yard of my parents' house, right on the horizon line. The sun set behind it. When night came to Simpson Road, she came from that barn. At least, that's how it looked to me.

It stands to reason that that barn was where Night spent the day, sleeping. Don't know where she sleeps now that it's been replaced by brick-and-vinyl palaces decked out in shades of builder beige. Perhaps the urban planners provided her with a condo under Section 8.

I'll tell you a secret: I never went in that barn. It was abandoned the entire time I knew of it. The cornfield around it was one of my favorite places to play. We played hide and seek among the rows when the corn was high. When the corn was harvested, leaving the fields mud-caked and barren, I would go alone and pretend I was exploring an alien world on which some ancient disaster had wiped out all life. Cheerful cuss, wasn't I? But I never went inside that barn, at least not that I remember. Some little voice in my

head always called out, "Don't go in the barn!" Well, after all, Night was in there, waiting to claim you. Truth be told, I was probably just afraid of snakes.

But here's an update of a story I wrote in 1983, inspired by my beloved barn that I never dared enter, about Johnny, the wind, and how Night decided to take a bride... er, groom.

———————

"Don't go in the barn, Johnny!"

The phrase had echoed in his head down through the years. They had taunted him with it, when he stared at the old building.

"Why not?" he would ask, and they would only say, "Because you'll never come out again."

Stupid kids. It was just an old empty barn. A barn on which the sun set every night, dropping, orange and swollen, behind the rotting, gray timbers. Once the sun entered the barn, night came. That was all. What was there to be afraid of?

But Johnny never went in…not then.

Johnny was afraid. Fascinated, but afraid. He couldn't look away from the barn, but he didn't dare go near it. The other kids picked up on this, and they made the taunt a condemnation of his fear:

"Don't go in the barn, Johnny!"

Meaning, *you won't go in the barn, Johnny! You won't, because you're afraid. But what was there to be afraid of?*

Blackness. Darkness. Death. A chasm of inky black that swallows you whole, swallows your soul. In the dark, you can't see, you don't know what's touching you. You can't see your own hands in front of your face, don't know if you have hands anymore.

In the dark, you go mad. It steals your mind. It steals your soul.

So Johnny didn't go in. Not then. Then he'd been afraid of the dark. That was before.

And now he drew his light jacket up around him and swore at the flashlight as it struck him. Its batteries dead, the useless instrument, lodged in his pocket and weighing his jacket down, banged painfully in cadence against his hip as he ran against the fierce, icy wind.

Why had he carried it? Old habits. He didn't need light. The night was perfect and black.

No moon shattered the darkness of the old road, nor paced him as he jogged. Only the wind followed him, chased him. Rude and forceful, it threw branches in his path, tossed dust in his eyes. It howled through old trees and shacks by the roadside, making Johnny wonder briefly if the wind had a voice it was even now struggling to make heard.

Everything was alive tonight, a paradox. The road and all around it was dead, the only sign of life and warmth the sweat forming a sheen beneath his hoodie and track pants. The wind sang in atrocious harmony with itself. The trees, old and cynical, laughed wildly at his youth.

But no bats cried for attention; no black cats dove for shelter in rotted sheds. No rats or possums came from the ancient, secret places to claim any portion of their meager rations.

Apart from himself, there was only one kind of life afoot tonight, the kind that was fit to live no other night, the kind whose existence depended upon belief, upon the imagination. Ghosts, phantoms, spirits, demons… you could only believe in such things on a night like this.

It was these kinds of creatures that Johnny preferred. He had grown up with them. They clung to the shadows, hid in the darkness, watching, waiting. He had always known they were there. He had been afraid. He wanted to know them, wanted to know what they wanted. But he didn't dare go near the places they would be, the dark places.

It was talked about, Johnny's fear of the dark. He slept with the light on. He wouldn't go in the basement. He wouldn't go in any dark place.

"Don't go in the barn, Johnny!"

Oh yes, the other kids had noticed, of course. Kids notice everything. They haven't yet been trained not to notice. They notice the dark things, waiting to feed. They notice who's afraid of the dark things. Some kids, like Johnny, react to fear by staying away. Some try to make peace with fear by offering sacrifices. Give the darkness someone who's afraid, and maybe the darkness will leave you alone. Maybe you'll look strong.

They made Johnny a sacrifice.

It was just a closet at school, a closet with two doors that opened in two rooms. They'd gotten on either side and shut him in, holding the doors shut. An old school, with old doors, it didn't have lights in the closets, or louvres in the doors. It was pitch black in the closet. Johnny was alone in the dark for a lifetime.

Thinking of it, he felt the rawness in his throat from the screaming. The bite of his nails in his palms. After a while, the wetness, as his nails pierced the skin and blood flowed. He'd begun to tremble and shake. His throat had closed up. His chest had seized in pain. He didn't remember the teacher opening the door, or the ride to the hospital. He'd woken up on a table, with his mother watching him, eyes red.

It was a problem, now, his fear. His parents were scared, and the doctors had scared them more. It was a problem, so they'd fixed it. They'd fixed it with a new technique in deep brain stimulation. "Less invasive," they'd called it. Surgery without incision. They hadn't even had to shave his head, they'd just put him under and injected transmitters into his brain.

And now he wasn't afraid anymore. Now he loved the dark, and everything that lived in it. The doctors had told his parents not to worry that he now stayed up at night, or when he'd taken up midnight jogging. "Carry a flashlight at least, Johnny!" So Johnny carried a flashlight, even after the batteries in it had died.

Now, Johnny lived for the darkness.

Though the ghosts of the dark still made him uneasy within himself, he felt truly alive in their presence. They didn't speak. They didn't show themselves. He knew they were there, all the same. Defiantly, silently, he would state the case for his kind of life to them. Always they would listen, offering him no understandable verdict. Perhaps the song of the wind held the answer, if only he could discern its music.

Ahead of him now was the barn, which he passed every night as he jogged the old road. In Johnny's eyes a dignified residence, its original owner and its former bestial occupants were a century departed. Now it was a place for that which governed the night.

Its rotting planks, the gaping holes in its walls like worn holes in the knees of jeans, frayed and ragged, marked it a truly sacred place. He took particular notice of the song the wind sang about it. It was a different song than the song for the trees or the song for the road. It had no tragic tone of melancholy. The wind held no pity for this place, only the deepest reverence. The song proclaimed the untarnished beauty and withstanding dignity of the spirit within.

He had passed the barn every night since he'd come home, since he'd started jogging this road. He had not gone inside. Despite his newfound love of the dark, the remnants of old fears had lingered, keeping him from within.

But tonight, the wind sang. Chilling, icy, it numbed his ears, squelching earthly sounds, but letting him hear in a new way. He heard the call from within the ancient walls, an alluring siren's song. A generalized eroticism swept over and past him and drew him in.

Tonight, tonight he would go inside.

"Don't go in the barn, Johnny! Don't go..."

The voices of the past, of the earth, of the living, faded.

He would go inside.

He moved toward it. It was a masterwork of the horrible. In the radiant black-blue of the sky he could see the overgrowth, all of it dead, which blocked the path, warning away the living, the heretics who would not pay the homage this sacred place deserved. Sharp broomsage and wicked briars conspired together to protect their charge.

Ahead of him, the darkness had laid a trap for the unwary. A hole, a threatening pit of black, yawned before the maw of the building. Johnny halted, peering in. Was it bottomless, endless? Within it, was there a vacuum of blackness, waiting to dislodge his soul and claim it as a prize?

Fear flitted about him, darting like an insect, trying to annoy, to draw a reaction. A traveler, alone with no source of light, should beware such a hole, should fear it.

Fear held no power over Johnny. His driving need now was to enter the place of shadows, to discover the secret Night was keeping only for him. And so Night revealed the truth about the hole to him. It was merely a shallow pit of rotting timbers and blackish mud, a dugout place where once there had been a well, now filled. Her ebon veils had made it seem so much more. He knew, should she have so chosen, she could have made the pit bottomless. It could have swallowed him forever. Any other it would have swallowed, but Night wanted him to come further.

The song grew louder. Another voice had joined the wind in its chorus, a light voice, a voice from his oldest dreams. It touched his ears. It drifted, weaving and dancing, from within the barn. The song touched every part of his body at once, exciting every nerve. Ahead, through the black of the doorway, Night smiled seductively.

He caught the briefest, most furtive of glimpses of her... or was it a glimpse at all? Was it not something his eyes had witnessed, something objective, but just a phantom from his own subconscious? Seeing her, seeing her smile, he still could not describe her.

Whatever it was, it was enough. Now he knew what was inside: inside was his goal. The shadows held her in waiting. He plunged into the massive cavern of the opening, almost leaping into the dark. He searched, not with his eyes--which were of no use here--but with his being.

In the corner was the voice, the one that danced on the wind. It beckoned from above, drawing his eyes upward. Night was perched atop the loft, waiting.

Night was not dark, far from it. She had skin like the milky surface of the moon and hair pale gold as the haze which adorned the moon on misty evenings. He realized that this was what he had expected. Her ethereal white robes blew around him on the wind, entangling him.

Night smiled. She was the most beautiful thing he had ever seen.

He was cold no longer.

In fact, he found he was uncomfortably warm. Night nodded, and he tore off his jacket, flinging it away. The weight of the dead light carried it to the corner. His t-shirt, slick now with sweat, he peeled off. He kicked away his shoes. The clothes were things of the day. He rejected them.

Naked he stood before her, and the dark reflected off his skin. He had not known dark could reflect, but it did, no doubt on wavelengths the human eye could not detect. But Johnny saw the reflection. In Night's gaze his body was smooth and young and perfect.

She held out her arms, causing her robes to flow and billow and engulf him. He was lost within their folds, and she drew him closer.

And Night smiled.

There was no heat, only a passion cold, but fierce. Night, as incredibly old as he was young, drew him to her. He gave himself entirely, unthinking, un-sensing, only feeling in a way he had never known.

His breath grew short, and stopped completely. Night smiled.

———

As he woke, it was light. The wind had gone. He shivered, feeling the absence of true life around him. Straw pricked his naked flesh, and he felt the coarseness of the old floor boards with every nerve in his back and legs.

He wanted to get up, to stretch, but the girl was nestled against his shoulder. Her breath, even and perfect, tickled his neck and riffled his hair. Pinpoints of light shone through holes in the old walls and painted patterns on her ivory flesh. Just pinpoints, like starlight. Not enough to disturb her. Not enough to burn away the perfect flesh.

Last night, her flesh had been icy. To him, she now felt soft and warm. He pulled her to him; and together they slept, waiting until the time was ripe for them to come alive again. It was not so very long from now, before the other kind of life would walk: Ghosts. Phantoms. Demons. That would be their time, the time after the sun went away.

For now, Night had no place in the world. In this dead world.

In the daytime, they would try to find him, the living. They would not. He was not there, not in the light, no longer in the light. After days they would give up, the living would. After years, they would tear down this shrine, where Night and her consort slept the day through. It did not matter. They would find another place. Night slept in many places. Night never went away.

And he was hers.

Because Johnny wasn't afraid of the dark anymore.

EVELYN
by Michael Critzer

The walls were covered in red fabric with black arabesque patterns, illuminated and animated by the twitching flames of gas lamps. The tables were filled with gentlemen wearing Venetian masks, and they were waited on by young women in corsets and burlesque skirts that exposed their legs in the front. They sat upon men's laps, shared hookah pipes, and led them behind the black curtains in the back of the room.

On the stage, a man in an elegant cravat played a dark waltz on a tall stringed instrument. It was connected to an automated contraption with gears, steam, and glass tubing that chimed like a macabre music box. The woman next to him had painted eyes and moved in place like a graceful marionette. She sang a haunting soprano that floated through the room on the opium-tinged air.

A young man emerged from the entranceway, overshadowed by the apelike doorman, and looked around nervously as he took a seat at an empty table. His shirt was stained, his waistcoat disheveled, and there was a week's worth of stubble on his face, but his youthful, refined features presented it all with a bohemian charm.

A portly gentleman in a frock coat watched the young man from a distant table. He rested his chin on a pink fist surrounded by a lacey cuff as he admired the strong jawline beneath the young man's beard. One of the girls, with a black feather in her hair, approached the young man, and a few moments later he cried out and pushed her away.

People from the surrounding tables stopped to stare as the girl gripped her arm where the young man had clutched her. The doorman stepped forward, and a woman floated towards the table in a long full skirt. "Is there a problem?" she asked. She was older than the other girls, with her dress cresting over the back of her shoulders to clasp at the neck.

"He's only come to gape, ma'am," the girl with the feather said indignantly.

The woman looked down at the young man and said softly, "The cabaret is for paying customers only, sir. Perhaps you'd like to begin with a drink?"

The bohemian looked nervously from the woman to the doorman, who took another step forward. "I—I came to see Evelyn," he eventually stammered.

A murmur of laughter spread around the room, and the woman's face became stern, but just before she spoke, all heads turned to the sound of a bell ringing.

When the portly gentleman had their attention, he put down the service bell and announced, "The young man is with me, Madame. I apologize for his manners, but he'll be no more trouble." Then, to the girl with the black feather, he said, "Bring us a bottle of absinthe, and we shall be purely ornamental." Everyone returned to their business, but the girl gave the young man an anxious glance as he made his way cautiously over to the gentleman's table.

Once he got there, he stood for a moment, unsure.

The gentleman laughed and said, "Please, sit. You've nothing to fear from me. I could merely use some company, and you looked so desperate to avoid expulsion."

"I was at that," the young man said, taking a seat.

"Anton Jacobus," the gentleman said, extending his hand.

"Tarun Adams," the young man replied. "And thank you for the help."

As they shook hands, Anton took note of the muscles that flexed beneath the young man's clothing. "Did I hear you mention Evelyn?" he asked.

"Yes," Tarun said, withdrawing his hand and looking down at the table. "I must see her again."

"May I ask why?"

Tarun looked up at him in shock. "You don't think she's beautiful?"

"That and more," Anton said, "though, I confess, not in the manner I suspect you do. You see, Evelyn is like a daughter to me."

"I beg your pardon, sir! I meant no disrespect!"

Anton waved the supposed offense aside, and the young man continued, "I only first saw her last week, performing on this very stage, but I've been unable to think about anything else since."

"Was it her movements? Her voice? Her expressions?" Anton asked, leaning in eager for the answer.

Tarun shook his head. "It was everything. She has an otherworldly beauty—so familiar and yet so foreign—so touchable and yet so distant."

Anton leaned back with a satisfied smile, and Tarun began to blush. "Forgive me," he said, "Again, I mean no disrespect."

But before Anton could respond, the girl with the feather approached, carrying a bottle and two glasses. "Thank you, my dear," Anton said in form of a dismissal once she had placed them on the table.

But she did not leave. Instead she looked at Tarun tentatively. "No hard feelings, then?"

He looked at her for a brief instant and answered, "No. And I'm sorry about before, ma'am." But when he dropped his gaze, it fell to the flesh that swelled out of her corset. She noticed, and Anton watched amusedly as she sat down slowly next to Tarun. He stiffened, now staring only at his folded hands on the table.

"Don't worry about it, love," she said leaning in and trying to position her chest beneath his gaze once more. "And, please, call me Lyla." She waited for him to respond, but he did not offer up his own name. "Why don't we seal our new friendship with a private massage?" she continued, motioning to the black curtains at the back of the room." She rested her hand on his and whispered, "No charge."

"I said no!" Tarun snapped, jerking away.

Anton erupted in laughter, "A fine effort, my dear, but your cards have been played. Now leave us."

She gave Anton a vindictive glare as his amusement continued, but she turned to Tarun with an expression of concern as she reluctantly left the table.

Anton's laughter faded slowly, but before either man could say anything, the couple on stage finished their song, and the room filled with applause as a curtain descended.

"I believe your Evelyn is up next," Anton said, as a shuffling was heard backstage.

Tarun became wide-eyed and leaned forward in his chair. Anton poured the young man a glass and watched him drink until, finally, the curtain rose once more.

Music could be heard, yet there was no one on the stage. Tarun became visibly agitated, but then the rising curtain revealed a young woman's bare legs, crossed at the ankles. She was seated on a trapeze that faced the audience, hanging from two green vines. A black silk robe covered her body, with fur cuffs and collar. Though it revealed her long, fair legs, it was closed tightly around her torso, where it provided contrast to her pale and flowing blonde hair. Her face was elaborately painted for the stage and remained eerily still as her body swung to the slow rhythm of the music. Eventually, she opened her mouth to sing. Her voice began softly, with an angelic timbre, but swelled gradually with emotion and an unearthly resonance. She sang of secret gardens, lost love, and loneliness.

Anton watched a tear make its way down Tarun's cheek and poured him another drink. "I trust she does not disappoint?"

Tarun accepted the glass and wiped the moisture from his beard. "She's even lovelier than last time," he said. "God never made a creature so beautiful . . ."

As the song progressed, Evelyn moved both of her hands higher up the vines, and in a motion that looked effortless, she lifted herself up to stand on the bar. She sang of helplessness as she raised one arm above her head and let it descend behind her, allowing the robe to slide away from that half of her body. Then she sang of cruel destiny as she repeated the movement with her other arm and the robe fell to the stage.

Tarun mopped the sweat from his brow as he stared at her. Green leaves covered her breasts and between her legs, while her skin around them looked porcelain in its beauty. His vision blurred as the song came to a finish, and he blinked rapidly to clear his eyes.

"Something wrong?" Anton asked.

"No," Tarun sighed, as the curtain descended to more applause. "Just the price of gazing at perfection, I suppose."

Anton laughed. "Would you like to meet her?"

Tarun jerked his head up. "You can arrange that? I mean, yes, more than anything! You don't know what that would mean to me."

"Wait here," Anton said, as he stood and walked through the curtains at the back of the room.

Tarun waited at the table for what seemed like an eternity. Lyla was seated with a gentleman across the room, but she tried anxiously to get Tarun's attention when he would look her way. He refused to give it, though, and remained staring at his glass until Anton finally emerged and beckoned for Tarun to follow him before disappearing once more.

Tarun left the table and passed through the still-swaying curtains just in time to see Anton turn left at the end of a hallway. From rooms on either side came the carnal sounds of pleasure from patrons and their chosen girls. Tarun became dizzy from the echo, but he pressed on until he rounded the corner and saw Anton holding a door open.

"She's expecting you," the older man said with a wink. Tarun took a deep breath and stepped inside as Anton closed the door behind him.

There was only a single lamp suspended from the ceiling, and to the side of the room, Tarun saw a machine like the one that had kept time for the man and woman performing the waltz. It thumped and hissed quietly, and beside it, Tarun saw Evelyn seated in her robe at a dressing table that faced away from him.

"Ms. Evelyn?" he began as he took a step forward. "I apologize for the intrusion. I'm sure you hear this very thing all of the time. But when I first saw you perform, you struck such a chord within me." He took another step closer. "I've never been good with people, but watching and hearing you perform with such beauty, I knew I had to meet you."

When he was a step or two behind her, he noticed that her mirror was covered with a black cloth, so he stepped around to see her face. It was unmoving and stared into the covered mirror.

"Are you alright?" he asked, placing a cautious hand on her shoulder. But as he did so, her head tilted back from his touch. The room began to spin as he felt the blood drain from his face. He pressed his fingers to her neck to check her pulse, but he felt something hard and sharp. When he brushed her hair aside, he saw a flesh-colored gear that enabled her head to nod up and down. Then he jumped as part of her song, music and all, poured out of her open mouth before cutting off abruptly.

Tarun stepped back in horror and shame as he looked around, waiting for Anton, and maybe the rest of the cabaret, to step out and laugh at his expense. But he saw no one. The room was still swimming in his eyes, so he walked as determinedly as he could back to the door. He slowly became aware of two figures on either side of it and stopped cold as he recognized the man and woman performers from the stage. They too were unmoving.

The door opened then, and Anton appeared. "Still standing?" he asked. "You do hold your liquor well."

Tarun felt a sudden fear of the man and turned around to escape, but heard the slow footsteps following him.

"Are you piecing it together yet?" Anton chided. "Maybe you should look down."

Tarun fell forward and caught himself on Evelyn's table. He was unable to take another step. On the floor beneath him were tubes filled with a dark substance, and they ran from the machine up and into the sleeves of Evelyn's robe.

"She's very old and must be maintained," Anton continued, "but she is very much alive. That is what drew you to her. Both suspended and animated, she has been given everlasting life."

Tarun turned his head with his last bit of strength to see Anton approaching him with a handful of tubes and needles, and just before losing consciousness, he heard the words, "But it is not good for her to be alone."

FORM AND SUBSTANCE
by Susanna Reilly

Alindra soared across the darkening sky, reveling in the freedom of flight. Nothing matched the pure ecstasy of gliding through the air hundreds of feet above the ground, a gentle wind buffeting her body, carrying her higher and farther with each movement of a delicate wing. The dark brought temporary relief from the intense heat of the day, fueled by the dual suns now setting on either side of the horizon. So she hurtled toward the desert floor, allowing the tip of her wing to graze its surface, sending a puff of dry dust into the air, before pulling up again to soar into the deepening night. It was wondrous how the wings responded instantaneously to her thoughts, as though they had always been a part of her.

Ahead, the flock drifted toward the desert floor and began dropping from the sky. Four spindly legs carried each across the hard-packed surface until the texture changed to loosely packed grains of sand. Joining them, Alindra pushed her long curved snout through the loose sand until it reached the hidden spring below, and she gratefully sucked up the sweet green liquid, suchara, that gave nourishment to this body. Her hunger sated, she raced across the desert floor until the curved wings carried her back into the air.

The light gravity of this world allowed for daring aerial acrobatics and Alindra took full advantage, swooping in tighter and tighter loops toward the ground, and then breaking off to head straight up into the sky again. It was exhilarating and terrifying at the same time, but she could not imagine any place she would rather be.

A long, piercing screech from below sent her heart racing. Instinct took over as she dipped and curved away from the sound, hoping the predator would not catch sight of her. The Batlans' size made them slow and cumbersome compared to the smaller and more graceful Ludiki, but it did not pay to underestimate them. Alindra's heart settled into a more natural rhythm as a quick glance down showed the beast had found other prey. She turned away, not wanting to watch as the Batlan stuffed a Ludiki into the mouth that took up most of the center of its body. It was natural selection at its most basic. As an explorer, Alindra accepted that basic tenet of life, but that did not mean she had to watch as it happened.

The creature below finished its meal, unfolded its huge, dark wings and reached for the sky. Alindra stretched her own wings as far as she could to boost her speed and banked left toward the Ludiki habitat in the far off mountains. A screech rent the air, much too close, and she twisted her body, barely avoiding the writhing tentacle of the Batlan that had taken advantage of her distraction with its brother's meal. A higher-pitched screech just below signaled that the creatures had teamed up for the hunt. Her heart tried to pound its way out of her chest as Alindra forced more speed from her straining form. But the Batlans had locked onto her and were closing in.

Flight easily won the battle against fight and she allowed herself only a moment of regret as she concentrated on the sky in front of her. The darkness dissolved in a shimmer of light. As she strained toward its glow, a tentacle smashed into her wing. She shrieked in agony as her body tumbled out of control, forward momentum the only thing that prevented the grasping tentacles from reaching her before the shimmering expanse engulfed her.

Elation and relief turned quickly to regret as the delicate wings melted into her body, leaving only small fins, and the four spindly legs merged into a thick tail. She could feel the heavy press of liquid against her now, but there was no fear at the radical change. Fear had been left behind long ago, the changes that accompanied her travels now second nature. The portal's energy was fading quickly, and she used the last of it to absorb information about her new environment before the shimmer disappeared completely, leaving her in solid blackness.

Alindra swam for some time, cruising effortlessly through the cool, thick liquid. This species, which called itself Krattak, had no optical nodes, so she was forced to rely on the impressions sent back by its primitive sonar. Occasionally another Krattak would pass by, but they were creatures of limited intelligence, with little desire for interaction unless it was time to mate, so none of them approached her. She swam upward, searching for the surface of the liquid and any other environment that might exist above it. But there was no change—only the sensation of the liquid pressing against her or the occasional sonar echo of other Krattak.

Bored by the monotony of this world, Alindra concentrated on a point directly in front of her. Although she could not see the shimmer that signaled the portal's appearance, she sensed its energy and swam directly into it. As she passed through, her fins elongated into two jointed arms, each ending in five grasping appendages, the thick tail divided and morphed into two long jointed legs that each ended in five short stubby appendages similar to those at the end of her arms. The gills melted into a throat topped by an oval-shaped head with a face that featured two eyes, a small stub of a nose, a mouth and ears on either side of the head. Dark hair cascaded from the top of the head down past her shoulders.

———

Alindra stretched her new limbs tentatively, testing their strength and agility. She flexed the appendages at the ends of her arms—the word "fingers" came to her—then did the same with the—again a word came—"toes." She touched the delicate skin on her arm and felt the tingle of soft, light hair that coated it. Not wings. It was a humanoid form. There would be no flying here.

Ignoring her disappointment, Alindra focused on her surroundings. There was little time before the portal closed completely, and she needed more information regarding this world and its inhabitants. Humanoid cultures were much more difficult to infiltrate than those of less-sentient beings like the Ludiki and the Krattak. Language, customs, technology–the smallest mistake in any area could lead to discovery. A shiver ran down her spine at the thought of detection. Humanoids were unpredictable, their reactions at times extreme. Capture could not be allowed.

The room the portal had deposited her in was small and piled high with storage canisters and containers of varying sizes and shapes. The only uncluttered area was a small alcove against the far wall. Alindra sighed in relief as she crossed quickly to the computer access terminal nestled in the niche. Calling on the last of the portal's energy, she placed her hand on its surface. The hand shimmered, then disappeared as it interfaced with the computer. Knowledge regarding this place–a research vessel called *Callisto*–and its inhabitants began filling her, but there was simply too much information and not enough time. The portal's energy was dissipating too rapidly to handle a full data transfer and there was one more thing she had to do before it was gone. She discontinued the data transfer and sent a final pulse of energy to the central processing core, containing instructions that it accepted without question and immediately began to implement.

A sudden loud beeping pulled Research Specialist Jason Garvey's attention from the project at hand. He grabbed his tablet and almost dropped it again when he saw the message it displayed, "Anomaly matching designated parameters detected." He stood there for a few moments before the shock wore off, then raced out of his lab, eyes glued to the map on his tablet screen.

Alindra looked down at her naked form and frowned. These beings required coverings. Scanning the storeroom quickly, she located a crate full of clothing in various sizes, styles and colors. She accessed the data provided by the computer and quickly selected a light blue jumpsuit favored by females on the ship and pulled it on.

The fabric was uncomfortable against her skin—most of the forms she assumed required no such coverings. Perhaps undergarments would make it less uncomfortable, but they would have to wait. Her brief interaction with the computer had included its security measures, so she knew that the ship's protectors were already on their way. Taking a deep breath, she triggered the door release and quickly stepped out into the hallway beyond.

Footfalls pounded toward her as she approached the corner. Her heart raced as it had when the Batlan were chasing her, but this time she did not summon the portal. The knowledge she had obtained from the computer suggested that these beings would not harm her unless she tried to harm them first, and, if the command she had given the computer to create an identity for her throughout its systems had been effective, it would be some time before anyone realized she did not belong here.

Jason Garvey rushed down the main corridor, his heart racing. He didn't care what the sensors said now, he'd seen the initial message about the anomaly. Even if it was gone now, he was determined to see for himself if it had left any evidence behind.

As he rounded the last turn, trying to beat the security officers he knew were on the way, he almost knocked over a young woman coming from the other direction. Registering only long, dark hair and one of those form fitting blue jumpsuits that a lot of the women wore, he muttered a quick apology and kept going.

"Explain yourself, mister!" Head of Security Damon Jarvis demanded, angrily pacing back and forth in front of a recalcitrant Jason Garvey. Ryan Daniels, the head of the Research Division and Garvey's immediate supervisor, remained seated behind his desk, his gaze severe and unwavering.

"I've been working on a theory about dimensional conduits–portals between dimensions. I've had monitoring equipment going round-the-clock for the last month, looking for signs to support my theory. This afternoon, I got a signal on my equipment indicating a dimensional conduit had opened."

"I thought I knew about every experiment being run on this ship," Daniels said, "but I don't recall this one. Perhaps a few more details will remind me. "

"Well, um, we never actually discussed this experiment," Garvey kept his gaze locked on his hands, which were clenched in tight fists in his lap.

"Do you mean to tell me, Mr. Garvey, that you have been running unauthorized experiments on this ship?" Daniels said.

Shifting uncomfortably, Jason muttered, "It's nothing dangerous, sir. Nothing that would interfere with the ship's systems."

"And you know that because you are intimately familiar with every system and every experiment currently running on this ship," Jarvis cut in.

Jason sighed heavily. This was going even worse than he had imagined.

When Garvey didn't respond, Jarvis resumed pacing, "So when your monitoring equipment went off, indicating a…"

"Dimensional portal."

"…you decided to take matters into your own hands and investigate this anomaly without any backup from Security."

"They would have run in with guns drawn and scared it!"

"It? Exactly what 'it' is that, Mr. Garvey? My security team found nothing in that compartment but you."

"I know, but my equipment clearly indicated a life form of some kind, but then it just disappeared. I had to see for myself if something was there!"

Daniels' exterior remained severe, but he softened a bit at the young man's passion. Although fairly new to the ship, Garvey didn't have a record as a troublemaker. He was extremely bright, if not very ambitious, according to his records, and had not been a problem at all—until today. "You should go to the brig for what you've done ..." he said thoughtfully.

"Definitely," Jarvis growled.

"...but since this is your first offense, I'm going to give you an opportunity to redeem yourself."

"What?!" Jarvis's eyes went wide.

"Consider yourself on probation under my direct supervision. You are to share all of your research with me. If I decide your experiment has merit and is not detrimental to the ship in any way, I may allow it to continue. But one more incident like this and you are off this ship. Is that understood?"

"Yes, sir," Garvey muttered.

———————

Two hours later, a frustrated and abashed Jason Garvey headed toward the central lounge, wanting only to get his hands on some alcohol to help drown the memory of this miserable day. Not finding an alien or any sign of a dimensional portal, followed by the humiliation of the subsequent dressing-down by Daniels and Jarvis and the delegation of his research to Daniels' oversight had been bad enough, but having Daniels discover a problem with his equipment that might have affected the ship's systems under battle conditions had been excruciating. Daniels had come up with a change in the configuration of the equipment that would eliminate the problem and had even complimented him on the experiment, but that was little comfort.

Jason knew that his greatest flaw was his ego. He was the smartest person in his admittedly very narrow field of study, and had no patience for those who could not keep up. He had spent many years working alone in a research lab to perfect his theories and equipment. But once the theoretical part of his research had been completed, application of the theories required travel among the stars to prove their merit. Unfortunately, privately funded research vessels had their own protocols, one of the primary ones being cross-training and redundancy so vital data would not be lost in the event of a crewmember's death or disability. The idea of sharing his research had been so repugnant, he had hidden it away. While on duty, he performed, to the best of his ability and with a smile, the research projects assigned by his supervisors, safe in the knowledge that at the end of his shift, his personal work awaited him out of sight of the rest of the crew. But now the most important project of his life had been taken out of his hands.

Jason's thoughts were in turmoil as he barreled around the final corner leading to the lounge. A sudden jolt knocked him backwards and he staggered, trying not to trip over his own feet. A high-pitched cry of surprise brought his attention to an attractive, dark haired woman who seemed as disoriented as he was.

"Are you okay, miss? I'm really sorry. I should have been paying better attention."

"Just a little shaken up. I'll be fine."

"Good, that's good. I'm really, really sorry."

"It's okay, I believe you," she said, allowing a small smile. "Although I'm beginning to wonder if this is your way of meeting women."

"I'm . . . I'm sorry, what?"

She laughed lightly. "You ran into me earlier today, too."

Embarrassed, Jason tried to remember when that had been and had a brief flash of a dark haired woman in the corridor leading to the storage area right before his entire world had crashed down on him.

"I'm sorry," he repeated, "and no, it's not. It's just been that kind of day." Impulsively, he added, "Although I'd like to do something to make up for being such an oaf. I'm headed to the lounge for dinner, and a good stiff drink. Would you care to join me?"

She gazed at him for a moment before responding, "My mother taught me never to accept invitations from strangers—"

"Oh, right, sorry…"

"—but if you were to tell me your name, I suppose you wouldn't be a stranger anymore."

Jason had never been much of a ladies' man and her impish smile completely unnerved him. "Oh, sure. Garvey, Jason Garvey, Astrometrics –at least for the moment," he added ruefully. "And you are?"

"Alindra. Alindra Duvane."

Alindra was not sure why she had accepted Jason Garvey's invitation or why she had reminded him of their earlier meeting. Even though he had no reason to suspect her, it would have been far safer to keep her distance from him. And while it was true that this body needed nourishment, it would be far safer to feed it away from the prying eyes of the crew. Still, she had spent the hours since her arrival exploring the ship and observing its occupants. She had listened carefully to exchanges among the crew and had easily picked up the rhythm of casual conversation.

Although she needed to access the portal soon to upload the information she had gathered so far, and to receive further information it deemed relevant from the earlier download, she wanted to put that off awhile longer. There were still small gaps in her knowledge, but she felt confident enough to test her skills, and Jason Garvey was a convenient test subject.

The lounge featured a long, sleek, bar in the center, surrounded by table and chair groupings of metallic silver that could seat couples looking for some privacy or groups of up to a dozen. They chose a table for two by an observation port. If the ship had still been docked at the space station, it would have provided a beautiful view of the stars. But since it was now streaking through space, protective shields had been lowered over the port. A built-in vidscreen could simulate the at-rest view but by unspoken agreement, they did not turn it on.

After they entered their orders on the vidscreen, an uncomfortable silence settled over the table. Jason had always had difficulty with small talk. Having been raised by a highly intellectual but extremely clannish alien race after the death of his scientist parents, he had spent ten years in an environment that cherished his intelligence but had crippled him socially. Talking about topics other than his work was difficult for him at the best of times. But now that they were seated at a table facing each other, words failed him.

Alindra noticed his sudden discomfort but, unsure of its source, decided to break the silence. "Tell me about yourself, Jason Garvey. Where are you from?"

"Jason is fine, and there's not much to tell. I'm just a boring old Earther." He felt sweat breaking out on his brow as he forced the words out. "What about you?"

"I come from a long line of scientists and explorers, so I've spent most of my life traveling. There's no one place I call home."

"What's your specialty?"

"I have a great many interests, but right now I'm focusing on botany."

"So, you're a botanist." Jason heard the words coming out of his mouth and wanted to slap it shut. *Very intelligent, Mr. Obvious.*

"Primarily, but I find all life forms interesting," she said, a soft smile playing at the corners of her mouth. "You said in the corridor that you're in Astrometrics 'for the time being'. Are you thinking of changing careers?"

Garvey winced at the memory of his encounter with his boss and the security chief and responded glumly, "I may not have any choice."

He hadn't intended to tell her the story, but she was such a good listener that it spilled out of him. "So anyway, now my research is being babysat by my boss and I'm this close to getting booted off the ship altogether. I don't expect it will look too good on my service record to have been kicked off the premiere research vessel in the galaxy after only two months."

"I just got here myself," she responded, "so I can sympathize. This place is amazing. I hope to be able to stay here for some time."

"When did you come on board?"

Hoping that the computer had completed its secret work and her new identity had been fed throughout the system, Alindra replied, "This morning, during the crew transfer at the space station."

He stared at her in surprise. "I was there as part of the greeting party for the new people in our department, but I don't remember seeing you."

She pouted. "I guess I'm not that memorable."

He looked at her–a clear, light skinned face, framed by dark wavy hair that spilled in waves past her shoulders, brilliant blue eyes and soft, full lips. Definitely a face he would have remembered.

She smiled to sooth his look of consternation. "I was overseeing the transfer of some fragile botanical samples, so I didn't come in at the same time as the others. Anyway, what is this research that's gotten you into so much trouble?"

"It's kind of technical. I wouldn't want to bore you."

"Why don't you give it a try and I'll let you know if I get bored."

Garvey shrugged and responded, "Okay, you asked for it."

He told her his theory about the existence of fixed portals between dimensions and his attempts to detect them. She listened attentively and, to his surprise, asked several intelligent questions.

Before he realized it, his life story was tumbling out. "My parents were sociologists. They volunteered to go to the planet Luton, a world on the farthest edges of explored space, in a solar system that's otherwise barren of life, to learn more about Luton history and culture and act as intermediaries for their interactions with other races.

"The Lutons revere knowledge and learning above all else, but are clan-oriented to a fault. Each Luton knows his relationship to every other Luton in the community, and an insult to one member of a clan could cause a blood feud that would last for generations. That led to many unnecessary wars and conflict over the centuries that kept the Lutons from working together to reach their full potential. Only in the twenty years prior to our family's arrival were the Lutons able to pull their disparate clans together to work toward the goal of exploring space. Having spent so many years fighting one another, they were reluctant to trust strangers, especially those of a different species, so aliens like us were initially treated with suspicion.

"But my parents won the respect of the Lutons, not only because of their keen intellects, but also their dedication to their own small clan, which included me and my younger sister. I guess that's why they took me in after my parents and sister were killed."

"What happened to them?" Alindra asked.

"There was a flare up of hostilities between two of the clans. We were visiting one of the clans and there was an explosion. I was the only one in my family who survived. The clan took me in as a ward of the community until a ship could be sent to pick me up. Because Luton was so remote and of no military importance, it took almost eight years for that ship to come."

"I'm so sorry," Alindra whispered.

Jason remained quiet, lost in his memories. Being shuttled from family to family among the Lutons, learning all they had to teach him, then passed along to the next family. During the triennial family festivals, when the clans of related families gathered to celebrate their history, being left alone at the home of his current patron to fend for himself. An orphan on a world that celebrated family connection, he had always felt like an outsider, waiting anxiously for the day when he could return home to his own extended family, and be among people with whom he truly "belonged."

Unfortunately, that dream had been shattered when he found himself returned to a world that didn't celebrate family connection the way the Luton had. His only remaining blood relative was his mother's sister, a dedicated scientist with no time to waste on a 13-year-old boy. Her response to the problem of Jason had been to send him away to the science academy until he was old enough to go out on his own. At school, the knowledge and skills he had gained from the Luton had put him intellectually many years ahead of those his own age, resulting in his being placed in classes with students much older than himself and not much interested in a teenage boy. There had been a few friends and mentors along the way, but

Jason had learned early the difficult lesson that he had no one to depend on but himself.

The gentle squeeze of Alindra's hand reminded him he was no longer alone. "It was the Luton who taught me that other dimensions existed. I didn't know the stories were just Luton fairytales, but the dream of one day visiting those other worlds was my lifeline. I buried myself in my studies–all types of math, physics, astrophysics and anything else I thought might even remotely help. I even spent some time studying the folklore of various cultures to see if they had stories like the Lutons. And there were some. But it wasn't until last year that the theory about the gateways came to me one night out of the blue."

Alindra reached over and squeezed his hand again. "Thank you for sharing your story with me, Jason. I very much enjoyed spending this time with you and hope we can do it again soon. But I must go now and get some sleep before my duty shift starts."

Jason watched her go with a smile then left the lounge whistling. He'd never had much luck with girls in the past, but something told him this one was different–and he hoped to have an opportunity to see her again soon.

———

Alindra moved through the halls purposefully, with no intention of wasting her valuable time sleeping. It was extremely bad luck that Jason had been present for the crew transfer that was part of her cover story, but she thought she had been convincing enough to divert him from wondering about it. His research was a bigger problem. If he began to suspect that an "alien" had indeed come through the portal he had detected, it wouldn't take him long to figure out who that alien was. This was a fascinating world and Alindra was determined to continue exploring it for as long as she safely could.

———

Jason dragged himself out of the dream, trembling. In it, he walked down a corridor, turned the corner and came face to face with a door, nothing but blank walls on either side of him. Quickly pulling on some clothes, he raced down the hallway, took a quick ride on the lift and ran down the final corridor to the corner he had seen in his dream–the one where he had collided with Alindra the first time. Slowly, he turned the corner. Straight ahead was the door to the cargo hold. On either side were –blank walls. The only place she could have come from was that cargo hold.

As he slowly retraced his steps to his cabin, Jason thought about the inconsistencies–not seeing her at the crew transfer, her knowledge of technical issues way outside her field–but he kept coming back to the incontrovertible fact of her being in that particular corridor at that particular time. He thought briefly about taking his suspicions to Ryan Daniels, but knew he'd either be found wrong and look like a fool again or be taken seriously and have the entire matter turned over to the Captain or, worse yet, Security. No, if Alindra really was an alien and really had come through a dimensional portal, Jason Garvey wanted to know why, how and, most importantly, what was on the other side. Stopping at a computer access terminal, he snapped, "Provide location of Alindra Duvane."

It took a second or two longer than usual for the computer to respond. Finally, the screen changed, displaying a small section of the ship with a pulsing red dot.

The Botanical Garden.

Jason approached Alindra cautiously, his steps slowing the closer he came to her. She seemed so normal, so human, seated on a bench in the middle of the garden, looking at the plants, that he could almost convince himself he had been wrong about her.

She was examining the plant in front of her so intently he didn't think she'd heard his approach, so he jumped when she suddenly said, "I can tell by your hesitation in approaching that you've figured it all out."

His heart sank as he responded, "Not all of it, but enough. Who are you really? Where are you from and what are you doing here?"

All good questions and she gave him honest answers. "My name is Alindra. As for where I come from, I don't really remember, to tell you the truth. I've been traveling for so long and visited so many different worlds in so many different dimensions that I can't really remember where I started out. This one is particularly fascinating. I wish I could stay here longer."

"You're not going to leave, are you?" he asked with genuine alarm.

"I have no desire to be your next experiment," she said, looking him steadily in the eyes. "As for what I am doing here, I too am a scientist— traveling from place to place, learning all I can in each before moving on to the next—and I want to continue exploring, to see all that is out there, not remain a prisoner being poked and prodded to find out what I am and how I do it."

"I would never do that," Garvey said earnestly, "I swear if you stay I won't tell anyone. I do want to know how it all works, but I promise not to tell anyone else and I certainly won't poke and prod you. Is that your natural form?" He slid onto the bench beside her without conscious thought.

Her smile dimmed. "Right now, I am human. When I cross the portal into a new world, my body adapts to fit in with the environment of that particular place. The portal provides me with information and the ability to interface with certain systems right after the crossing, but once the portal's energy dissipates fully, I am just like every other member of the species whose shape I took. Your sensors and other equipment will read me as human, because I am human for as long as I remain here."

"What is your natural form? Are you humanoid or . . . something else?"

She frowned, contemplating the question, then gave an uneasy laugh. "It has been so long, I do not remember."

"You don't ever change into your original form?"

"I suppose if I ever go back to my home world, I would, but I have not done so in so long, I do not even remember which world is the one of my origin. The portal retains that knowledge and will provide it to me if it is needed. But when I am elsewhere, I retain whatever form the portal gives me in that place until I leave it."

"What are the portals? How do you find them?"

Her smile widened at his fascination. "Your mistake is in thinking that they are localized phenomena. The portal is a living thing. It is everywhere. All I have to do is will it to open and it appears."

"You mean you could open one right here, right now?"

"If I choose."

Garvey's amazed silence was interrupted by the bleep of his wristcomm. The tense voice of Damon Jarvis came through the device, "Mr. Garvey, you are needed on the Bridge immediately."

Garvey looked at the device in annoyance and snapped, "I'll be there shortly. I'm in the middle of something," and closed the connection.

It was Alindra's turn to look at him in amazement.

"What?"

"You just told the head of Security you're too busy to be bothered with him."

"I am."

"Don't you think he'll find that suspicious?"

"I suppose."

"You'd better go."

"Not until you answer some more of my questions."

———

Alindra's wristcomm bleeped as she walked with Garvey toward the main entrance to the hydroponics garden. "The Captain has requested the service record for Alindra Duvane," came the computer's tinny voice.

"Damn," Alindra stopped. "I'm going to have to go."

"No," Jason said, "you can't. "Wait and talk to them. Captain Roberts isn't the 'shoot first, ask questions later' type. She's an explorer, too. And Lt. Daniels will be interested in learning about you and your people."

Alert klaxons began blaring all around them. The doors to the hydroponics garden swished open revealing Captain Roberts, Lts. Daniels and Jarvis, and four security guards with weapons drawn.

Roberts demanded, "Who are you and what do you want with this ship?"

"She's not an enemy, Captain. She's an explorer just like us," Jason broke in, "she's just trying to learn about our world."

"Friends do not generally break into my computer and try to reprogram it," Roberts responded coldly.

"I was trying to remain anonymous, Captain, until I was sure your people wouldn't attempt to harm me," Alindra responded coolly. "I have had unpleasant experiences during my travels and have learned to be cautious."

"Then you will understand my desire for caution and agree to go into quarantine in sickbay until we can be sure you are not a threat to this ship or its crew. Once that has been determined, I will be happy to talk to you more about our respective worlds."

"I don't think so," Alindra said. "I will be happy to speak with you if you wish, but I'll skip the quarantine. I dislike confinement of any kind."

One of the security guards sighted his laser rifle on her. She immediately turned away and concentrated on the space directly in front of her. Jason vaguely heard Roberts shout, "Lower that weapon," as he watched Alindra, and was astonished when he saw the air in front of her begin to shimmer. Realizing what she was about to do, Jason cried out, "Wait! Take me with you."

Alindra glanced at him in surprise, and, seeing the determination in his eyes, grabbed his hand and quickly pulled him through the now brightly shimmering portal.

———

There was a strange sensation as Jason passed through the portal. He felt Alindra's hand slip out of his as all went dark for a moment, like a camera shutter closing then immediately reopening to an entirely different view. Although the scene around him was amazing, Jason could not tear his gaze from the wondrous creature before him. It resembled nothing more than a dark sack with thick, leathery skin. There was no sign of limbs, only a thinning in the membranes around its sides. His eyes began to burn and he blinked to clear them, but the pain continued. His breath became raspy and his nasal passages and throat began to burn. He lifted his hands to cover them. Blinking his eyes open and closed rapidly, he realized with growing horror what the problem was.

Alindra gazed out over the vast purple field, struggling to adapt to the limited vision provided by the single eye in the middle of her new form and the gelatinous membrane that soothed and protected it from the acidic environment. She spun her awkward form around to see how Jason was reacting to this new world and his new form, but froze in shock at what she saw—a very human Jason Garvey doubled over, gasping for breath, the skin on his face darkening as he crumpled toward the ground. The fading outline of the portal shimmered behind him.

She struggled to move toward him, then the word *bounce* entered her mind. She crouched this new legless form and sprang forward, knocking Jason back through the portal. The shimmer brightened momentarily as he passed through it, then began to fade again. She stared at it, contemplating. The time she had spent with Jason had been enjoyable and the thought of having a companion in her travels had been unexpectedly pleasing. The word *lonely* briefly flashed through her mind. She was confused by the fact that he had not changed as she had, and the thought that he might have been injured because she had brought him here troubled her. But there were also people with guns in his world who wished to confine her.

Alindra started to crouch to bounce toward the portal, when the sounds reached her—beautiful and ethereal, they came from above. She turned her single eye to the sky and gasped with delight. Above her were thousands of creatures just like her, swooping effortlessly through the air, using the thin membranes at the sides of their otherwise thick bodies to steer themselves.

The portal momentarily forgotten, she bounced tentatively away from it, realizing that gravity on this world was practically non-existent, enabling the otherwise heavy, cumbersome bodies of the Didkana, as these creatures were called, to leave the ground. Delighted by the thought of flying again, Alindra bounced off the ground and joined the creatures in the sky above.

———

"How is he?" Ryan Daniels asked Doctor Lillian Bentley as he looked through the window of the isolation room.

Bentley shrugged noncommittally, "As well as can be expected. The environment he was exposed to was extremely acidic. Luckily the acid didn't remain on his skin when he came back. His eyes were badly damaged, but I was able to save part of his sight. He'll need to be sent back to Earth to see if the specialists can do anything else, but I doubt it. The burns on his body are healing, but it'll take time. Dermal regeneration on wounds this extensive can't be done overnight."

———

Daniels entered the room and went to Jason Garvey's bedside. The lighting was low and the patient was wearing dark glasses to protect his injured eyes. He had lost most of his hair and dermal patches covered much of his face to protect the healing skin.

"Jason, it's Ryan Daniels. May I sit with you for a while?"

Garvey simply shrugged and it was clear even that simple movement caused him pain.

"Doctor Bentley says you're improving steadily. We'll be able to return you to Earth for further treatment very soon."

"Great." Even through the hoarse croak of his injured throat, the word was limp and lifeless.

"Would you like to talk about what happened?"

"There's not much to tell. She was wrong. She thought it was the portal that changed her form, so we assumed it would change mine, too.

But it didn't." He was silent for a long moment. "It was the most amazing thing I've ever seen. The land was purple... and Alindra, she changed into this thing that looked like a big, leathery sack. I was so excited to be there, to be part of such an incredible experience. Then my eyes and my throat started to burn and I looked down and saw my hands, my arms, and I knew...I knew it was...over...that I was going to die."

"But you're not dead."

"No," he responded flatly.

"There are plenty of strange new worlds in this dimension to explore," Daniels said. "Your life isn't over because you couldn't go with Alindra."

"I know, it's just that..."

"Yes?"

"For a minute, when she pushed me back through, I thought she was going to come back with me. There's so much we could have learned from her. She's one of the few people I've ever been able to talk to who understood..." The word *me* froze on his lips and, suddenly self-conscious, he finished, "...the work that I do."

"Maybe she'll come back some day."

"Maybe."

"I noticed in your service record that you don't have much family. We've notified your aunt about your injuries and your expected arrival date back on Earth, but we haven't received a reply yet. Is there anyone else you'd like me to notify?"

A lone tear slipped out from beneath the dark glasses. "No, there's no one else".

"I understand your parents and sister died on Luton and you spent several years there before returning home. I've never had an opportunity to visit that particular world. What was it like growing up there?"

"They're a very intelligent but extremely clannish people. Everything revolves around family. They did the best they could for me, but after my family died, I never really felt like I belonged. But I learned a lot from them."

"About things like dimensional portals?"

He smiled thinly. "No. They told me stories about other dimensions, but the only way they knew to reach another dimension was to die. One of their most ancient legends tells how the spirits of the dead pass on to another plane of existence where they wait for their loved ones to join them."

Daniels nodded. "A similar belief is held by many races. And since dying is a rather extreme way to test the theory, you decided to find another way."

He nodded.

"Why?"

Jason's brow furrowed over the bandages. "Why? Why not?! Anything would be better than the life I have here. No family except an aunt who doesn't want to be bothered with me, no friends, a dead-end career. . ."

"Not so dead-end anymore. Alindra's appearance has made your area of research very hot. I'm anxious to hear what you've learned and I expect you're going to be very popular in the scientific community."

"Great," he responded with much less enthusiasm than Daniels had expected. "If you don't mind I'd like to try and get some rest now."

Sensing he was pushing too hard on this first visit, Daniels responded, "Certainly. Call me anytime you need to talk."

Jason nodded distractedly and looked toward the window, but instead of the darkness of space his mind's eye showed him a bright purple world and an amazing creature that looked like a big, leathery sack. He couldn't help but wonder if the being called Alindra had ever found the dimension where the Luton dead existed and, if so, whether there had been three humans among them. He longed for the chance to find out.

APARTMENT HUNTING
by Daniel Patrick Corcoran

The apartment bedroom was dark, lit only by the silver wash of the lights from the surrounding city. A slight breeze through the open balcony door ruffled the sheer curtain and the black silk cape worn by the tall man framed in the doorway. He stared at the sleeping form of the woman.

He stood stock still, his unwavering gaze locked on his prey as the wind rustled the long cape around his evening tuxedo. The only other movement in the room, ever so slight, was the faint pulse in her throat caused by her life's blood coursing through her body. It was that which held the man's fixated attention.

When he finally moved, it was with a predator's step—silent, sure, coiled to spring into action. His eyes never lost their focus. She was in his sight, and there she would remain. His eyes were long adjusted to the twilight of the room, but he only stared at a single spot and did not let his eyes fall once from his intended destination.

The edge of the wooden coffee table met his shin hard, and it nearly flipped over as he raised his leg in a sharp motion and caught the edge with his foot. Aside from a sharp hiss, he refrained from crying out, but

grabbing the pained leg caused him to lose his balance. He was forced to make several quick hops over to the bedside table, where he put his hand down for support. A stack of magazines slipped out from under his hand, bringing him crashing down onto the table. His arms shot out for stability, and they achieved success in wrapping themselves around the telephone before his weight brought himself, the telephone, and the rest of the table's contents clattering to the floor.

The light on the other side of the bed flipped on. "Is someone there?"

He sat up with a quick motion and spoke in a deep, suave voice. "Good evening."

"Who are you?" Pulling the sheets up to her chin, the woman drew herself away from him.

"My name is unimportant," he answered with a dismissive wave. "It's Conrad."

"What do you want?"

He pulled himself up to sit on the edge of the bed. "To look into your eyes and see the passion that burns behind them."

"You broke into my apartment to do that?" Her hands were still clutched tight on the blankets, but her expression began to harden.

"I was drawn to the deep desire in your heart, as I could sense it was an echo of my own."

"What does that mean?" She crossed her arms and almost pouted. "What kind of attacker are you?"

"I do not wish to attack you. It is my hope that you will share your essence with me," he lingered over his next word, "willingly."

"You barge in here, wake me up in the middle of the night and expect me to just let you ravish me?"

"Of course not." He leaned towards her, putting a hand down on the mattress. He made a quick study of the distance that separated them. "Uh, look, do you mind if I came over there?"

"I like you just fine right where you are. You'll find I'm not going to be that easy to deflower."

"It is not the flower that attracts me," he leaned forward, his arm trembling to maintain his balance as he stared directly into her eyes, "but the water in the vase."

She brushed a lock of wavy brown hair out of her eyes as she tilted her head. "That has to be the stupidest metaphor I've ever heard."

His whole body was shaking with the effort to maintain his position. "I think you'll find it's a simile."

"Only if you're predicating a specific feature of comparison." She threw up her arms in exasperation. "I mean, it's obvious what the flower represents, but for the vase and water to have an objective relationship, you'd have to mean-"

He made a stern effort to hold still as he watched her gaze wash over him, taking in his manner of dress, his pale complexion, his dark, slicked-back hair groomed into a meticulous widow's peak, and his waggling eyebrows.

"Oh my god, you're a vampire!"

"There are many terms for my kind." He did his best to switch his weight to his other arm without tipping over. "That one I have never enjoyed."

"What do you prefer?"

"'Midnight Lover' has always been a favorite."

It took her a few moments, but her expression cracked and she burst out laughing. Her fit of giggling continued and renewed itself over several minutes. He sat up straight and turned his profile to her, looking at her askance. Finally, she held up a hand as she took a deep breath.

"Sorry, just give me a second." She burst out laughing again and covered her face with the duvet.

Turning to the wall, Conrad reached into his jacket with a sigh and pulled out a cell phone. He pressed a button and held it to his ear. "Carol?" he said a moment later in a voice several octaves higher than earlier. "It's happening again…Of course it's late, that's when I do this…No, I didn't break a window. Her patio door was unlocked…That's right, a big city like this and she left a door wide open."

He stood up and started pacing along the length of the bed. "Sure, she's on the eleventh floor, but come on, that's just asking for troub-"

His shoulders slumped as he muttered, "I'm deflecting...No...Well, no." He glanced over his shoulder at the woman on the bed. Her laughter had subsided and she returned his glance with curiosity.

"I can't ask her that," he hissed into the phone.

His shoulders slumped again. "All right."

Turning to face her, he took a deep breath. "I don't suppose, I mean, would you consider—do you mind if I come in?"

Her look of curiosity moved to outright puzzlement. "Now you ask me that? I don't even know you."

She barely finished speaking before he whipped the phone back up to his ear. "Yeah, she said 'no'...I know, I know, but look. I do it this way for a reason. I mean, I'm a vampire, right? There's no way to just bring up the whole 'drinking blood' thing. The least I can do is to put them at their ease and make them as comfortable as possible. However things wind up, at least they've gotten some enjoyment out of the process, right?"

The woman on the bed crossed her arms and leaned back against the headboard with her head cocked to one side. "Huh. You know, I never thought of it like that."

Conrad's eyes swiveled to stare at her for a moment. "Call you back later." He snapped the phone closed and almost threw himself across the bed. "So, where were we?"

She held up a palm. "Now, hold on a second. Let's talk about this drinking blood business. I don't know how much seduction you plan to lay on, but how could you expect anyone to go along with that?"

He eased up the bed to lean against the headboard. "As you say, seduction. It is an art designed to inflame the passions of the heart. When desire burns hot enough, no sensation will stand in its way."

"Okay, I get that, but it still seems like it would hurt."

"Perhaps, but if one is determined to have an experience, pain is unimportant. It can be minimized, regardless."

"Really?" she asked. "How?"

He held up his hands. "You know, I think we're getting a little technical here. Can I go back to describing your eyes or something?"

"Sure, sure, but hang on. This just occurred to me." She sat up fully, the blanket dropping to her lap. "We are talking about the exchange of bodily fluids. Aren't you worried about AIDS or STDs or anything?"

"I've got that covered." Pulling a wallet out of his back pocket, he extricated a plastic card and held it out to her. It showed his picture and a stamp from the state Board of Health with the words "HIV FREE" in bold letters with a recent date.

She gave the card a cursory examination before handing it back to him. "Well, that puts my mind at ease somewhat, but what about me? You don't know me from Adam. I could have anything."

He lowered his voice, almost whispering. "An Eve of your beauty and spirit? I believe you must be very discerning in your choices. You would not be with anyone you did not... trust, would you?"

She looked deep into his eyes. "Well, no."

"Besides, I don't think I could catch a wooden stake or a shaft of sunlight from you, at least not directly-" He stopped talking to let her recover from another fit of giggling.

"Could you hand me my robe, please?" She pointed to the corner of the bed. Conrad scooted over to the edge and passed her the light yellow robe. Throwing it around her shoulders, she got up and started to walk out of the room. "Would you like some tea?"

"No, thank you," he replied, as she paused in the doorway. "I don't drink... tea."

Covering her mouth to stifle more giggling, she turned and headed out of the room.

"Here, let me give you a hand with that," he said with a smile as he followed her.

Her kitchen was small and cramped, and while she boiled water and prepared the teacups, he arranged some crackers and cheese on a plate that she handed him. After a few minutes, they moved to a table in a spacious breakfast nook where they sat across from each other.

"So, how long have you been a vampire?" she asked.

"My spirit has always yearned for the night, an eternal longing that I could not deny. I did not become a vampire, so much as release my true self…"

She stared at him and cocked her head.

"But, not long, as time is measured."

A knock on the apartment door startled them both. He looked from the front of the apartment back to her.

"I wasn't thirty seconds behind you from the bedroom. Did I trip an alarm?" He stayed in his seat as she went to answer the door. "I hope it's Officer Ramirez. He keeps his patrol car so clean."

"I didn't call anyone." Looking through the peephole, a startled frown crossed her face before she unlatched the door and opened it. "Can I help you?"

The middle-aged woman standing at the door was wearing a leather coat over a bathrobe that did not quite reach the ground, revealing sneakered feet without socks. Dark hair, dirty with gray, hung limply down to her shoulders.

"I'm sorry," the woman said, "My name is Doctor Carol Townsend. I'm Conrad's therapist."

"Oh, please come in."

Carol strode into the apartment with a purpose, and made a beeline towards Conrad when she spotted him sitting at the table.

She stood over him and crossed her arms. "You said you wouldn't do this anymore."

"Carol, the reason I started seeing you is because I do this. Did you think I could just suddenly stop?"

"You promised you would call me when you were tempted to do this again."

"I did call you." He stood up to meet her stern gaze. As soon as he did, he lowered himself back into his chair. "Before anything happened, anyway. Wait, how did you find me?"

"That phone I gave you has a GPS tracker. Did you call me because you were afraid you were going to go through with it, or because you were afraid you wouldn't?"

A light hand fell on Carol's shoulder. "I'm sorry, would you like some tea?"

Carol glanced at the young, beautiful woman. Slowly and deliberately, she raised her eyebrows. The hand was removed from her shoulder as if from a burning stove.

"What is your name, dear?" Carol asked.

"Tiffany," she stammered, rubbing the offending hand as if to soothe life back into it.

"Please don't apologize, Tiffany. You have two strangers in your apartment at two in the morning. I'm sure Miss Manners would applaud your decorum." Carol pulled out a chair at the table and sat down. "I'd love some tea, thank you."

"Gouda?" Conrad asked, picking up a plate and offering it to Carol. In response to her withering frown, he added, "I think there's some brie..."

Carol accepted a teacup of mint jasmine blossom handed to her. "Tiffany, on behalf of myself and my patient, please accept my apology for disturbing you this evening."

"Well," Tiffany said, pouring herself another cup, "it hasn't really been a problem. In fact, I think he's been kind of nice."

"That's right," Conrad said, placing his hand on the table. "I've been a perfect gentleman."

"Says the man who scaled eleven floors to break into a woman's apartment." Carol folded her hands and leaned back in her chair.

"Only eight. The third floor backs up against the parking garage next door." Carol's frown seemed to be absorbing all sound.

"He didn't really break in," Tiffany said, "my balcony door is open..." The sound absorption was not individually exclusive.

Carol relaxed her arms and frowned. Slightly. "I must say, Tiffany, you're handling this very calmly."

"Well," Tiffany said, clinking her cup onto its saucer and cocking her head to the side, "I've never been chosen by a vampire before."

"Chosen?" Carol placed both her hands flat on the table with a slap. "Do you think you won first prize in a contest?"

"Of course not, but all he's done since he arrived is explain things from his point of view. He hasn't tried to attack me or anything, and if he had I just would have used the shotgun I keep under my bed." Tiffany paused for a second before addressing Conrad. "Would a shotgun stop you?"

"Twelve-gauge?"

"Yes."

"Double-barrel?"

"Single. Pump-action."

"Just buckshot? Or-"

"It would slow him down," Carol cut in. "I notice you haven't pulled it out."

"Like I said, I haven't needed to, have I? If flattery and charm are the worst things he inflicts on me, then I'll call it a lovely way to spend an evening." Tiffany cocked her head to the side as she continued. "A late, unplanned evening, or maybe an early morning, but I don't have to work tomorrow, so whatever."

Conrad held up a hand. "Excuse me, I was crouched down next to your bed. The frame goes all the way to the floor. How would you get to your gun?"

"Oh," Tiffany replied with a bright smile, "I was bluffing about that. I don't really own a gun."

"No, really?" Conrad asked.

"Nope. I only thought of it just now."

"That's amazing. I completely believed you."

"Really?" Tiffany lowered her eyes without losing her smile.

"Absolutely. Why, if you had brought that up in the bedroom I would have scampered straight out the window."

"Would you have turned into a bat?"

He spread his arms wide under his cape. "Well, you would have seen a lot of flapping!"

Tiffany put a hand over her mouth as she laughed.

Carol started patting her jacket and checking her pockets.

"What are you looking for?" Conrad asked.

"A blue ribbon for Tiffany. I think she's earned it."

There was a heavy knock on the door, followed by a deep voice on the other side announcing "Police!"

"Oh! There's my ride." Conrad started to brush the crumbs from the table into a napkin.

Tiffany furrowed her brow as Carol stood up and headed for the door. "I called them on my way over, dear. I was hoping they'd beat me here but I couldn't be sure."

Carol undid the latch and opened the door. Two police officers walked in as she beckoned them towards the table. A Hispanic officer walked up to Conrad with a smile.

"Conrad! How ya doing?"

"Just fine, Rico," Conrad held his hands close together in front of him as the officer pulled out a pair of handcuffs. "Yourself?"

"Can't complain." Officer Rico slipped the handcuffs onto Conrad's wrists and pulled him to his feet. "Trudy graduated."

"Already?" Conrad asked as he was being led to the door. "So she's a nurse now?"

"A nurse practitioner. Okay if we Miranda you in the car?"

"Whatever's easier for you. How are Lucy and Juan?"

"Growing like weeds. I have their school pictures."

"Can't wait. Hang on a second." Conrad turned in the door to face Tiffany. He held his right hand to the side of his head with the thumb and pinky extended as he awkwardly pointed to her with his left hand and mouthed "I'll call you." Then he turned back to continue his chat with the police officer as he was escorted out the door.

The other officer spoke briefly to Tiffany and Carol and left a card with instructions on making a statement for the police. After an assurance that both women were fine, he left as well.

Tiffany looked down at the small card in her hand. "Wow. I guess he does do this a lot."

"Unfortunately so, yes." Carol started heading for the door once again.

Tiffany laid the card down and leaned back in her chair. "I know you think I'm silly, but he was really charming. You don't think he really would have hurt me, do you?"

"Impossible, dear." Carol pushed the door closed and threw the latch with a loud snap. "A vampire can only harm you when you invite them in."

PHOTOS FROM THE ATTIC
by Phil Giunta

I swear on my father's grave that everything you're about to read is true. It happened three years ago, around the holidays, bringing to a close the worst year of my life. I'd almost completely put it out of my mind until I came across my diary last week while moving to my new house.

With Christmas almost upon us yet again, and since enough time has passed, I feel compelled to reveal what happened. After you read this account, feel free to tell me I'm full of crap, but I know what I experienced was real.

It had to be.

———————

Three weeks before Thanksgiving, cardiac arrest had sent my Uncle Rawley to his grave along with nearly a lifetime of bitter grudges. He was my dad's younger brother, but you'd never have guessed it from their personalities. Whereas my dad had been gregarious and sociable, Rawley had been a loner almost his entire life, especially after turning his back on almost everyone in the family over the last fifteen years.

Now, Rawley was six feet under, and, to my surprise, he'd willed his house to me. Call us chickens, but neither my daughter nor I were keen on living in a place where someone had given up the ghost. I'll sell and take the money elsewhere, thank you very much.

Truth be told, I was probably the only family member that Uncle Rawley had never quarreled with. Of course, we hadn't seen each other since I was 21. I remember the incident well. A few days after I'd come home from college, my father died suddenly. At least he'd lived long enough to see me graduate. Near the end of that summer, Uncle Rawley had come to visit a few times. I remember that blistering August night when my mom and Uncle Rawley ended up in an argument in our living room. From the top of the stairs, I'd caught the tail end of an explosive screaming match that ended when mom threw him out of the house. I never saw my uncle again.

Later, my mom explained that the argument had been about some matter concerning my dad's will. To this day, I'm not convinced of that, but at the time, I was too busy missing my Dad to press her for details.

With that history in mind, it hadn't entirely surprised me when my mother refused to help us clear out Rawley's house before putting it up for sale.

"Why don't you and Grace take care of it?" she had said. "It's not that much, and it'll be good therapy for you both. Get your mind off the divorce and give you two some quality time together."

As if I didn't have enough to do as a single parent with a full-time job. My ex and I had just finalized the demise of our marriage two days after I turned 38, and exactly one month before Uncle Rawley passed away. I was no longer Claudia Paulino, I was back to being old Claudia Adamski. Joy.

So, on one of the coldest Black Fridays on record, I found myself crawling around a freezing attic, my nose, ears, and fingertips completely numb after just twenty minutes. I slid a tattered cardboard box across a filthy plywood floor toward the steps. It was the last thing to go, thank God. I wanted a hot shower and coffee in the worst way.

"Mom?"

"Up here."

My fifteen-year-old-going-on-thirty appeared at the bottom of the pull-down ladder. I still wasn't accustomed to her two-tone black and blonde hair, let alone her exposed neck. Grace thought the short do made her look older and more sophisticated. As far as I was concerned, she was too young to worry about "sophisticated" and as for looking older, I'd told her not to rush it. Someday, that's the last thing she'll want.

"Did you get everything out of the kitchen?" I asked.

"It's all in the truck. What about the furniture?"

"The movers will be here on Monday to take it all to storage. Mom was right. Rawley didn't have much, thankfully."

"It's a small house." Grace started up the steps, but stopped halfway into the attic. "Cold up here." She nodded toward the cardboard box. "What's in there?"

"Probably more junk. Can you take it down? Be careful, it's a little heavy. It might bottom out."

Grace tilted the box as she carried it down, causing its contents to slide and shuffle.

"Sounds like a lot of paperwork." She carried it into the nearest bedroom and set it down atop the antique dresser. After wiping it off with a dust rag, she unfolded the flaps and peeked inside.

"What is it?" I asked, relieved to be back in a room with heat.

"Old photos."

No sooner had she spoken than the wall clock behind me stopped. Even weirder was the draft that swept into the room and ruffled the curtains. Grace and I looked at each other.

"You felt that?" I asked.

"Yep."

"Maybe it came from the attic." Of course, I said that more for my own sake than Grace's.

We stood statue-still for another moment, anticipating something more, but all was quiet. Finally, Grace reached into the box and pulled out a handful of photographs. She set them on the dresser and began sifting through them. Some were stuck together face-to-face and had to be peeled apart.

"Careful," I said. "They've been up there for God knows how long in extreme temperatures and humidity."

Grace separated two photos and held them up for me to see.

One was actually an old postcard from Assateague, Virginia, showing an aerial view of a calm blue ocean and crowded beach. The other was a Polaroid of a smiling little girl, eight or nine years old. She had long black hair and a one-piece powder blue dress. It took me a moment to recognize—

"Margot." I snatched the photo from Grace's hand and sat on the edge of the bed. "God, this has to be mid-eighties. I haven't seen Margot since high school. She lived two houses up the street until her parents moved to who-knows-where after we graduated. This looks like it could have been a birthday party. Yep, that was our picnic table there in the background. Looks like there's a cake on it."

I glanced at the cardboard box. "Oy, sorting through all those will be a drive down memory lane. I don't think that's a trip I want to take, but I bet your grandmother would love it. We can drop the box off at her place on the way home."

"Actually, these are kinda cool," Grace said. "What if I salvaged what I could and put them into an album? I could give them to Grandmom as a Christmas gift."

I thought it was a good idea. Money was a little tight and the project might distract Grace from the divorce. As a teenager watching her family fracture and being helpless to stop it, Grace did an admirable job of hiding her pain most of the time. She got that strength from her dad—and I got it from her.

I'd come to the conclusion a long time ago that grocery stores in the Northern part of the country must love winter. At the mere mention of snow in the forecast, milk and bread become more valuable than gold and checkout lines turn into the neighborhood hangout.

And there I was, staring through the freezer door and debating the four-pack of crab cakes, when someone called my name. I'd heard it, but it didn't register until the voice was suddenly right beside me.

"Claudia Adamski?"

I turned to look at the woman, half-expecting her to serve me a court summons from my ex-husband. Instead, she thrust out an empty hand. "Tina Reese from high school."

I shook her hand out of reflex and I think my eyes almost popped out of my head. It took a moment before I recognized "Two-Ton Tina," the heaviest girl in our class. I'd never called her that, of course, but I'd overhead other kids say it.

There's no way that slur would apply today, though. Now, she was more like "Teaspoon Tina," slim and buff. The weight loss even made her seem taller than I remembered. I had to admit, she was gorgeous. Dammit.

"Oh my God, you're skinny!" I blurted. I do that a lot, blurting. I'm blonde. It happens. "I mean, you look great."

Tina laughed. "It took a lot of work. So how are you? Getting ready for Christmas?"

I nodded. Emphatically. It seems I always do that before I tell someone that everything's wonderful when I'm not really feeling it. It's like I'm trying to convince myself, too. I probably looked like a bobble-head.

"I'm doing great. Well, now I am. Had a rough patch earlier this year. Got divorced."

Tina nodded solemnly, not like a bobble-head at all. "Sorry to hear that. Do you have any kids?"

"My daughter Grace is fifteen. Doing very well in school, thankfully. She's taking martial arts, piano lessons, archery. I get exhausted just talking about it."

"We have two boys, thirteen and ten. Between the two of them, we have almost every sport covered, plus guitar and drum lessons. It's non-stop. Didn't life seem simpler when we were kids?"

"You ain't kidding. Do you keep in touch with anyone from the old days?" I don't know why I asked. I'm the least nostalgic person on the planet, but it was the only common ground between us.

"A few here and there. Do you remember Margot Hansen?"

"Absolutely! Last week, I came across a photo of her when she was a little kid from the old neighborhood."

"She's dead."

I had to consciously close my gaping mouth. An awkward moment of silence passed before Tina spoke again. "Her family moved to Florida after she graduated high school, and Margot still lived there. Married into money, had three kids, big house, private beach, all that. Went swimming two days ago and apparently went out too far. They say she had a seizure before she drowned."

"Seizure?" *Drowned?*

"Margot had epilepsy."

"I never knew that."

"Neither did Margot until she was sixteen, and even then she didn't tell anyone. Kept it under control with meds."

"That's unbelievable."

We chatted for another minute before Tina wrote her email address on the back of my grocery list. We wished each other a Merry Christmas before parting ways. I turned back to the freezer and the crab cakes, realizing that I'd lost my appetite for seafood.

The snow still hadn't started yet by the time we finished dinner. Grace went off to her room to finish her homework, filled with hope that there would be no school the next day.

I didn't say a word about Margot, but her photo was still on the coffee table on top of a pile that Grace had pulled from the box yesterday. I said I'm not the nostalgic type, but I was curious so I scooped up a small stack of pictures, dropped onto the sofa and started flipping through them. There was a mix of different sizes, but most were 4x6 or Polaroids. Some were familiar, though it had been years since I'd seen them.

It's always interesting to see your parents when they were your age or younger. They'd actually had a life before I was born—vacation pictures, their first house, first car, the usual stuff. There was one picture of my parents and Uncle Rawley at the log cabin that my Aunt Josephine used to own. She's my mom's sister and still with us, God bless her, but she sold the cabin about a year after her second husband died in 1982.

At the bottom of the stack, I found two pictures stuck together like the ones with Margot and the beach. I managed to peel them apart without tearing them, although slivers from each image left their mark on the other. Still, Uncle Rawley's sky blue Mustang brought back memories. I don't remember the car's exact year, but it was early seventies with a white interior. I remember riding in it a few times when I was a kid.

The other photo was a Polaroid of Aunt Josephine dining at a fancy restaurant. I couldn't tell what the occasion was, but there were other people in the background that I didn't recognize. Judging by the clothes and hair and age of the photo, it was clearly the sixties. The image was faded and the photo was frayed around the edges.

"Taking over the project?"

I nearly jumped out of my skin when Grace appeared and picked up another stack of photos. I guess I was too focused on, well, nostalgia.

"Finish your homework?"

She rolled her eyes and gave an exasperated "yes." Ah, teenagers.

"Dad texted me. He wants me to help him pick out a Christmas tree this weekend."

"Real or fake?"

"Fake."

How appropriate. I kept my mouth shut and went into bobble-head mode again.

"He wants a white tree with blue lights," Grace said as she sifted through her handful of photos. She came across two more that were stuck together and started working on them. "He asked me to help put it together."

"That'll be nice. I'm glad he wants to spend some quality time with you."

Grace successfully separated the photos. She glanced at them both before handing one to me. "Is that Dominic?"

I took it and turned it right side up. "Yep." It was my cousin at his college graduation, complete with cap and gown. Dominic had been two years ahead of me at Lehigh University and had graduated *summa cum laude*. At the time, I'd hated him for it. Aunt Josephine spared no opportunity to inform the family of her son's latest achievements, like making Dean's list again or earning yet another award or generally walking on water. OK, maybe Dominic hadn't done that last one, but you get the idea.

He'd moved to Tulsa three years ago, after accepting a promotion to VP of Operations at whatever Fortune 500 company he worked for. Last I'd heard, he was dating some rich, high-powered attorney who had started her own firm.

"What's the other photo that was stuck to this one?"

Grace held it up. "A couple of antique airplanes."

Two single-pilot prop planes to be exact and straight out of the 1930s. Sunlight gleamed off perfectly polished silver wings. Both of them were side by side on a massive concrete pad.

"Must have been a museum," I yawned. "Or an air show."

By then, it was nearly 9:30 and I was fading fast. I pushed aside the curtains behind the sofa and took a quick peek outside. Sure enough, it had started to snow.

"You might just get your wish after all."

"It'll be nice to sleep in."

"And then you can help me clear the snow at Uncle Rawley's house."

"I think I'd rather be in school. I'm sorry, but that place creeps me out. I mean, he died in the living room."

"People die in their homes every day. It isn't like we're going to live there."

"It's probably haunted."

"Only if you imagine it to be."

"I didn't imagine that draft we felt in the bedroom when we opened the box of photos. I didn't imagine all the clocks in the house stopping at once."

I had to admit, I had no answer for that. Grace was right. It wasn't only the clock in the bedroom that had stopped when we'd opened the box. Afterward, as we checked the house one last time before leaving, we noticed that every clock had stopped.

Great, now my imagination was starting to run with the idea. Just what I needed before going to bed.

————————

With Christmas just two weeks away, death had struck our family again.

I sat at my mom's dining room table, picking at the breading on cold chicken fingers as the sheer, cruel absurdity of it ran through my head. Across the room, Aunt Josephine and Dominic stared at me, waving, smiling, hugging. A combined 112 years of living had been reduced to a collage of photos taped to poster boards. Grace had volunteered to create them for the double funeral, using the photos from Uncle Rawley's attic.

Aunt Josephine had been killed by a drunk driver while leaving the post office in the middle of the afternoon. The little prick had tried to make a turn on the cross street, but had had cut to the right too soon, plowing into Aunt Josephine and crushing her between his car and a brick wall.

To take the pressure off of Mom, I'd volunteered to call Dominic. I remember the quivering in my chest as I dialed his number. It had occurred to me that I'd never broken that kind of news to anyone before. To be honest, I don't even remember the conversation now.

Dominic had jumped on a plane the next morning—but he never made it.

His connecting flight from Tulsa to Dallas-Fort Worth had crashed somewhere outside of Wewoka, Oklahoma.

Dominic's remains had been cremated and buried in an urn with Aunt Josephine.

Mom was devastated. We all were, of course, but she was the oldest of three sisters and now, the last. The youngest, Aunt Wendy, had lost her battle with cancer over a decade ago.

As I continued staring at the poster boards, I heard my Mom's voice in the living room. Her tone was hushed and detached as she chatted with Grace and a few of my cousins. She was doing an admirable job of holding herself together, which only meant the dam would burst once everyone had gone. I'd inherited that trait from her. Grace is different. She'd been my rock since her father and I separated, and now she was doing the same for her grandmother.

Hard to believe she's my kid.

"Your daughter reminds me of Dominic."

The silky, southern drawl snapped me back to attention and I realized that I'd been focused on the photos to the exclusion of anything else around me. I'm not sure why I couldn't look away. Something was troubling me, beyond the obvious. I filed it for later and glanced up to see Elaina taking a seat to my left. Dominic's girlfriend had flown in two days ago. She was quite the exotic beauty, with narrow, hazel eyes and luxurious brown hair that framed high cheekbones and a flawless olive complexion. Her waist was so damn narrow I wanted to offer her my cold chicken fingers. Above the waist, she was rather well endowed. I wondered if they were—

"Real...I mean really?" I gave up on the chicken and wiped my fingers on a napkin. "How so? I hadn't seen him in years, just heard about him from time to time."

"Well, Dominic never let circumstances get the best of him. He had broad shoulders, literally and figuratively. A lot of people leaned on him, both professionally and personally, but his attitude never faltered, even when he was stressed out. He was always there when needed."

I smiled despite myself. That was my Grace to a tee.

Elaina sat back in her chair and turned her gaze to the poster boards. "I never thought I'd meet his family under these circumstances."

"How long were you two dating?"

"About three years. We talked about marriage." Elaina wiped her eyes. "But I wasn't ready for that yet."

I didn't know what to say, so I changed the subject slightly, and because I was curious. "How did you two meet?"

Elaina let out a short laugh. "Through mutual friends, although we recognized each other the minute they introduced us. Dominic and I had crossed paths several times before that during evening runs at LaFortune Park." She gave a weak smile. "Apparently, he noticed me as much I did him."

"I didn't know he was a runner."

Elaina nodded. "Dominic loved exercise. He was the picture of health."

And that's when I realized exactly what was bothering me.

The next week and a half was filled with overtime, Christmas shopping and decorating our apartment. The latter two were mostly an attempt to put me into a holiday spirit that I just wasn't feeling. Still, Grace had bounced back from our family tragedies and for that, I was grateful. We'd been so busy, that I'd nearly forgotten about the box of old photos from Uncle Rawley's attic until I noticed Grace's album lying open on the coffee table. Just beside it was a short stack of photos, presumably queued up for processing. There were still empty pages to be filled.

I took a seat on the edge of the sofa and picked up the album, just to see how much progress Grace had made since last time. Before I'd even moved it to my lap, my fingertips started to sting so badly I dropped the album on the cushion beside me.

Grace bounded into the room. "Mom, what happened?"

"Did you leave that outside or something? It was like picking up a sheet of ice." I rubbed my fingertips on my jeans to warm them up.

"What?"

"I'm telling you, it's frozen. I could barely touch it."

Grace frowned in that usual condescending teenager way and walked over to the sofa. She spread her hands over the open pages. After a moment, she picked it up, sat down, and placed it on her lap.

"Feels fine to me."

Just then, a frigid draft swept through the room. The stack of photos toppled across the coffee table. Some fell to the floor. My entire body jolted as a shiver tore through me. I looked at Grace. Her shoulders were hunched as she crossed her arms over her chest.

"You felt that, right?" I asked.

"Just like at Uncle Rawley's house—only colder."

I nodded toward the photo album. "And it started with those."

"What do you mean?"

"It didn't occur to me until after the funeral. Three people have died so far—Margot drowned, Aunt Josephine was hit by a car and Dominic was killed in a plane crash. We found photos of all three of them in that box."

Grace leaned forward. "We also found pictures of you, Grandmom, some of our cousins, Aunt Wendy and other people."

"There's a difference. Remember how we found the photo of Margot? It was stuck to a postcard of the ocean. The Polaroid of Aunt Josephine was stuck to a photo of a car—"

"And Dominic's photo was peeled off a picture of airplanes," Grace finished hastily. "I get it, Mom. I just think it's a stretch. Are you trying to say that the photos are killing people? It's coincidence, that's all."

I took a deep breath. I did that a lot when dealing with my daughter. "Whatever you think of the idea—"

"*Ridonkulous* comes to mind."

"Let me rephrase that. Regardless of what you think, I want all of these photos picked up, put back in the box, and left alone for a while. Can you do that for me?"

Grace rolled her eyes. "Mom, they already closed school for tomorrow. They're calling for, like, two feet of snow. I wanted to finish the album for Grandmom."

"I don't care. Put them away and don't touch them again until I say so. Is that clear?"

Grace sighed. "Fine."

"Besides, if you're off from school, you can help me clear the snow at Grandmom's house tomorrow."

"Joy." Grace gathered up the photos from the floor and heaved them into the box before plodding off her to room, muttering. "Merry-freakin-Christmas…"

Ah, teenagers.

"Burn them all."

"Hm?"

It took me a moment to realize that I'd heard a voice. It jarred me awake and honestly, I thought I'd dreamt it. It was just after 3:30 in the morning and I'd had a miserable night of tossing and turning. I don't think I'd slept for more than twenty minutes at a time. Just before waking up for the final time, I'd had a dream that there was a party in my apartment. No idea why, but there had been people everywhere—including recently deceased members of my family. Even Uncle Rawley! In fact, it was his voice that woke me.

That's also when I realized that my throat was sore. For me, that means I was coming down with something. I'd had my flu shot, but I was prone to colds or worse, bronchitis. Yeah, just what I needed right now. Merry-freakin-Christmas.

I tossed aside the covers and plodded my way to the kitchen for a glass of orange juice. As I stepped out into the living room, I heard the voice before I saw the face.

"Burn them all."

I couldn't scream. I had no voice. It came out as a squeal.

Even in the dim amber glow of the streetlight through the window, the dark baggy eyes, thick salt-and-pepper hair and long, narrow nose were unmistakable.

Uncle Rawley was sitting on my sofa.

"I'm so sorry," he said. "Just burn them all."

Finally, my brain kicked into gear, and I slapped the light switch to my right. The floor lamp turned on to reveal an empty living room.

"Mom?"

Now this time, I yelped with authority. I also spun around and pressed myself against the wall as my inner freaked-out-drama-queen came out.

Grace squinted against the light. "Whoa, Mom, chill out. What happened?"

"Nothing," I croaked. It seemed that my yelp took what was left of my voice. I decided to whisper as I collected myself. "I just thought I saw—uh, heard—something."

"Like what?"

"Voices, but it was probably the neighbors above or below. You might want to keep your distance, sweetie. I think I'm getting sick. I came out here for some orange juice."

"I'll get it for you."

"Don't worry about it. Why don't you go back to bed?"

"I can sleep late." Grace made her way to the kitchen and opened the fridge. "Look out the window."

I knelt on the sofa and leaned forward to part the curtains. There was easily a foot of snow on the ground already. It wasn't until I peered into the light of the streetlamp that I saw snowflakes the size of half dollars.

"Here you go—whoa."

I took the glass of orange juice from Grace and watched as she picked up a 4x6 photo from the floor. It wasn't until she turned it over that we realized it was yet two more photos stuck together face-to-face. Grace dropped onto the sofa and started peeling them apart.

"No, wait," I said, or tried to. I leaned over in a feeble attempt to pluck them from her grasp, but I wasn't quick enough. Grace twisted away from me and inspected the pictures. I slid down to sit beside her. I figured that if she got sick, too, then she had it coming.

"Wow." I saw myself at about eight years old, with my Mom and Santa Claus. We stood beside a fire truck that had been decked out for Christmas. A wreath hung on the passenger door, and pine garland was looped around the ladder hanging on the side. The picture had been taken on the street at night. Multicolored Christmas lights, the kind that flashed and chased, had been draped around the back of the truck.

I recognized the scene instantly as the Christmas parade that used to happen in my old neighborhood. Seeing this picture again made me miss those days far beyond mere nostalgia. The fire company had continued the parades for a few years after my father passed on, but it hadn't been the same with someone else playing Santa.

A much younger Uncle Rawley stared back at me from Grace's other hand. I stifled a gasp at what I knew was far from coincidence. Grace had found the photo right in front of the spot where his apparition had been sitting. Of course, I wasn't about to tell her that.

At the time the picture had been taken, Bella had still been alive. In the picture, the Rottweiler sat obediently beside Uncle Rawley in his side yard. My parents had forbidden me from going near her, but to be honest, she'd been far more pleasant to deal with than her cantankerous owner.

"This doesn't fit the pattern," I muttered to myself. Grace didn't believe my theory anyway. "All of the photos so far were one-to-one. One person, one object. This is different."

Grace shrugged. "Well, either you or Grandmom are going to be attacked by a dog, or hit by a fire truck. Should we flip a coin?"

I glared at her. No respect from my offspring. On second thought, if she were to get sick, she'd be home from school and whiny. "Thanks, I appreciate the support. I'm going back to bed."

———

The snow had stopped by dawn. By ten o'clock, the plow trucks had been through twice. Mustering all of my resolve, I took my life into my gloved hands and set out for Uncle Rawley's house to clear the snow while Grace ate cereal and checked Facebook. The realtor was coming to show the property to two buyers, one in the morning and other in the afternoon. And here I thought the holidays were a lousy time to put a house on the market.

Oh, what fun it was to ride in a front-wheel-drive sedan in the snow. I slid off-course about three times, including a 180-degree spin that sent me sideways into a mound of snow on the opposite side of the street. Thank God I was the only one on the road. Did I mention that my sore throat was now accompanied by a slight fever?

By the time I stopped at the top of the hill two blocks from the house, all confidence in my survival was out the window. As I rode my brakes down the slope, I heard the sirens and blaring horns of fire trucks in the distance. They were approaching fast. I glanced at my rearview mirror hoping they wouldn't be screaming down my back in a second, but the street behind me was empty.

As I neared the bottom of the hill, I pressed the brake pedal. The car slowed, but didn't stop. I tried pumping the brakes. That didn't help. I was sliding toward the intersection—right into the path of the approaching fire trucks! By this time, I was practically standing on the brake pedal, but the car continued dashing through densely packed snow on a collision course. The first truck passed in front of me with room to spare. I had my eyes on the second truck.

"Shit, shit, shit," I said. I don't know how many times I actually said that, but I'm sure a few justifiable "F-bombs" were also dropped. The second truck blared its horn at me. I replied by screaming at the top of my lungs, sore throat be damned, and it's debatable as to which one of us was louder.

Then my car stopped.

The second truck blew past my front bumper with about six inches to spare. I sat there for a few moments as both trucks turned out of view and disappeared. I closed my eyes and exhaled the breath I'd been holding. The sirens faded into the distance as I continued on.

The power was out at Uncle Rawley's house, which meant I had to walk through the place to open the garage door manually. I turned the key in the front door lock, but hesitated before opening it. What would I find inside? Would Uncle Rawley make another appearance? The fact that the sun was occasionally peeking out from behind the drifting clouds provided some comfort. I sure as hell wouldn't have the guts to go in there at night.

Once inside, I locked the door behind me and hurried through the family room, past the bathroom and spare bedroom and into the laundry room. It wasn't until I opened the door to the garage that I heard the ticking. I looked over my shoulder at the small plastic wall clock. I realized that we'd forgotten to take it with us last time, but that didn't bother me. What made the blood drain from my face was that it displayed the correct time, even though it had stopped last week along with every other clock in the house. *You got a job to do. Get it done and get the hell out.* I forced myself to turn away.

The musty two-car garage was so damn cold, I could have stored perishables in it. Uncle Rawley's year-old Chevy Impala was still parked on one side. He'd left that to me, too. Since Grace would be able to drive next year, I'd planned to let her use my car and I would take the Impala. I was comfortable with that. After all, it wasn't like anyone had died in it.

On the other side of the garage were Uncle Rawley's workbench, tools, tractor mower and most importantly, the snow blower. It was a large machine with levers that moved in every direction. I'd been smart enough to research the model online from my phone when Grace and I were there last. I'd figured out how to start it and mix the gas/oil fuel it needed.

I reached up and pulled the red rope to open the garage door. It barely budged. I walked backward, putting my weight into it—which wasn't much, I might add. Finally, after a crackling of ice, the door began to rise and I pulled it over my head until it stopped.

I looked out to the driveway—or I would have, had I not locked eyes with a full-grown Rottweiler that erupted in a tantrum of vicious barking and growling. I fell back over the snow blower and landed on my ass on the concrete floor. The Rottweiler, muscular and apparently angry as hell, paced back and forth just outside the garage, as if it had been waiting for me. I expected it to lunge at me, but it never moved beyond the concrete threshold. It just glared at me with black eyes that narrowed threateningly as it bared a set of long, pointy pearlies.

"Ike!" a deep voice called out. The demon dog turned to look, but continued its patrol in front of me, launching into a second tirade of barking the minute I tried to pick myself up.

A plump old man in a red-and-black checkered coat and red knitted cap stepped into view and leaned over the dog. "Ike, shut the hell up!"

And with that, the Rottweiler fell silent.

The man looked at me. Between bushy white mustache and matching beard, his mouth opened in surprise.

"Oh my God, I am so sorry, sweetheart." He hurried into the garage and extended a black-gloved hand, which I gratefully accepted. He pulled me to my feet as if I were a rag doll. "Are you hurt?"

"Just my pride."

"I'm sorry about Ike. He must've gotten out when I was clearing the snow. I'm Nick. I live two houses up."

"Claudia Adamski. Rawley was my uncle."

"Really? He never talked much about his family. Hell, Rawley never talked much about anything. No offense, but he never really seemed like a happy fella."

I nodded. "Yeah, that was Rawley."

"Well, he's in a better place. Can't say I'm too far behind. Then again, who is?" As he chuckled, his whole body shook like a bowl of—hey, wait a minute. I suddenly remembered the pictures that Grace had peeled apart last night. Fire truck, dog, Santa Claus?

Nick walked back outside. "Anyway, take care and sorry again about old Ike."

"No problem, sir. Merry Christmas."

"You, too." Nick waved then snapped his fingers at the Rottweiler. "Get moving, Ike!"

Ike and I exchanged parting glances before he turned and bolted up the street.

Well, Grace, you called it—almost. There ain't gonna be another death in this family today!

———

After clearing the sidewalk and driveway without further incident, I called my Mom to let her know that I was coming over to do the same for her, but there was no answer.

Thirty minutes later, I stood on her porch and rang the doorbell for the fourth time. Finally, I pulled the key from my purse and let myself in. I heard the electronic screeching as soon as I stepped through the door. It was the smoke alarm on the second floor! I ran to the bottom of the steps and looked up into a thick gray fog. The stench of burning plastic and wood was just beginning to permeate the entire house.

"Mom!" I called out to no avail. I lifted my scarf over my nose and mouth and charged up the stairs. To the left, the master bedroom was empty as was the bathroom. That's when I heard the dog barking. Yes, another one. I turned right and peered into the haze. Near the end of the hallway, a Rottweiler stood whimpering over my mother's prone form. As I ran toward them, the dog backed away—and vanished into the smoke.

The spare bedroom was on fire. Mom had used it as a storage room for years, everything from holiday decorations to old books to spare linens, you name it. Obviously, some of it was flammable.

I grabbed my mother under her arms and dragged her to the top of the stairs. She had always been petite, and I was never more grateful for it as I lifted her and carried her down to the first floor. Something made me turn and glance up the steps. The Rottweiler was there—along with Uncle Rawley. They seemed to form out of the smoke.

I said the first thing that popped into my head. "You did this, you fucking bastard!"

Belle lowered her head and whimpered again.

"I'm sorry," Rawley said. "It's out of my control. If you want to end this, either burn the photos," he pointed to my mother, "or make her tell the truth."

And with that, they were gone.

Christmas Day

The women in my family had always been tough broads. My mother recovered from smoke inhalation with no respiratory issues. She'd been reading in bed when the hallway smoke alarm sounded. By that time, the spare bedroom had already been ablaze for several minutes. Apparently, I'd arrived seconds after my Mom had passed out.

According to the investigators, the fire had been caused by faulty wiring in the electric baseboard radiator, which was odd considering that my Mom had never turned on the heat in that room.

Of course, I had my own theories on what—or who—had ignited the fire, but I kept those to myself.

Nevertheless, we made a valiant attempt to put our worries aside on Christmas Day. After morning mass, I dropped off Grace and Mom at the apartment. I had one last errand to run.

The drive to Uncle Rawley's lacked the death-defying adventure of the previous trip. In fact, all was quiet as I pulled into the driveway. I popped the trunk where I'd stashed the box of photographs on Christmas Eve—along with a bottle of lighter fluid and a pack of wooden matches. Uncle Rawley had a metal burning barrel in his backyard, and I intended to take his advice.

I stuck around long enough to watch the photos shrivel into blackened scraps. It occurred to me then that Uncle Rawley hadn't simply dumped old photos into a box and put them out of sight. He'd also packed it full of deep bitterness and hatred that had festered during the last fifteen years of his life. I honestly wished I knew why. I couldn't help but to think of that summer night after my father's death, when my mother and Uncle Rawley had exploded at one another. As I started back toward my car, I resolved to find out the truth about that.

Halfway across the yard, I stopped at the sight of the Rottweiler that suddenly appeared in the driveway. Without turning my head, I looked right and left for Uncle Rawley, but he was nowhere to be seen.

"Ike! What the hell are you doing?"

I let out the breath I'd been holding and shook my head. The dog ran off.

I cranked up the Christmas tunes all the way home, thankful that it was finally over—

———

—and then I remembered the album that Grace had put together. By the time I stepped through the door, Mom was already paging through her Christmas present.

"This is wonderful, Grace," she said. "I can't believe Rawley had all of these hidden away."

"There were others." Grace shot a sidelong glance at me. "But they were stuck together and kinda ruined."

I nodded to her as I made my way into the kitchen. Grace wasn't happy that I had denied her the chance to complete her project, but Mom was tickled with what she had. As far as I'm concerned, it was a win-win.

"I already looked in on the chicken, Claudia," my Mom said. "Have you seen this album yet?"

"I'll look at it later."

"Oh, I know you're not the sentimental type, but would it kill you to look at a few pictures?"

Grace cleared her throat.

If only you knew. That reminded me. There was one last nagging question that only my mother could answer.

I asked Grace to join me in the kitchen. "Did you call your dad yet and wish him a Merry Christmas?"

"I'm going to see him tomorrow."

"I know, but I think he'd like to hear from you today. Besides, I need to talk to your grandmother about something."

Grace sighed as she reached for the cordless phone on the wall. "Fine. Then can we open the rest of the gifts?"

I kissed her on the forehead. "Absolutely."

With that, I stepped out to the living room and took a seat next to my Mom on the sofa. "Mom, I have a question about Uncle Rawley. After dad died, I remember the two of you had a pretty severe blow out. At the time, you said it was about Dad's will, but you never told me the details. What really happened?"

The color drained from her face as she smiled awkwardly. "Claudia, it's Christmas. I don't want to talk about old family problems now. That's all in the past."

"Mom, please. I have a reason for asking."

She looked down at the photo album with a sigh. It was nearly thirty seconds before she worked up the courage to speak. "I had an affair with your Uncle Rawley."

"What?"

"I wanted to break it off when your father died." Tears welled up in her eyes as she continued. "I felt guilty, ashamed. Rawley took it hard. He was so angry. That's what the argument was really about, nothing to do with your father's will. I'm sorry I lied to you back then, but I didn't have the guts to tell you. I was afraid you'd hate me. I know how much you idolized your father, but we'd grown apart while you were away at college. You weren't around to see it. I never stopped loving him, Claudia, I swear. I was just confused and very lonely. I can't say that straying with Rawley was the best decision I ever made."

You ain't kidding! As my mind was trying to grasp what my ears were hearing, my stomach started tying itself into a giant knot. I wanted to puke. What the hell did she see in Uncle Rawley? "Did anyone else know about it?"

Mom nodded. "One of the neighbors...found out, let's just say. They blabbed to your Aunt Josephine. She confronted me about it, but I denied it at the time. I don't think she believed me. She shunned Rawley after that. Then those neighbors moved away."

"Which neighbors?"

"Oh, I don't remember their last name. You used to play with their daughter. I think her name was—"

"Margot."

"Yes, that was it. Claudia, I'm so sorry. I'll understand if you're disappointed in me. I'd hoped the subject would never come up."

Well, you asked for it, dumb-ass. Yes, I did. No wonder why Uncle Rawley had turned his back on the family, not that I'm defending him. He had betrayed his own brother, my father. Now, after a decade and a half, it all made sense.

Grace returned to the living room. "Dad's coming at nine tomorrow morning to pick me up. He told me to wish you a Merry Christmas."

Yeah, Merry-freakin'-Christmas.

PARALLAX
by Amanda Headlee

When we have lost everything, and we stand in the darkest hour of our lives, that is when fate will smile upon us, bringing us back into the light. Our sorrows and bad luck turn to fortune and happiness. Our purpose here on this plane is to live a life of understanding and knowledge, not to suffer an eternity of depression. We have but one life to live and we must experience all that this life has to offer.

This is what our mothers and fathers have taught us since birth. Sadly, our parents are not always right.

———

The musty oak doors are held slightly ajar by rusted hinges as he stands in front of their mass. They sway slightly in the midnight breeze, creaking as they shift to and fro. The crisp air would tingle the skin of anyone who stood in this place. The doors lead to the narthex of a desolate, abandoned abbey lost in the woodlands of County Kilkenny. The abbey's bulk stands out, massive and black, against the starlit sky. Yet, when the fog rolls in, the abbey becomes a shadow concealed by a veil of gloom.

On this silent night, no creatures stir. Not even the lone soul who stands at the abbey's doorway.

Silent, lost in the rhythm of his breathing. His exhalation mimics the sound of the wind as it rattles through the barren trees outside the abbey. He contemplates why his feet tread so lightly upon this hallowed ground, so far from civilization. So far from the place that was once his home.

The reverberation of years gone by makes seismic waves within his brain. He gasps in pain and collapses to the stone floor as memories flood back from a place where he had dammed them up. Life, happiness, love, sadness, anger, death. His memories always follow this cycle. Whenever he finds a place that offers respite, the black reaper comes to take it all away. She follows him wherever he goes, making his life a faded dream. Why just the other day, as he worked a newsstand in Kilkenny, she appeared again.

———————

"Parallax. 'Tis me favorite word." The balding man grinned at Ciarán from the opposite side of the newsstand counter. "Ever heard of it before?"

"Nah," Ciarán mumbled as he counted back the man's change.

"It's the apparent shiftin' of an object against a background," the man explained, "as viewed from different angles."

"I don't understan'," Ciarán said, confused, then curious. For once, someone was paying attention to him. Someone was actually speaking to him as a living person, not just a shell of a soul.

"Okay." The man set down his newspaper and coffee on the counter and held his hand up with the palm facing away from his face. "Ya ever play that game when you're a kid where ya hold yer hand in front of yer face and open yer eyes back and forth?"

"Yeah," Ciarán uttered, bemused, watching the man open and close each eye independently.

"You see how with the openin' of me right eye I can see ya standing to the right of me hand? Yet, when I close me right eye and open me left eye, ya disappear behind me hand."

"Nah, I don't see, because yer lookin' at me."

"Oh, give me yer hand," the man grumbled, grabbing Ciarán's right hand and holding it up in front of Ciarán's face. "Now, blink yer eyes back and forth. No, not that quick. Take yer time and examine the background behind yer hand." He paused to take a sip of his coffee, watching Ciarán blink his eyes back and forth. "Okay, you seem t' be enjoying this a wee bit too much." The man said with a smile.

"And this is parallax?"

"You got it, me boy," the man beamed. "Use this as a reminder that not everythin' that you see with yer eyes is real. Sometimes our eyes distort reality."

"Makes life seem like a giant illusion," Ciarán mumbled.

"Exactly. Like when our true purpose on this Earth turns out to be not what we expected."

"I'm sorry?" Ciarán quavered.

"We never realize our purpose in life until we die. We walk through life seein' illusions of what we think our meanin' of life is. We'll never be told why we're here until the day we die."

The man smiled and picked up his coffee from the counter.

With a nod, Ciarán smiled back at him in silent gratitude.

"Anytime, paperboy." The man turned, coffee in hand, and walked towards the street. Ciarán was left in awe.

He acknowledged me, Ciarán thought. It was at that moment that he looked down to the newsstand counter and realized that the man had left his newspaper. Ciarán quickly picked it up and headed towards the departing man.

"Sir, SIR!" Ciarán yelled and waved his arms in the air at the man.

The man stopped halfway across the street and turned to see what the commotion was about. Suddenly, he was pitched into the air by a passing motorist. Ciarán watched in horror as the man's body twisted in a gruesome midair somersault. His face contorted in sheer pain as blood bubbled from his lips. The coffee cup burst apart in the air above him and the liquid rained down on his body in black droplets.

When the man's aerial ballet ended, his broken body struck the ground, face to God.

Lost in the horror of the accident, Ciarán shivered, chilled by the presence that appeared standing over the man in a mass of flowing black. The details of her body were indistinguishable, but her reason for being in Kilkenny that day was unmistakable.

This was not the first time Ciarán had seen the specter in his short twenty-three years of life. He would never forget the first time she had appeared...

———

In the hospital, Ciarán sat on his father's lap beside his mother's bed. He held her rough hand with his tiny, insignificant one. He could hear his father's voice rolling lightly, like the distant sound of thunder, as he spoke to the nurse. Ciarán watched as she injected a solution into the IV catheter attached to his mother's hand.

"Maybe I should take him down to the cafeteria to get some ice cream," the nurse suggested.

"No, he needs to be wit' his family. He needs to be here wit' me," his father vacantly responded.

"But do ye want to expose a child to this at such a young age?"

"Ye cannot run from death." Those words reverberated through Ciarán like needles pricking his skin.

That was when the dark lady appeared, sweeping into the room with an air of grace and priority. Blackness, like mist, swirled around her shadowy form as she looked down upon Ciarán's mother, who lay dying in a hospital bed after giving birth to his younger sister. Her approach went unnoticed by all but Ciarán. The sudden coldness of his mother's hand made his small body tremble in sadness and fright.

Ciarán slowly turned to look at his father, while keeping the dark lady in his peripheral vision. His father was oblivious to her arrival as he chatted with the nurse about his mother's medication.

"Da," Ciarán whispered.

His father placed a hand on Ciarán's shoulder, which meant not to interrupt. His father continued talking to the nurse, who was now standing right next to the dark lady. Neither of them saw her.

"Ciarán." His name hissed upon the dry air as he was called out.

The dark lady stood on the opposite side of his mother so that she could stand over both of them. Ciarán's father and the nurse faded into the background and ceased to exist. This was a lesson meant only for Ciarán.

He watched in awe as the lady leaned over his mother and stroked her stomach with a glowing hand. His eyes darted up to the lady's head. In the black hollow of her face, he stood transfixed by her eyes. They swarmed with a sparkle of stars and galaxies, bursting supernovae and collapsing black holes. Life flowed warmly through Ciarán's veins as he gazed into the eyes of Death. But ice quickly encased his heart at the echoing scream of his mother as her womb convulsed and her life hemorrhaged out onto the floor.

———

Those eyes haunted Ciarán wherever he went. He saw them at the passing of every life with whom he shared an emotional connection. He could not gaze into the eyes of others without seeing her, seeing what she did, how she harvested.

How she reaped.

———

Niamh giggled at him from somewhere within the barn.

"Niamh, ye come out here before I git angry," Ciarán demanded of his sister.

"Nay, Ciarán, I am livin' here with Embarr now." A flowery voice trilled behind the slatted barn door.

"What now?" he asked her, perplexed. "Embarr, who be that?"

"Why, my magical white horse that will whisk us off to Tír na nÓg." The door to the barn flew open. "Come, brother, run away wit' me."

She stood looking at him, dressed in a white flowing smock, hands placed pertly on her hips. The noon sun caught her curly red hair, making it shimmer with its rays. Behind her, safely in his stall, stood Mister O'Neill's prized white steed, chomping away at the oats Niamh had fed him. The horse stared at Ciarán with its big black eyes. Like burning coal they were, Ciarán shivered. He turned his attention back to his little sister. Had he not known she was only six years old, he would have sworn the voice that came from her lips was that of a much older girl. Young Niamh's world was just as affected as his. The tragedies that they had both experienced wore on their young lives.

"Ah, Niamh," he groaned. "I'll not be fancying yer dreams again."

"They are not dreams, Ciarán," she protested. "I am the real Niamh. And this be me Embarr." She pointed to the horse, trying to convince Ciarán that she was one of the queens of the fabled land of the young, Tír na nÓg. His sister fancied herself as the Niamh of myth. It is said that the fabled queen had crossed the Western Sea on her gallant white steed, Embarr, to seek out the mortal poet Oisín. For Niamh had been in love with him and wished to take him back with her to Tír na nÓg. Eventually, Oisín agreed to go, but not before promising his father that he would someday return. With that, the star-crossed lovers had traveled to the land of Tír na nÓg .

After three years in the realm of eternal youth, Oisín decided to return to the mortal world to keep his promise. Niamh had given Oisín her steed, Embarr, to ride to the mortal world, but warned him that should his feet touch the soil, he would instantly wither with age and die. For each year he had spent in Tír na nÓg, one hundred years had passed in the mortal world. Upon his return, Oisín found his father's house abandoned and in shambles. After mourning his father, the poet left the ruins of his childhood to travel across the land. During his journey, an unfortunate accident triggered Embarr to break, causing Oisín to fall—and suffer the fatal consequences of his decision to leave Tír na nÓg.

Ciarán noted that his sister's dream of becoming the mythical queen had come into full effect about a month ago, though she'd always loved hearing the story the way their father told it.

———

After Niamh's birth, their father brought his children home from the hospital to a silent, empty house. The death of their mother just a few days before had worn on Ciarán and his father. They could not comprehend that she was gone. Ciarán would never again hear her angelic voice or smell the hint of lavender about her. He would especially miss the lullaby she had sung to him every night.

She would start by humming as she tucked him in, giving him his worn teddy to hold. Then she would sit on the bed next to him and sing the Ballyeamon Cradle Song while lightly running her fingers from his temple around the back of his ear. His eyes would grow heavy as her song whisked him away to dreamland. He could never stay awake until the end of the song, but deep down he would always hear her whisper "I love ya, me sweet boy," as she kissed his check.

———

Ciarán's father had been unable to cope with a newborn and a young boy of five. There were occasions when he would disappear into the living room, sit in his tattered blue armchair, and just stare at the wall. When these spells had first started, Ciarán was able to stir his father by screaming at him. Later, only Niamh's cries of hunger or attention would rouse him. Now, not even the baby's needs would bring him into the present. With his disheveled black hair, unshaven face, and unwashed, rumpled clothes, Ciarán's father looked barely alive.

Within three months of their mother's death, Ciarán and Niamh's Nan arrived. She was their mother's mother. She cooked, cleaned, and took care of Niamh. Despite her cheerfulness, something about the way she talked made Ciarán believe she was hollow and on the verge of coming under a spell like his father. A few months after Nan had come to live with them, their father moved to his bedroom and never came out until after midnight. It had nearly been six months since Ciarán saw his father awake and walking about the house.

Most nights it would take Ciarán hours to fall asleep. Without the love of his mother, insomnia would prevail. On the rare occasions when he would drift off, he saw his mother's beautiful, full smile. She spoke to him, reached for him, and then suddenly screamed at the top of her lungs, "Run, run!"

A swirling black mist coalesced at her feet and boiled up around her body, overtaking her until the Lady Reaper materialized. She stood beside his mother, stroking her stomach.

"Ciarán… Time has come." Her voice rasped in his ear, sending him into panic. He screamed for his mother to no avail.

"Her time has passed, your time has come. Come, come with me, Ciarán." The wraith's glowing hand reached out, grasping his wrist. All feeling drained from Ciarán's small body.

"No!" He screamed, waking with a start.

The same dream visited him every night. Tonight was no different, yet Ciarán was especially bothered by it. For this time, when he awoke, there was a small bruise around his right wrist.

As he began to inspect it, trying to shake off the nightmare, Niamh began to wail. After a few minutes of listening to her cries, Ciarán realized that no one was waking to get her. He slipped out of bed and walked down the hall to her room.

She stood in her crib, her tear-streaked, red face looking at him. The tuft of red hair on her head was disheveled and her blue eyes were glassy from crying.

"Kirn," she cried when he walked into the room. His name had been her first word, though technically it was not pronounced correctly. "Up." She held her arms out wanting to be held.

"Niamh, I can't git you out," he said to her. He was still too small to reach the top of the crib and not quite strong enough to lift her. "Why don't ye lie down and rest yer wee head."

She began to whimper at him and stomp her right foot. It was her new thing to do when she did not get her way.

"Come on now. Be a good lass." He laughed at her antics. "If ye be a good wee sprite, I'll sing ye a song."

She seemed to like the attention. She cooed at him and fell back on her bum in the crib. She rolled over onto her belly and looked at her older brother. Ciarán pulled the old wooden rocking chair from the corner and positioned it next to the crib. He put his arms through the bars and pulled her pink blanket up over her body.

"Now, be a good lass." He said to her as he sat back in the rocking chair and began to sing.

Rest tired eyes a while
Sweet is thy baby's smile
Angels are guarding
And they watch o'er thee

Sleep, sleep grah mo chree
Here on your mamma's knee
Angels are guarding
And they watch o'er thee

As he continued to sing the lullaby, he reached through the bars again and lightly stroked from her temple around her ear.

———

Their father stood in the hallway, watching his son and daughter. A lump formed in his throat as he listened to the lullaby that his wife had once sung. He slid his jacket from his shoulders and quietly walked into the nursery, not wanting to disturb the scene. He stood behind his son and became lost in the lyrics, lost in the memories of his wife. It had been over a year since her death and he had allowed the moments of his life to slip away since the day she passed.

As Ciarán finished his song, Niamh's soft breathing was the only sound in the room. Her face was calm, at peace, a face he had hardly looked upon since the day she was brought into the world. He realized what he had nearly lost. Ciarán turned in the wooden rocking chair and looked up at his father.

"Da?"

"I'm home, me boy. I'm home."

The spell had been broken.

"Now Da, please tell me th' story again," whined Niamh.

"Oh, come now, lass. Ye've heard the story a hundred times."

"But it's such a lovely story and I want to hear it every day, for the rest of me life."

"Not the Queen Niamh story," Ciarán groaned as he pulled away from the refrigerator.

"Is there any other?" His father chuckled.

Since their father had come out of his depression, he had finally taken on the responsibility of raising his children. In return, Ciarán and his sister had grown to love him, for he was once again the man Ciarán knew before their mother died. Niamh, now truly smitten with her father's love, never left his side. Wherever he went, Niamh was not far behind. Ciarán had come to respect his father and understood the spell that he had fallen under. He never harbored any ill will toward him and had immediately forgiven his father when he had finally recovered. Their lives were whole once again. Ciarán finally felt like he was home.

Nan had eventually returned home, but not before making their father promise to call her if the depression threatened to overwhelm him again. Even though he had assured her that he would never be bewitched again, Nan's expression had made it clear that she did not believe him.

Before she departed, Nan had left Ciarán and Niamh with a note and made them promise to call her everyday so that she would know that they were okay. Once Nan was gone, they ran up to Ciarán's room to read the note. Ciarán allowed Niamh to open the envelope and pull out the slip of paper contained inside. In her feathery handwriting, Nan simply wrote "Always remember where your home is".

Ciarán returned to the kitchen after his daily phone call to Nan.

"Does the old biddy approve that ye two are still breathin'?" His father asked him.

"Aye, and she sends her love."

"Aw, isn't that lovely."

"Now will ye tell the story?" Niamh demanded, her long red curls bounced as she stomped her right foot on the floor.

"Ah, this young lass always gits her way." His father rolled his eyes. "Ah, well. There is a love story from the old world about the beautiful Niamh, daughter of the great sea god Manannán mac Lir, and the Irish poet Oisín ..." His father began the story that he told Niamh every morning. She was enthralled and dreamed of running away to Tír na nÓg to be the real Queen Niamh. For that was her namesake. Their mother had been fascinated by the religion of the old world, and since their father had chosen his son's name, she had taken it upon herself to name their unborn baby girl. Niamh was the name she had chosen because she so loved the tale of Tír na nÓg. Ciarán believed his mother had fantasized of running away to the land of the young, a trait that seemed to be passed on to his sister.

"Ah, now ye kiddies, isn't it be time that ye were off?" His father finished telling Niamh her morning tale, and hurried to get them ready for the day. Ciarán was in the Sixth Class of primary school, while Niamh was in the Senior Infant class.

"Da, that was the best telling of Queen Niamh ever." Niamh's blue eyes shone as she looked at her father with adoration. She was right. Their father had been so animated and had held Niamh tightly as he wove the tale. His grey eyes had looked back and forth between Niamh and Ciarán, ensuring that he had a captive audience. Though Ciarán was overjoyed to see how happy Niamh was this morning, he was ever so curious as to why his father had changed his whole tone in telling the story. His voice was usually filled with a little annoyance. The storytelling had literally become a chore over the years as it was recited daily, but this morning it was like he was telling the tale for the very first time.

Lost in his thoughts, it took Ciarán several seconds to notice, and when he did the pit of his stomach sunk to his feet. Even in the bright light of the kitchen, a black shadow passed behind his father. Ciarán quickly closed his eyes and willed the dark lady away. When he opened them again, she was gone.

Me eyes are playing tricks again, he thought, but was not fully convinced. Deep down, he knew he should not leave his father's side today.

"Da, I don' feel too well. Can I stay home?" Ciarán whined in an attempt to make himself sound ill. His father did not even turn to acknowledge him.

"Nay," his father said sternly. He stood with his back to them and gathered the children's coats and bags. "Take Niamh and go right to school. No funny business this morn."

A lump formed in Ciarán's throat. His father's face became hollow and pale. Ciarán feared that he was falling under the spell again.

"Ye kids are… well, I just want ye to know that I love ye," their father said as he handed them their jackets. He assisted Niamh with hers and once it was on, he hugged her tightly. "Ye know, sometimes adults do things and there are no explanations for our actions. Just know that we have always loved ye both."

He kissed Niamh on the head and she beamed, blissfully ignorant to what her father was really saying.

"Da?" Ciarán frowned. His eyes panned across the kitchen, praying that the sight of her was only his imagination.

"Ye are growin' into a fine man." His father placed a weathered hand on Ciarán's head. "Th' world is yer oyster, me boy." A tear escaped the corner of his father's right eye. "Now be a good lad, and take care of yer sister."

Niamh giggled. "Da, Ciarán is only walking me to school."

"Right he is, me lass."

"Da? I…" Ciarán questioned again, trying to find the words to convince his father to allow him to stay at home. He did not understand the sudden change in his father's behavior, coupled with the fear that he may have seen her.

But she was nowhere in sight. Aside from the three of them standing in the kitchen, all was quiet. Nothing was wrong. *Da's just showing us love. You're just overthinking things because you're afraid.* Ciarán brushed off his fear. He knew full well that there was nothing wrong with his father. The spell had been broken and it would not return. He grabbed his father around his waist and hugged tightly.

"I love ye, Da."

Ciarán closed the door behind them and led his sister to the front gate, allowing Niamh through first. Once through, he turned and slowly closed the gate, latching it behind them. He looked up at their home. The stone mortar was cracked and desperately needed repointing, but still held strong against the elements. The shutters were a crisp blue, but the paint was slowly peeling. It had been Ciarán's mother who painted them last. As such, his father would never restore them. The garden bloomed brightly and was a distraction from the sight of the house. Gardening was something that Ciarán had taken up two years ago in memory of his mother. Yes, all was quiet and quaint. His father must have walked up to his bedroom to get ready because the light shone through the window. Ciarán stepped back on the sidewalk to gain a full view of the house.

He looked up at his father's window and saw his shadow move across from the left side of the window to the right. A moment later, a second shadow followed.

"No!" Ciarán cried out.

"What?" Niamh looked to her brother in alarm.

"Niamh, I need you to run to school as fast as ye can and get help. Do not stop for anything." He grabbed her by the shoulders and burned his gaze into her. "Do ye understan'?"

"Ye-yes," she stammered. Tears began to stream down her face.

"God, not again." Ciarán swore as he threw open the wrought-iron gate, ran across the front yard, and burst through the front door.

"Da!" He screamed as he raced up the stairs towards his father's bedroom. *Please no, not again,* his mind cried as he ran down the hall.

He grabbed the doorknob, wrenched it hard, kicked the door open and stopped dead in his tracks. In the far corner of the bedroom sat his father. The Lady Reaper stood next to him, glowing hand on his disheveled, greying hair.

"Get away from him," Ciarán growled. His eyes were like daggers staring into the blackness of her face.

"Ciarán, come." She beckoned him with her free hand. "Watch." Her voice was a dry hiss upon the air.

"I told you—"

"Ciarán," his father sobbed. "Leave now. Don't come back in here." Tears streamed down his father's face. "Ye cannot see me like this."

Ciarán locked eyes with his father, but could already tell that he was not in the present. Taking a step back, he fully observed the scene. That was when Ciarán noticed the gun in his father's right hand.

"Me boy, just leave. I cannot hold on any longer. I cannot do this anymore for you kids. I ain't strong enough. I need yer ma." He sobbed as he raised the barrel of the pistol to his right temple.

Atop his head, her hand continued to glow in soft pulses of light.

"Stop makin' him do this!" Ciarán took a step closer. He was prepared to attack, even if it meant ripping her arm from her body. She had taken his mother. He would not allow her to take his father.

"Always remember where your home is." His father said as he locked his eyes onto Ciarán's for the last time. "Ye cannot run from death."

"No, silly," Ciarán said in a soothing voice, trying to pull Niamh back into reality. "You are just Niamh, me Niamh, me sister."

"Nay!" She shouted at her brother as she slammed the barn door shut. "I'm leaving for Tír na nÓg without you. I don't wanna be here anymore."

He could hear her sniffling on the other side of the door. And then the wailing began. Ciarán could hear Mister O'Neill's horse snort in annoyance at the high-pitched crying. Her tears were for the father that she had lost and the mother that she had never met.

Almost one month ago today, Ciarán stared at the bloodied, lifeless body of their father on the floor. She had been there, and Ciarán knew it was she who had forced his father to kill himself. He cursed her every second of the day. Raw hate seethed through his body at the thought of her. She had taken his mother and his father, and taunted him as she stole them. After their quick deaths, she had vanished into thin air, as though she had never been there.

He had stood in his father's bedroom for what seemed like an eternity, staring at the bloody corpse crumpled in the corner. He couldn't bring himself to move closer or turn away. He had just stared, lost in his anger and fear. *Always remember where your home is.* The words were on the note from Nan and among the last his father had said to him. Home. Ciarán's home was gone. It was nothing more than an empty building now, a shell that had once housed happy souls. Home would never be seen by his eyes again. It would be forever out of his reach.

The silence that came from within the barn shook Ciarán from his memories.

"Niamh?" He called out.

The girl and the horse were silent, save for a little shuffling here and there.

"Niamh?" He called again. He drew himself closer to the barn door and peeked through a crack in the slats. Though it was dark inside, every so often he would catch a flash of white moving about. On the ground, he saw the board that was normally used to hold the door closed. The silly lass hadn't even locked him out, just slammed the door in his face.

"Ciarán." The sound of his name on the wind made him stop cold before pushing the door open.

"Ciarán."

"No…" He breathed. "No, ye fuckin' bitch!"

He threw open the doors and in the middle of the barn stood Mister O'Neill's horse with Niamh mounted on his back. With her hand on Niamh's leg, the black wraith looked at him. Her undulating form swirled about the ground, entwining the horse's hooves. The horse's eyes were so wide that the whites flashed as it looked about the barn in fear. Ears twitching and nostrils flaring, the horse looked to bolt any second.

Torn between attacking the reaper and pulling his sister from the horse, Ciarán boldly took a step forward. The wraith watched his every move. Niamh was stroking the horse's neck and speaking to it in low, hushed murmurs. She was oblivious to the imminent danger.

"Please, just let her go," Ciarán said through gritted teeth, trying to barter with the wraith.

"Ciarán," she hissed, grabbing his full attention. Her hand began to glow with a familiar soft, pulsing light.

"God, no!" He screamed and jolted forward to rip her away from his sister.

The horse whinnied.

"Embarr, go!" Niamh ordered as she kicked the horse's flank. The white steed bolted past Ciarán, knocking him to the ground. He quickly jumped to his feet and took off after his sister across the meadow towards the lake that lay behind Mister O'Neill's property.

Niamh crossed the Western Sea on her gallant white steed, Embarr, from the mortal world to Tír na nÓg. He could hear his father's voice reciting the myth.

"Niamh!" Ciarán screamed as it dawned on him that his sister was riding the horse towards the lake. "Niamh, no!"

"I'm runnin' from death!" Her voice yelled back at him. "Go home, Ciarán."

His heart pumped in his chest as he ran faster, in a gallant attempt to catch the horse. The reaper had touched his sister—and everyone she touched had died. *Oh God, not Niamh. Please not me Niamh.*

Blood pounded in his ears as he pushed himself past the point of exhaustion. His breath became ragged and his peripheral vision blurred, yet he never slowed. He was focused on his sister, racing toward the cliff that overlooked the lake.

And then Niamh and the horse leapt into the air.

Ciarán continued to chase down his sister, but watched in awe as the horse began to run on the wind. Is she really Queen Niamh?

He burst through the tall grass of the field at the edge of the cliff in time to see the horse and Niamh begin their descent. The horror suddenly dawned on Ciarán. The horse, fearing that it was being chased by a predator, took a leap of faith from the cliff.

Queen Niamh and Embarr crashed through the crystalline surface of the lake, never to walk in the mortal world again.

The stone of the abbey is cold and crudely hewn by human hands, built in a time before modern machinery. Outside, surrounding the vacant yard, broken remnants of what was once a stone barrier marks the abbey's property. Inside the barrier, the only things that belong to the abbey are the small, moss covered graveyard and the bodies that rest there. The stone path that once led to the large oak doors is broken and overgrown. Small steps, uneven and crumbling with age, lead up to the façade where Ciarán sits. Bits of smashed stone shingles from the steeple lay strewn about the ground. The smell of must and decomposition rises out of the moist soil.

The aroma of the decay makes the bile rise in the back of Ciarán's throat. He cannot escape. Everywhere he turns, looks, smells, there she is. His life has continued to follow the same circle since the first time he looked into her eyes. Life, happiness, love, sadness, anger, death. She controls it;

he has no power. He sits cold and alone at the door to the abbey, hugging his knees to his chest. His breathing mimics the wind blowing through the woodland's branches. Fog rises from the warm, damp earth and forms a ring about the full moon. *A halo*, Ciarán thinks as he smiles wanly upon the light that shines through the darkness.

He sits for hours, cold and stiff upon the abandoned abbey's façade. Loneliness engulfs him like it would a lost sailor swept out into the dark, glacial Arctic Sea, where crashing waves merge with the night sky, snuffing out the horizon of land, making home undistinguishable. Damn the parallax of the Earth, he curses in his mind. Home was just a figment of his imagination. He could circle the Earth hundreds of times, but home would always lie in shadow, hidden beyond his sight.

From his pocket, he pulls his last cigarette and nestles it securely between his lips. He pulls a match from his shoe and strikes it against the stone. It sizzles for a second and casts a brief light on his face. He lifts the small flame to his mouth, burning the end of his cigarette. He breathes in, then exhales toxins into the night sky.

With four drags, he grows tired of the stale, smoky taste and rubs out the spark on the façade's stone. An icy breeze trails the smoke of the smoldering cigarette up Ciarán's right arm. It tickles the hair by his ear and rushes past with enough force to slam shut the large oak doors. Ciarán leaps to his feet and looks about, confused by the noise that has shattered the silence. He pulls his jacket tightly around his body and searches for the source. All is silent except for the moaning of the wind in the trees. Mumbling to himself, he settles back down outside the doors, hugs his knees to his chest, and hangs his head.

The whisper of his name on the wind sends ice through his heart. Bewildered, he snaps his head up and looks around again. Through the darkness, his eyes comb the area. He takes in a long, slow breath as he looks toward the graveyard. There, he finally finds what he seeks. Haloed by the moon, encased in Earth's mist, she stands atop the hallowed grounds, beckoning to him.

"Enough! What do you want from me?" Ciarán demands.

"Ciarán, Ciiiaráaánn," she whispers hauntingly upon the wind.

"Please," Ciarán whimpers. "Just leave me in peace." He crumples to the ground, protecting his head with his arms. "Have ye not caused enough pain in me life?" Tears begin streaming down his face.

"Come with me, Ciarán."

"No. *Never!*" He jumps up and with a shudder he turns, throwing open the abbey's oak doors, escaping inside.

"Please, I need sanctuary." His cries echo through the narthex and nave as he slams shut and bolts the doors behind him. They begin to buckle and rattle as though a freight train was on the other side. Terrifying screams, like those of harpies, fill the air as Ciarán stumbles between decaying pews on his way to the altar. The golden cross, which once presided over the heads of the congregation, now hangs tarnished and upside down on broken brackets.

"Please…" He cries with his hands clasped together in prayer. "I need sanctuary."

Silence echoes around him as he turns and looks across the now quiet decrepit nave.

"Thank you, thank you," he whispers to unseen ears.

Ciarán settles down upon the steps of the altar and begins to weep. The thoughts of dead loved ones fill his mind. He replays in horror the deaths of his mother, father, Niamh, his Nan, his ex-girlfriend, the man on the street… everyone with whom he once shared an emotional connection. Memories of their deaths begin to play out before his eyes. He sits transfixed, watching the greatest curse of his life replay before him.

Then, out of the dark memories, an image forms of his childhood home. The stone house with the blue shutters and red door stands tall and alive before him. The lights in the windows are on, and grey swirls of smoke billow from the chimney. Warmth takes Ciarán as he watches his father step out onto the front porch, followed by his mother carrying Niamh.

"Home." The word unfamiliar on Ciarán's lips. He crawls closer to the image and reaches out to touch it. To feel the warmth. *Niamh, Ma, Da, I am ready to come home.*

As he draws near, one of the abbey's oak doors slowly creaks open. A bone-chilling breeze whips through the nave to the altar and spirals itself around Ciarán's home, extinguishing its warmth. The image suddenly plunges into the floor of the altar. Darkness triumphs over his memories. Surging from the cracks in the altar's floor, a murky, black liquid rises upward to its ceiling. It stretches as it gyrates into a vortex. Out of the whirlpool of gloom steps the wraith.

"Time, time, time has come." The whisper resonates loudly upon the silence of the atmosphere.

"No! Please, leave me in peace!" Ciarán cries out. "I don't wanna go with you."

She reaches out her dark arms and encircles Ciarán, trying to hold him close, but he backs up further on the altar.

"Time."

"No! I want nothin' to do with you."

The wraith continues to advance upon him as he stands tall against her.

Dark hands reach out and caress his neck. The coldness of the touch runs down Ciarán's spine. Instantly, he recalls sitting in the hospital room beside his dying mother. He sees the wraith's hand begin to glow against his skin just as it had on his mother's stomach, his father's head, Niamh's leg, Nan's chest…

An intolerable pain grows sharp and hot in the left side of his chest. He looks at his left arm as it begins to lose all feeling. Her glowing hands seep into his neck, merging her body with his. Her black mass engulfs his arm, across his chest, slowly creeping up to his face. He gasps in pain, stumbling back against the wall under the upside-down cross. He pulls at her, trying to tear her infection from his skin.

Ciarán's eyes begin to roll into the back of his head. He feels compelled to give into the darkness eating away at him.

In the recesses of his mind, he hears his father's last words, *Ye cannot run from death.*

"Why? Why can't I run away?" Ciarán voice cracked.

We never realize our purpose in life until we die. The words from the man on the streets of Kilkenny echo off the walls of the abbey, bringing to light the reason why Ciarán was really granted the right to walk this dimension. All of the deaths that he witnessed were like a school lesson, and she was the teacher. The wraith was instructing him. He is to become a reaper, just like her.

Summoning whatever strength he has within his body, he pulls himself even further out of her grasp, despite the painful weight that wrenches his heart.

"I will not die. I'll not go wit' ye," he snarls, looking deeply into the black vortex that serves as her face. He will not accept his life's purpose.

She shudders, slowly releasing the grasp on his body.

"Ye are death!" he spits. "I'll not go wit' ye and become a stealer of souls like you!"

Her black mass ripples and shudders. He screams in pain from what feels like his heart exploding in his chest as her glowing hands tear away. His pain is quickly replaced by satisfaction as he watches her crumple to the ground, writhing in agony. The wraith's darkness melts into the floor of the abbey, flowing back into the vortex that had eaten Ciarán's image of home.

———————

He sits on the steps of the altar, relishing the silence. Ciarán looks upon the blackened spot on the floor where his home and his ghosts had faded from existence. He is numb, everything is gone. So, what is his purpose in life now? He has nothing to live for, yet there is so much unfinished business. He needs to find his home.

After an hour of brooding, a smile forms on his face. Even though everything he has known until this point of his life is dead, it is time to go out into the world and live. He has defeated a terrible foe that haunted every step of his life. Now he can walk out into the world without having to fear catching a glimpse of death.

Still smiling, he stands up and walks through the abbey to the oak doors leading outside. Where is he going to go?

"Anywhere that feels right," He says out loud to the walls, placing his hand on the left side of his chest and breathing in deeply. He fears that the emptiness in his heart will always remain, but now he has his life to live. A life no longer haunted with the worry that he will again lose something he loves.

He places his hands on the oak doors, still bolted from when he first ran into the abbey's narthex. Perplexed, Ciarán frowns at the locked bolt. She unlocked and broke through this door to get to him, why was the door still locked?

"Who cares!" He laughs out loud to no one. "I am free!"

Reaching for the bolt, he grasps the rough, tarnished metal. His face briefly contorts. He cannot feel the texture of the rusty bolt in his hand. *I may still be a bit numb from when she tried to overtake me.*

He clutches the bolt between his thumb and forefinger and tries to slide it open. Nothing. The bolt holds tight. When he had locked it earlier, the bolt slid with ease. Now it is stuck fast. He begins to panic for fear that he is stranded in this desolate place, for there are no other doors visible from within this central part of the abbey.

Ciarán begins to search for an alternate route out. The windows along the walls of the nave are suddenly too high to break and climb out. His eyes rake over the interior of the building. Breath catches in his throat as he grimly looks towards the altar. The cross that hung upside-down is now upright in a blaze of a gold. The ambiance of the abbey's interior lightens and, warmth fills the large room. The soft sound of choir music dances upon the stillness of the air, but instead of being at ease with this new haven, Ciarán is overtaken by dread. He fears the wraith has returned.

At the very end of the narthex is a low-hanging window with a red velvet chair, embellished with gold tassels, sitting beneath it. He runs over to the chair, lifts it by its arms and throws it hard through the window. Turning, he shields his face.

But there is no crash of glass.

Ciarán lowers his arms from his head and turns around. The chair is still sitting beneath the window as though he never moved it. He grabs the chair again and pulls. It does not budge. The chair does not move even an inch, no matter how much of his weight he throws at it. He runs his hands across the seat cushion. The velvet should feel soft under his fingertips.

Instead, there is no sensation at all.

Ciarán stumbles back, away from the chair, finally realizing his situation. Slowly, he raises his left hand and palpates the left side of his neck. A sickening *snap* echoes through the interior of the abbey as the crucifix falls, crashing to the ground. The plush velvet chair behind him turns black with rot. The atmosphere of the abbey's interior once more turns dark and dissolves back into decay. A stagnant silence fills the air. His expression hardens at the numbness under his fingers. There is no warmth, no pulse.

Ciarán crumples to the ground, screaming within the walls of the abbey that he will forever haunt.

DEAD AIR
by Lance Woods

"*She'll* kill *you!*"

The dead guy on the radio tried to warn me.

"*She's just waiting for the right moment. Don't give it to her!*"

I didn't know who he was, or why he was talking to me, but it didn't matter.

He said those words almost sixty years ago. He couldn't know.

"*If you do, I swear, she'll kill you!*"

Not if she died first, I kept telling myself.

At least, that was the plan.

On the radio, I mean.

"*Intensity!*"

I think I started to nod off when the guy got shot by the woman who sold him out to the gangsters in exchange for the plans to the bank—

"*For the next 30 minutes, experience new worlds of danger from the edge of your seat as we spin another tale of—Intensity!*"

No, wait, that was a different show. *Suspense*, maybe, or *Crime Classics*. I'd never heard this one before.

"Tonight, presenting Miss Magnolia Fallston as Karen Griffith and Mister Randall Meriwether as Steven Flint in Albert Rush's taut mystery, 'The Widow's Rest', a tale packed with suspense, thrills, and—Intensity!"

MUSIC: ORCHESTRA UP & UNDER NARRATION

A new old show. That should have been my first clue that something weird was going to happen. But I was too bored reviewing program schedules for the next week to make that connection right away.

Then, why did this "new" show seem somehow familiar?

Maybe it was the first scene ...

"The girl who walked out of the cold rain and into my slightly warmer office was a small, thin, pretty woman I guessed to be in her early twenties, and the older style of her clothes reflected the frugality of the working class."

"Excuse me, are you Steven Flint?"

"He's not here, missy."

"I need to speak to him. Who are you?"

"Cleaning woman. You dirty?"

"Why, no, certainly not!"

"Can't help you, then."

"Please, Mister Flint. My name is Karen Griffith. I need you to help my aunt find someone."

"Yeah? Who?"

"Me."

So much for "new." That's how most of those old noir mystery programs started: nice girl or femme fatale strolls into the private dick's office and plunges him into a cesspool of intrigue. And that poor guy Flint would be taking several cruises in this cesspool, because that's how the schedule at the Golden Age Radio Channel was constructed. Every program played at least three times a week during different parts of the day, so whatever audience we had always had a shot at hearing them.

And chances were that I'd hear each one at least twice during the 40 hours I sat behind my desk at channel 82 on your satellite radio dial. My duties: answering the phone on those infrequent occasions when someone called; playing receptionist on those even more infrequent occasions when someone visited the studio in person; typing up the program schedules and logs for each week; running out for pastries and coffee and other stuff for the boss; watching said boss hustle his pastry-fueled girth between the reception area, his office, and the glass-walled studio where he spent most of his time; and other duties as assigned.

So how did a nice 21st Century girl like me get stuck in a small office with neutral-colored walls decorated with black-&-white photos of long-dead radio actors, listening to said actors on 70-year-old radio shows for eight hours a day, five days a week?

Because I needed work and, it turns out, I'm not that nice.

Well, I wasn't nice at one time. Ask my parole officer.

"She'll kill you, Alex!"

What? Who said that?

"Hiiiiii, Aleeeeex."

As she called to me, the petite woman with short, blonde hair and the middle-aged, motherly face opened our office doorway and set off the chime. That woke me up right after the death warning. But that didn't come from this woman, Teri. She wasn't threatening at all.

I smiled, sort of, and tried to shake off that voice I'd heard. "Teri. Hi. What's up? You're not here to take me back to prison, are you?"

"No, no, no," she said. "I had another appointment nearby and thought I'd pop in."

"Checking to see if I had a real job in a real place?"

"Oh, no. I verified the address months ago. I've even talked to Mister Finch. He says he's very happy with your work, very glad to have you."

"Excuse me?"

"To have you here, working for him," Teri corrected. Then she became serious. "He hasn't tried to 'have' you any other way, has he?"

"Please." I glanced across the office at the studio, where the subject under discussion sat on an office chair that was far too small for him, even with its arms removed. Ogden Finch busily sat there with his headphones on, adjusting audio levels on ancient radio shows, and making the center piston of that office chair cry for mercy.

"When he makes the chair squeak, I pretend I'm at the aquarium listening to whale song," I said.

Teri looked at him, too. "He sounds thinner when he introduces the shows on my car radio. I guess that's why they call it 'Theatre of the Mind.'"

"Sometimes I wish my hearing aid batteries would die more often so I didn't even have to hear that," I said.

"How are they holding up?"

"I didn't expect much from the prison infirmary, but they're okay. I suppose that was one good thing about that experience. I didn't know I had a hearing problem until the doctor told me. I thought the rest of the world just started talking funny. That's what I get for sitting too close to the stage at concerts."

"Diagnosed with hearing loss and you end up in radio," Teri said. "Funny how that worked out, huh?"

"Hilarious," I said. "Guess I can thank community college for that little twist in my life. I took a theatre class for an easy A. One week, we read some old radio scripts for voice exercises. If I hadn't heard one of the shows I read back then on this channel after I got out, I never would have thought about applying. Good thing I did. I guess."

Unexpectedly, Ogden jumped–yes, jumped–off his chair, exited the studio, and bounced across the tiny lobby to my desk. "Alex, I've finished mixing the lead-ins and lead-outs for next week. Can you stay a little late tonight and help me log them in? It'll be one less thing for us to worry about this weekend."

"Yeah, I guess."

He realized we weren't alone and rapidly brushed off his shirt (in case crumbs from the morning's bear claw remained), followed by his graying goatee, and his thinning blond hair. "Pardon me, miss. May I help you?"

"Teri Glasgow," she said, extending her hand. "We've talked on the phone, Mister Finch."

"Oh, yes," Ogden said during the handshake. "You're Alex's, um …"

"Warden," I said, smiling at Teri.

"Parole officer," she said. "I thought I'd check in with Alex instead of vice versa, for a change. Sounds like you're busy."

"We're getting ready for this weekend's Golden Gate Nostalgia Convention," Ogden explained before turning to me. "Oh, I have the standby engineer coming in tomorrow morning and after I brief him, we can load the van and be on our way to San Francisco."

Teri turned to me. "You're going to San Francisco?"

"Certainly," Ogden said. "Alex will bring some extra beauty and class to our booth."

"You're not going to tell me I can't leave town?" I asked Teri. "You'd sound like this moldy old cop show we're running now."

"What cop show?" Ogden asked. "This is Benny."

"Benny?" I listened to the office speakers.

Sure enough, Jack Benny and his valet Rochester were throwing jokes around while they got Jack packed for a cross-country trip on the Super Chief. The live audience from nineteen-thirty-whatever howled with every punch line.

There was no *Intensity* to be found.

"You can move freely within the state," Teri said. "But call me when you get there and let me know where you are, just to quiet the mother hen in me."

"Starting tomorrow evening, you can reach her at the Faulkner Hotel, Miss Glasgow," Ogden said. "Not to worry. The only things we'll be selling at our booth are CDs and T-shirts, not mortgages, so there won't be any loan documents to tempt our girl's forgery skills."

"You're really looking out for me, Ogden," I grumbled.

"Alex is not a forger," Teri insisted. "She was convicted only as an accessory for helping her bosses forge those documents, which she wouldn't have done if one of them hadn't seduced her into it."

I put on my best contrite face as I flashed back to how many months of oral sex it had taken me to maneuver "one of them" into seriously considering divorcing his wife so he could cut me in on his plan to steal company funds, which he said he'd do after I helped him forge a few documents. You can read the rest in my criminal record, available for download from *www.lasuperiorcourt.org*.

"I know, I know," Ogden said. "That was a cheap shot, kid, I'm sorry." His middle-aged eyes actually showed a little regret, and I almost apologized for comparing him to a humpback a few minutes earlier, but kept quiet because I needed the paycheck.

"So, what cop show did you think was on?" Ogden asked.

"Some mystery show with a guy, a detective, what was his name…?" It was on the tip of my tongue, but I couldn't remember it. Instead, I remembered, "*Intensity!* That was the show. *Intensity.* I remember because I'd never heard it before."

Ogden burst out laughing so hard he looked like an earthquake. The sight seemed to give Teri a scare, too.

"I'm–I'm sorry." He pulled a handkerchief out of his pocket and dabbed his eyes. "That's so funny."

"Why?"

"Alex," he said, "you could not have heard *Intensity* on this channel. Or any channel. We don't have any of the episodes. Nobody has them. The rights to the transcriptions have been tied up for decades. Don't you remember? I wrote an entire chapter of it for *The Golden Age Radio Channel Companion*. You proofread it for me." He turned to Teri. "Retails for twenty bucks, but if you'd like a copy, I can sell it to you for the convention rate of fifteen. Signed by the author!"

Before Teri could tell him what he could sign instead (she wouldn't have, out loud), I jumped in. "Ogden, you're telling me that I imagined hearing a radio show that I've never heard of before now?"

"'Sounds' like it," Ogden quipped, pointing to one of my ears and chuckling in case I didn't get the pun.

I got it, and I turned to Teri.

"If I quit, will the prison library take me back?"

———————

Actually, I was pretty lucky to have my boring job, or any job. Even when you have office skills and are pleasant to look at, hard time for a white-collar offense tends to disqualify you in the eyes of most employers. But Ogden Nash Finch (he told me his mother was a lit professor, and Nash was her favorite poet) took a chance that I wouldn't rob him blind, which would have been hard since he never kept any cash in the office that I knew of outside of the pastry jar. I think he just wanted someone to do all the boring tasks that prevented him from spending hours in the studio cleaning up and restoring ancient audio, or talking on the phone to lawyers or old-time actors about scoring the rights to their shows.

Or maybe he just wanted something cute to look at. I mean, at 28, I'm still in decent physical condition, even after 18 months in minimum security. Or maybe because of it; I made good use of the exercise yard. Either way, I figured I was strong enough to shove Ogden's bulk out of the way if he ever tried to take advantage of my situation. He hadn't. The only times I ever saw even a hint of drool from his mouth was when I brought him the biggest bear claw from Marshall's Bakery every Wednesday.

That didn't mean I was looking forward to riding with him in his van for six hours from L.A. to San Francisco. That happened the next morning, Thursday. The van was clean, and so was he. He didn't chatter incessantly, not in person. The radio did it for him. He had it tuned in to the channel, which spat out one old show after the next, each featuring a lead-in and lead-out pre-recorded by Ogden. That might have freaked out anyone else, but I knew he was big enough to occupy two places at once, so it didn't faze me.

The scenery helped. Thanks to more than the usual number of construction advisories and backups on I-5, Ogden's GPS plotted a longer, but more scenic course up the 101. You've probably seen it in movies and on TV, but if you can drive it for yourself, you should. Twisting roads, mountains, the ocean. Very relaxing.

Maybe that's why, about a third of the way into our trip, I was starting to feel a little drowsy.

Gunsmoke was on. Marshall Dillon was tracking down a couple of bullies who roughed up his pal, Chester, and then... And then...

"So, that's my story, Mister Flint. I spent my last dime on those blood tests from the Hollander Labs and genealogy charts from Professor Gomez to confirm that I am Roberta Whitfield's niece. All I need for you to do is use your resources to conduct an impartial review of the documents I've given you and verify that what I say is true."

"And what if it isn't, Miss Griffith? Well?"

"Well?"

"Huh?!" I jumped. That wasn't what's-his-name's—Flint's—voice.

Ogden was talking. "The photos? You're sure you packed all of them?"

"Wh-what?"

"The photos? Of the actors who'll be at the show? You packed all of them, right?"

I forced myself to calm down. "Yeah, yeah, they're in the suitcase you loaned me. Nice and flat. They'll be fine."

"Good, good." He let out a sigh. "Sorry if I startled you. I just want to be sure they're in good condition for the contest next week. It could give our ratings a nice boost."

There were several old radio and TV actors appearing at the Golden Age Nostalgia Convention, and Ogden had made arrangements for them to sign some photographs that we planned to give away to our listeners. Since our target demographic ranged in age from 65 to 1,000, I thought he might be right about the ratings potential.

"How long—" I never finished my question. The radio answered it for me.

Gunsmoke was still playing. Judging from the time on the car's clock, the western had another five minutes to go.

"How long what?" Ogden asked.

"Um, how long until we hit San Francisco?"

"If traffic's good, about four hours. We should get there by six, seven tonight. Why, you have some action lined up when we get there?"

A loud, nervous laugh popped out of me. "No, no, just wondering how much longer we'll be able to enjoy the ride. It's nice."

Ogden nodded as he drove. "I always liked the 101. A girl I knew studied biochemistry in San Francisco when I was at UCLA. I used to drive up to see her on weekends."

"You must have liked her a lot to make that haul," I said. "I hope she appreciated it."

"Yeah, maybe. When she noticed me, I'd tell her I was haunting the libraries, researching something I couldn't find in L.A., you know ..."

"Wait, noticed you? You didn't tell her you were coming?"

He bit his lip and looked like he regretted opening his mouth.

"You never told her that you liked her, did you?"

He sighed, lowering his head slightly into his chins. "I never had a lot of close, solid female friends, Alex. I know that's hard to believe, looking at how much of me there is to go around, but it's true. Casey was special to me and I didn't want to do anything to risk screwing up our friendship. Besides, she was always popular and whenever I saw her she was usually hanging out with her college friends or a, you know, a date. I guess the right time never came. Or it passed me by."

I leaned back. "Sounds more like you let it pass you by."

"Pretty much. Of course, my standards weren't as high then. Nowadays, after spending so much time around these old shows, I keep hoping to meet someone with Myrna Loy's voice, Carole Lombard's sense of humor, and Hedy Lamarr's brains. But they don't make them like that anymore, do they?"

"I wouldn't know. Hell, I wouldn't have known those were actresses if I didn't work for you. And my *mom* was an actress."

"Really? Would I know anything she did?"

I shook my head. "Getting pregnant by a runaway father pretty much ended her career before it started, which might have made my fucking grandmother happy if she'd known, pardon my French."

"Feel free."

"Mom said when Grandma couldn't talk her out of being an actress, she threw her out." My voice rumbled. "The old bitch wouldn't take her back even after she was carrying me and the father bolted. So Mom ended up marrying a guy she worked with. He was okay, but he worked late a lot and she hardly worked at all, so we struggled and she did any drugs she could to cope with it. I used to sneak some of her stash out to school and sell it to the kids. I figured it kept some of the shit out of her hands and helped put me through community college. But it wasn't enough to keep her from overdosing one too many times. Her mother didn't bother to show up for the funeral. At least neither of them got to see little Alex become inmate 793019."

"I'm sorry," Ogden said. "I didn't mean to—we can talk about something else, anything else."

"Maybe later," I said. "Right now, I'd like to grab a nap, especially if we'll be spending most of the night setting up the booth once we get there."

"Sure. The view will still be there when you wake up."

I took one more look at the passing ocean and closed my eyes.

"And what if it isn't?" I whispered.

"And what if it isn't, Miss Griffith? Well?"

"Then you've lost nothing but a few days of your time."

"Which costs a few days of your money, Miss Griffith, and if you spent your last dime on these tests, how do you hope to pay me?"

"Well...maybe not my last dime. I might have enough to buy us coffee at the diner around the corner while I tell you more."

"Hmm...Miss Griffith, you've just made a down payment on my services. Come on."

MUSIC: LIGHT TRANSITION TO NEXT SCENE

When I woke up again, Ogden was navigating through Palo Alto on the home stretch of our ride. Less than half an hour later, we were rolling through the City by the Bay. Twilight was falling as the fog began to crest over the hills like the edge of a large white sheet being pulled over a dead—

Christ, I wasn't just only imagining that I was hearing a private eye, I was starting to *think* like one.

It wasn't until we arrived at our objective, the Faulkner Hotel, and parked the van in the garage that Ogden noticed my face. "Not carsick, are you?"

"Wha— no, no, I'm fine."

We climbed out of the van, grabbed our suitcases, and headed for the elevator to the lobby. "You remember yesterday when I told you I thought I heard that program, the one you said we didn't play?"

"*Intensity*? Yeah. That was pretty weird."

"You're sure nobody's playing it?"

"I've heard really bad bootlegs of a few episodes, but nothing restored. I'd love a crack at them. Maybe I'll get it after this weekend."

I pressed the button for the elevator. "Why this weekend?"

Ogden's eyes widened. "Alex. Where have you been for the last month? We've been playing promos for this convention. The guest of honor is Magnolia Fallston."

I must have looked like I'd been hit between the eyes with a hammer.

"Magnolia. Fallston," he spelled out. "The actress? One of radio's biggest stars, one of its first female producers, and the last living producer of …?"

The answer seemed obvious, but I didn't say it.

"*Intensity!*" Ogden barked like a frustrated teacher. "I wrote about her in *The Golden Age Radio Channel Companion*, too. Her lawyer's trying to get me some time with her this weekend. The old gal's realized at ninety-one that she won't be around forever and I want to convince her that our channel is the right place to leave her transcriptions."

We stepped into the elevator. Ogden pressed the button for the lobby. "So," I asked, "it's not possible for someone with a bootleg of the show to broadcast it over a frequency that might be picked up by someone wearing cheap, prison-issue hearing aids?"

Before that moment, the only times I'd seen Ogden Finch's jaw drop open that wide were right before his mouth docked with a pie. "You've been getting *Intensity* over your hearing aids?" he whispered.

"I don't know," I said. "If I were, I guess I'd be hearing it now, and I don't, so that can't be it."

"Could be because we're inside the garage," Ogden said.

"Maybe. And I'm usually drifting or nodding off when I do hear it. But I swear, Ogden, I never even heard of *Intensity* or Steven Flint or 'The Widow's Rest' before this started."

The doors opened, but Ogden rotated in front of me, blocking them. "What did you say? The title?"

"'The Widow's Rest.' You know anything about it?"

"Only by reputation," he said. "'The Widow's Rest' was the very last episode of *Intensity*.

"It never aired, Alex."

So not only was I hearing a radio show that nobody could broadcast, but I was hearing an episode that *nobody* had ever heard. Or *I was* imagining that I was hearing it? And if it was all in my head, what was my head trying to tell me?

I was surprised that Ogden didn't put me on the next bus back to L.A. or to any location at least fifty miles away from his home address. But he said, "This show's the biggest one of its kind on the West Coast. I need help, even crazy help," in that understanding way of his. I just thanked him and spent the rest of the evening in the Renaldo Ballroom of the Faulkner, helping him set up our booth of CDs from classic shows, Golden Age Radio Channel T-shirts and hats, and copies of *The Golden Age Radio Channel Companion.*

During the set-up, I sneaked a glance at a copy of the *Companion*. He was right; I'd proofread it after I'd been with Ogden for about a month, largely to get an idea of the kind of stuff I was listening to and logging in. Sure enough, he had a chapter dedicated to *Intensity*–how Magnolia Fallston, Randall Meriwether, and two other producers created the show in 1942; the kinds of scripts that they recorded (or "transcribed," as they used to call pre-recorded stuff, versus live-audience shows); and how the network pulled the plug on it in 1957 without even letting the last episode—"The Widow's Rest"—air. Unfortunately, Ogden only had enough information to write a short recap of the story, but not its ending:

"'The Widow's Rest', no air date; original story & script by Albert Rush. Cast: Magnolia Fallston (Karen Griffith), Randall Meriwether (Steven Flint), Brenda Grooms (Mrs. Whitfield), Scott Olesen (Lt. Regan), Alex Robinson (Dr. Finlay), Kelly Glenn (Librarian). Directed by Dean Merriman. Synopsis: Private detective Steven Flint is hired to verify the identity of Karen Griffith, a young woman who believes she is the sole heir to old Roberta Whitfield's fortune. But after he brings the two women together, Flint uncovers information that indicates Karen may not be what she seems."

So that helped me get an idea of what I was dealing with.

I was nuts.

It was after midnight before we finally got to our hotel rooms—our adjoining hotel rooms. Ogden put on a good show of not understanding why we didn't get completely separate rooms, but I knew how lonely guys like him worked. He even pretended to call the front desk to request another room for "the lady," but there were none. But he was quick to show me that the doors between our rooms had separate deadbolt locks, and I was quick to say good night, close my door, and show him how well my deadbolt worked.

That nonsense, setting up the booth, and the six-hour drive should have been enough to knock me out, but it wasn't.

Oh, I *was* beat, all right, but I didn't want to close my eyes.

No. I did want to close them, but not necessarily to sleep. I wanted to know what kind of trick my mind was playing on me, if it was my mind playing the trick and not someone with a pirate radio station, like Ogden suggested.

Only one way to find out.

Remove clothes.

Remove hearing aids.

Lie down.

Close eyes.

And sometime after that is when the old woman, Roberta Whitfield, showed up.

"Mister Flint, my train may not travel, shall we say, on your side of the tracks, but I know of your reputation from the newspaper accounts of your cases. On the strength of that, and of what I've seen in these documents, I would like to meet Miss Griffith as soon as possible."

"Mrs. Whitfield --"

"We're a very old family, Mister Flint, so old that I doubted there were any of us left. But I kept searching."

"I know, ma'am. Several 'colleagues,' to use polite language, would love to earn a fat fee by producing your 'heir.' I just don't want you getting fleeced. Before you meet Miss Griffith, please let me go over her documents again, just to be certain. That's what she's paying me for."

"Mister Flint, as I often tell my physician when he tells me to slow down: I can't take my time when I have so little of it left. Please bring Miss Griffith to me at once and I'll pay whatever she owes you -- with a **generous** *bonus."*

MUSIC: ORCHESTRA UP FULL

Music!

I slammed the off button on the hotel's clock radio by my bed when it went off at 6:30 Friday morning. I jumped partly because the radio scared me; I hadn't set it to a station other than the rap/hip-hop channel selected by the room's previous occupant, and partly because...

Because the other radio scared me. The one in my mind. Still, I wanted to go back to sleep and find out what happened next because the story was getting interesting, but I didn't want to start it up again because I really hated having all these people putting on a show in my brain. That was scary.

I tried to guess *about* what would come next so that it might move the story a little closer to the exit in my head. It was playing out the way Ogden had outlined it in the book. At this point, I knew Karen couldn't be Roberta's niece; that would end the story too soon, and I had a feeling I wasn't going to get off that easily.

But how would Flint know she was faking, and how would he prove it?

And why did he want to prove it in my goddamn head? And what if the fucking show didn't stop once he solved the case? At least Flint had clues, leads, people he could talk to in his make-believe world.

Then I remembered where I was, and that I might have someone I could talk to about "The Widow's Rest:"

Karen Griffith.

I was surprised that the Golden Gate Nostalgia Convention lived up to Ogden's hype when it opened the next morning. Over the genteel Muzak being piped into the ballroom, people chatted and laughed with each other, or talked and negotiated prices and trades with dealers of rare memorabilia from various media—the perfect vintage poster from a favorite movie, the clearest possible recording of an old radio show, or simply an autograph from a star of yore. It wasn't the mausoleum I expected to find.

I knew that someone in this room would be able to tell me the payoff to "The Widow's Rest" before listening to it in bite-size chunks made me scream.

From the moment the convention opened its doors at 9:00 a.m., Ogden and I were kept so busy selling merchandise and talking to conventioneers that I didn't have time to ask questions or nod off, so I couldn't hear "the show." When visitors to the booth felt chatty, I asked if they knew anything about *Intensity* (common response: "Ahhhhhhh, do you have those on CD?," followed by me saying "Nope") or "The Widow's Rest" (common response: "Ooooooooh," followed by them saying "Nope," followed by Ogden pointing out that they could read about it in *The Golden Age Radio Channel Companion*).

For the first couple of hours we were down there, I kept watching a row of tables that encircled the far half of the ballroom. There was seating for about 15 to 20 guests, mostly middle-aged or elderly actors, each identified by a colorful nameplate provided by the convention, a name badge, and any of their own photographs or decorations. I was surprised by how many of them I recognized from movies and TV shows I'd watched growing up. Had my mom broken into the business, she might have been one of them, selling her autograph for $20, and permitting herself to be photographed with willing attendees for $25. (That fee was occasionally waived if the request came from a cute member of the opposite sex; a few of the male stars even came by our booth to offer me such deals.) Other guests included authors who wrote about the actors and/or their works. Others were bloggers who wrote about the authors' works. Each set of guests was younger than the last, and the attendees standing in line and chatting them up reflected a similar range.

Everyone seemed to be the most interested in the table where no one sat. If this arrangement of stars was King Arthur's Round Table, this seat was the throne. An elegant, blue satin banner was draped over the front of the table. Simple, but stylish lettering stitched to the front said, simply, "Magnolia Fallston–Actress."

On the table was a small "Back at…" clock sign, with the hands set at 11:00.

I checked my watch. It was 10:55.

We'd been down in the ballroom with the rest of the guests since the room opened at 9:00.

"What's her deal?" I muttered under my breath. "Old bat's not good enough to open the room with the rest of us?"

"Shush!" Ogden said sharply. I didn't know he could hear me, and it was obvious from the look on his face that he was more worried about potential customers hearing me diss the belle of the ball. It wasn't keeping anyone from checking out our booth, so it looked like I still had a job.

"I talked with her lawyer this morning," Ogden continued. "This is the first show she's done in about fifteen years and she wants to make an entrance. It'll give her fans, and her, a special memory."

"Seems kind of rude. I mean, people are waiting to talk to her."

"She's the queen this weekend," Ogden said. "They'll wait. Why are you so worked up about it?"

"Huh? Oh, no reason. I was thinking about you, is all, whether you'd get an audience with Her Majesty."

"Working on it. Her lawyer's going to see about introducing me while she's down here," Ogden said. "Baby steps. We'll see where they take me."

"I hope you make the deal, Ogden. I know how much it means to you."

He gave a small bow. "Thank you, Miss Norris."

And if you get your fat little hands on "The Widow's Rest," I thought to myself, you'd better let me listen to it first.

Unless I hear the rest of it before you do. Or I can find out how it ends from—

Attendees and guests in the autograph section of the ballroom began to murmur, then there was clapping, then there was … the star.

Aided by a black cane in her right hand and a tall, middle-aged man in a suit & tie who gently held her left arm, the woman I'd come to know only as "Karen Griffith" entered the ballroom to thunderous applause. She stood up straight and moved pretty quickly for a 91-year-old, smiling, waving to the conventioneers and their cameras, and stepping over to the tables of a guest or two to shake hands, hug, or kiss them. Her skin looked like wrinkled porcelain. Her smile was radiant, probably due to very good dentures. She wore make-up, but every stroke had been carefully applied; she either had a stylist or very steady hands because she didn't look like Aunt Edna on bingo night at the Moose Lodge. Her red and gold pants suit looked like it was made about 30 years ago, but like her, it was well-preserved and it looked good on her. Her sculpted, silver hair (or wig; I couldn't tell at that distance) was accented by a thin, faint stripe of red that ran through the center. A small segment of the stripe dangled in front of her, as if it would make her look younger. She knew she was Hollywood royalty, one of the last treasures from a bygone age, and she was determined to make what might be her final bow a true event.

The dealers in our part of the ballroom, including Ogden, applauded as well. I didn't. I was too consumed with watching the guest of honor work the room. I figured I'd use Ogden as my foot in her door. He could get in to discuss *Intensity*, I could wrangle an invitation to sit in on the chat (if Ogden didn't want anything sleazy in exchange, because you never know), and I could ask her about "The Widow's Rest."

I started practicing what I wanted to say. Keep it simple, I told myself. Just tell her you've heard about her program from working at the channel and you're curious about how the last story ends. Not so hard. Maybe I'd even be able to…

Then she looked at me.

From across the room, Magnolia Fallston stopped and looked at me.

No…she studied me.

She was sizing me up.

I knew that look. It followed me everywhere for the first month that I was inside. Yeah, it was minimum security, but it was still prison, and when a new arrival showed up, all eyes stayed on her until the guards and the other inmates learned her story. I knew what it was like to be on both sides of that gaze, but I never shook the memory of when it first tracked me.

In real time, her look lasted only a second, maybe less. From my point of view, it lasted a month. Then, she turned away, quickly made her way to her throne behind her satin-draped table, sat down, and began welcoming her growing line of admirers.

Ogden brushed the stars from his eyes and pulled out his best pitchman's voice for the conventioneers near our table. "She looks great, doesn't she, folks? You can hear some of Miss Fallston's greatest performances on many of the fine CD collections offered here from the Golden Age Radio Channel, and you can read about them in my book, *The Golden Age Radio Channel Companion*, normally twenty dollars ..."

That's how it went for the rest of the day. Ogden pitched to the customers while I rang up purchases and acted like a nice young woman with no criminal record or obvious mental problems. But every now and then during the show, I couldn't help but glance across the ballroom at Magnolia Fallston's busy table.

And more than once, I glanced at her just as she was glancing away from me. Made me wonder what the old lady was really looking at.

Or looking *for*.

"Long story short, I contacted my bonus — er, Karen Griffith — and took her out to the old girl's mansion. Aunt Bertie fired off some questions about the family, Karen answered them correctly, and the next thing you know, the waterworks came on full blast. So with the last members of the Whitfield family reunited, and Aunt Bertie's generous check in my pocket, it looked like I had something truly special on my hands: a case that didn't end with me sending someone to the electric chair.

"Yeah, that's how it looked–until I decided to earn my pay and dig deeper into the niece's tale anyway.

MUSIC: ORCHESTRA UP FOR TRANSITION, THEN UNDER SCENE

SOUND: CITY STREET

"Hollander Labs wasn't in a part of town known for having squeaky-clean medical facilities. I parked the car, kept my revolver handy, and stepped up to the door. It was already open, but dark inside. So I turned on the light. That's when I saw that the guy who probably ran the place wouldn't be telling me about Karen's blood work because his own blood was all over the dingy tile floor!"

I awoke with such a jolt after finding the guy's body that I almost fell off the ladies' room toilet. Great way to end the only bathroom break I got after the 15-minute lunch Ogden granted me earlier that day. That was shortly before he left me at the booth for most of the afternoon, so he could participate in old-time radio panel discussions, promote the channel to anyone who would listen, and get the stars to sign the photos we brought. I noticed that he made an effort to steer clear of La Fallston's perch, probably because one did not approach her with a business proposition unless one was invited or commanded to do so.

After 6:00, the ballroom was closed in order to give the conventioneers their own food and pee breaks, and to let them get ready for some big banquet that was being held across the hall in the hotel's Grand Ballroom at 8:00. But Magnolia and the other guests who still had fans at their table refused to let convention security whisk them away until tomorrow.

After all, there was no telling what might happen to the old lady between now and then.

While Magnolia discussed some of her acting triumphs with a small group of devotees, her escort in the nice suit whispered something in her ear that made her frown momentarily. I wondered what it could have been.

When she nodded to him, and he rose, and he began to walk towards me, I regretted wondering. Had she noticed me noticing her? Would this guy tell me to avert my eyes under pain of death, or would he just take my eyes?

"Miss Norris?" The baritone voice came from a tan face that looked to be about 50, framed by just enough graying, sandy brown hair to make it look youthful and distinguished at the same time. It didn't matter. Whenever an official-looking guy in a suit walked up to me unexpectedly and said "Miss Norris," it usually meant trouble.

"Have we met, sir?" I asked calmly.

"Not officially," the suit said, extending his hand. "That's why I came over. My name is Bryan Burke. I'm Miss Fallston's lawyer. And you're Alex Norris of the Golden Age Radio Channel, unless you're wearing the wrong badge."

I looked down at my Golden Age Radio Channel T-shirt, read my Golden Gate Nostalgia Convention badge upside down, and laughed as I shook his hand.

"I'm sorry if I startled you," Burke said. "I imagine you're not too keen on lawyers."

"What do you mean?"

"Please relax, Miss Norris. I know about your, um, background. I found out about it when I investigated Mister Finch."

"Ogden? What's he done?"

"Nothing," Burke laughed. "I always do a background check of anyone that wants to do business with Miss Fallston, so when he inquired about the rights to *Intensity*, I did my homework on both of you. I hope working for him has helped...you know..."

"Make an honest woman out of me?"

He laughed again. "I'm not doing a very good job of this, am I?"

I smiled. "Depends, Mister Burke. What is 'this?'"

"An invitation to dinner. A business dinner. Unless you're going to the banquet?"

"You're not going with...?"

"One of the gentleman guests is relieving me. He and Miss Fallston haven't had a chance to hang out for decades. Thus, I've been dismissed for the evening."

"It sounds nice, but if you're looking to discuss the channel's offer for the *Intensity* rights, you'll have to talk with Ogden."

"In fact, Miss Norris, it has nothing to do with *Intensity*. It has to do with Miss Fallston. She, um, felt a little badly about glancing over at you so often today. Maybe you noticed."

"Actually, we were pretty busy."

"She thought you might be upset and she asked me to apologize on her behalf. Another reason for the dinner invitation."

Normally, older guys don't do it for me, but this one really knew how to bait the hook. "Why not just apologize and be done with it?"

"Because there's more."

There always is. But before I could ask for details, Karen Griffith called from across the ballroom: "Bryan!"

We turned in the direction of Magnolia Fallston's table. She stood in front of it with a tall, pudgy, dignified-looking man who looked to be about 10 years younger. Everyone in the immediate area turned and watched—no, listened—as she spoke. Her voice was slightly raspy, but her volume was impressive. Those ancient lungs were in great shape.

"Richard and I are going to the bar, and then to the banquet," she announced. She looked at me for a second, then asked Burke, in a slightly lower volume, "You'll be all right?"

"I'll be fine," Burke called back. "Have a wonderful evening. We'll talk at breakfast."

She looked at me again. "I hope so. Good night, Bryan." Then, she took Richard's arm and began her exit.

As we, and everyone in the room, watched her leave, I asked Burke, "Does 'more' include explaining why she keeps looking at me?"

"It does," he said. "Despite her energy, that voice you just heard is probably the strongest thing about Magnolia Fallston these days."

Now, why would he want me to know that?

SOUND: LIGHT RAIN OUTDOORS

"My aunt isn't feeling well and has retired for the evening, Mister Flint."

"You didn't retire her with that .38 in your hand, did you? Or is that what retired the guy who did your 'blood tests' at Hollander Labs—the guy I found bleeding all over the floor there an hour ago?"

"Why, whatever are you talking about? A girl has a right to protect herself and her poor, old aunt. How could I know it was you out here, skulking about in the garden?"

"Now you know, kid, so put the gun away."

"I will in a moment. André?"

SOUND: HARD HIT TO HEAD

<u>**SOUND: BODY HITTING WET GROUND**</u>

<u>**MUSIC: ORCHESTRA DRAMATIC CUE UP & OUT TO COMMERCIAL**</u>

I jolted when my face hit the mud–I mean, the top of the water in the bathtub. I was cleaning up and relaxing a little before meeting Burke for dinner, and I...oh, hell, you know the drill. I suppose I owed Karen Griffith a solid for having that André guy knock Flint out. If he hadn't fallen down, I might have kept sleeping and missed dinner, or slid farther down into the water and drowned.

At least I'd stop hearing the goddamn show.

Whatever. I climbed out of the tub, wrapped a short hotel towel around myself as much as I could, opened the bathroom door, and stepped into my room.

Contrary to what my mom used to say was a tradition in old movies, they don't cut you loose from prison with $20 and a new suit. If you work during your stretch, you get whatever money is in your prison account, but you have to buy your own new clothes when you get out. Thankfully, the prison held onto the dress I wore when I went in, which was a plain green number. It held up well enough in storage to serve as an interview dress when I was job-hunting, and would make me presentable enough for the hotel restaurant.

But when I took the dress out of the suitcase and brushed out the wrinkles, that's when this whole thing really started to get weird.

"She'll kill you!"

What the...? That was Flint. He was still alive. Why was I hearing him? Why didn't Karen kill him off? Why—

Why was I hearing him *now*?

I wasn't asleep.

"You're the only one who can stop her."

I wasn't wearing my hearing aids.

"She's just waiting for the right moment. Don't give it to her!"

But I was hearing Steven Flint talking in my head!

"If you do, I swear, she'll kill you!"

What I couldn't figure out was: who was he talking *to?*

"So what do you do at the channel?" Burke asked me over our steaks.

"I guess I'm sort of a librarian," I said. "Mostly I keep the logs on the shows, but I also help Ogden with the scripts he reads before and after each show, do general office work, nothing sexy."

"You like it?"

"Ogden treats me okay. If he's ogling me, I haven't caught him yet."

"You trying to catch him?"

"Sometimes, just to relieve the monotony. The everyday grind is kind of boring. I drift now and then."

"Sure. Everyone does that at work."

"Yeah, but they don't hear old radio shows playing in their heads whenever their minds wander." I was relieved to not be hearing it over our dinner. Thankfully, the Muzak that was being piped into Magda's, the hotel restaurant, distracted my senses.

"I know what you mean," Burke said. "Miss Fallston listens to recordings of the old shows all the time back in L.A., even when we're meeting on legal matters. After spending a few hours with her, I almost expect to walk out and see billboards selling war bonds on Sunset Boulevard."

"So I guess you're the only one who's heard the shows from *Intensity?* I mean, recently."

He shook his head. "She keeps telling me how proud she is of it, but she never plays it. I think it reminds her of Randall Meriwether."

"Oh. They had a thing?"

"They had a marriage, as well as a production company, the one that produced *Intensity.*"

"That's weird. I don't remember Ogden mentioning that in his book."

"Maybe he didn't want to risk Miss Fallston seeing it and cutting him out of any deal for the shows," Burke said. "Anyway, the series ended in

'57, and the marriage ended a few years later. He left her to go into the movies. According to her, he said that being married to a relic from radio was hurting his film career. Not being able to act very well in front of a camera might have had something to do with it, too."

"Jerk."

"And he left her pregnant. She had a daughter he never knew about, raised her by herself."

"Did she ever remarry?"

He shook his head again. "As time passed, she was sure that men were only after her money, which she's always been very good with. Not many radio stars knew how to save and invest the way she does."

"So she doesn't need to be selling autographs and pictures?"

"Nope." He took another sip of wine. "She just wants to get out and meet what's left of her fan base before they die. Or she does." One more quick sip. "That brings us to why I invited you to dinner."

"A business dinner," I reminded him, sipping from my glass.

"I don't know if you noticed, but Miss Fallston was, um, she was quite taken with you today."

"Yeah, I tried not to be rude and look back, but she's pretty hard to ignore."

"I've learned not to," Burke said. "In any case, she whispered something to me as she sat down at her table: 'That girl … she has her mother's eyes, Bryan.'"

"How the hell would she know what my mother looked like?"

"She wouldn't," Burke said. "She doesn't. As she's gotten older, Miss Fallston has been trying to get a few personal matters in order. One of them concerns her daughter, Francesca."

"Her and Randall's daughter?"

"Right. When the daughter was in her late teens, early twenties, she and her mother argued over something, and it ended badly. They didn't speak for many years. Miss Fallston won't give me all the details, only that she knows Francesca had a child and died several years ago."

"And she thinks I'm the kid?"

"You're not the first, just the latest. Thing is, she wants to meet you. And I think it could be very beneficial."

I leaned back in my chair. "Let me guess: you'll tell me everything I need to know about Miss Fallston and the family, I spit it back to her, she takes me into her arms, and when she finally dies, you and I split the estate."

Burke laughed again, louder than he *did* in the ballroom. In this more intimate setting, it packed quite a punch. "You've been hearing too many of those radio shows."

"Got that right," I muttered.

He didn't hear me. "In fact, I'd like you to meet her and convince her that you're *not* her granddaughter. See, our firm has spent years hiring investigators on Miss Fallston's behalf to try and find her daughter and granddaughter. We know Francesca died, but no one's been able to pick up the trail of the granddaughter. Miss Fallston's a lovely woman, Miss Norris, but she won't live forever. I hate seeing her waste money, even on our firm. If you can convince her that you're not Francesca's daughter, my hope is that she'll realize that the chase is over, and she'll get serious about putting her estate in order."

"I see where this benefits your client and your conscience," I said, "and that's very nice, but what's in it for me?"

"For starters, the rights to *Intensity*. Every episode from 1942 through 1957. Miss Fallston has yet to decide what she wants to do with the recordings, and acquiring them for your channel could get you a promotion or a raise."

"I doubt it," I said. "The only job above mine is Ogden's, and he's not going anywhere. Not very fast, anyway. Besides, he'd always be jealous that I bagged the shows and he didn't." I leaned forward and whispered. "Would those shows include 'The Widow's Rest?'"

"Naturally."

The idea of actually hearing the damn show for myself and finding out how it ended—and what, if anything, it had to do with me—made me want to shake his hand, but I stayed cool and curious. "So, Ogden gets something, you get something, and Miss Fallston gets something. What do I get?"

"How about twenty-five thousand dollars in cash? It'll be worth it to keep Miss Fallston from wasting any more time and money, and I imagine that a young woman trying to start a new life would find it helpful."

I wanted to shake his hand and have his baby.

Burke said that Magnolia Fallston planned to return to her suite from the banquet at about eleven o'clock. We finished dinner just before ten, so I told him I wanted to return to my room for some nose-powdering, and he promised to call when the queen was ready to receive me.

Truthfully, Burke was so nice I wouldn't have minded asking him to come back to the room with me. He wasn't unpleasant to look at, and he was certainly the nicest lawyer I'd met in a long time, and he wasn't wearing a wedding band, so maybe he'd be fun on a real date. Assuming he was 50, there weren't that many years separating us–or so I thought until I realized that those years equaled the age of a typical college graduate. Sorry, counselor.

So, as the clock radio ticked away the seconds—or made whatever noise electronic clocks make—I looked at myself in the mirror. I wasn't sure why I was so concerned. It wasn't like I was trying to impress the old crow; I was trying to—

"Mrs. Whitfield?"

I stopped.

It was Flint, whispering.

"Can you hear me, Mrs. Whitfield?"

"Mister...Flint?"

Old lady Whitfield didn't sound too good. I sat still and listened.

"We don't have much time, Mrs. Whitfield, so listen carefully: Karen Griffith is not your niece. She's trying to kill you to get your fortune."

"Can't believe...she would...she couldn't..."

"I bought her story, too, Mrs. Whitfield. I brought her here thinking she'd look after you. But when I did some digging, I found out that the blood tests she showed you were fake. So was the family tree. I tried to see you earlier, to warn you, but she's got André, your mountain of a chauffeur, in her pocket. But your hothouse, Mrs. Whitfield. The tropical plants. Any of them poisonous?

"P-poison?"

"That's right, Mrs. Whitfield. Karen works in a library. She checked out a book called 'Jungqvist's Guide to Cultivating Rare Hothouse Blossoms.' I think Karen's using this book and your hothouse to grow her own deadly flowers, or she's learned which of yours will do the trick. She's probably been putting them in your tea over time."

"Oh...help...me..."

"I will, I will, I'm gonna call an ambulance for you, then I'll call my police pals from the hospital. But she shut off the phone line to your room. Where's the nearest room on this floor with a phone? Can you tell me? Mrs. Whitfield? Mrs. Whitfield!"

"Don't move!"

Uh-oh. It was Miss Fallston—I mean, Karen!

"Look out, Flint!" Yes, I really said that to the air! I even stood up and looked for a place to hide!

"I spun around, reaching for my .38, only to see Karen in the doorway with hers cocked and ready to fire."

"You're a tenacious one, Mister Flint. I would have killed you outright in the garden but a dick of your reputation would be missed, not like my friend at Hollander Labs. I hoped André would be enough to discourage you, but I guess you'll be getting another look at the garden—from six feet beneath it."

Shit-shit-shit-shit!

"I only had one hope of saving the old girl, and it was a long shot—a real long shot. Now, listen to me...You're the only one who can stop her."

What the…? I'd heard this part earlier, but I didn't care. The music got louder, stronger, more threatening. I was getting scared, I was looking for a way out for me, for Flint—

"She's just waiting for the right moment. Don't give it to her!"

Who was he talking to? Old lady Whitfield? What was she gonna—

"If you do, I swear, she'll kill you!"

"She's killing her now, stupid, she's poisoned," I screamed at someone—the radio, the air, anyone, even though I knew no one would hear me because they weren't in the same room, or the same century. "Help her! Help her!"

"She'll kill you, Alex!"

"What?" I screamed.

I stopped.

"Flint? Flint!"

I listened for any kind of reply, anything that wasn't the sound of my heart pounding.

I tried a different approach. "Randall? Mister Meriwether?"

Nothing.

No music. No Flint. No gunshots.

Just silence.

What the fuck?

Who was going to kill me? Karen?

She was in 1957 and I was in 2013, and she wasn't even real! She was a character in a radio show…

But she was played by Magnolia Fallston.

Wait—was that what Flint was trying to tell me?

That *91-year-old* Magnolia Fallston would try to kill me? How would he have known, sixty years ago, that I was going to meet her? How would he have known my name? Hell, how would he have known anything because he was a *fucking make-believe character?!*

Call Burke, I thought. Just call the front desk, ring Magnolia's suite, where he said he'd be waiting, and tell him that dinner didn't agree with me and that I couldn't make it. Or just be honest and tell him I'd gone insane.

But what if he wanted me to meet her some other time during the convention? I couldn't dodge him for two days.

And there was the money.

Twenty-five large just for showing up.

If Flint was right, and Magnolia was planning something—although I couldn't figure out how or why she would—he didn't have to worry.

Like Burke said, she might not be around much longer.

"Hi," Burke said as he opened the door. "What kept you?"

"Just listening to the radio," I said. "In my room. I lost track of time, I guess."

"You're not that late. She got back from the banquet about twenty minutes ago. Come on in."

I walked into the large suite. The Faulkner didn't kid around when it came to pampering its guests. Off-white wallpaper with some fancy pattern in gold. Thick, red carpeting you just wanted to scrunch between your toes. Furniture that looked like it came from the court of Louis XIV, or Louis C.K., I don't know anything about furniture. And at the far end of the room, a set of white double doors, currently closed.

Burke pointed to them. "She's in the bedroom, winding down, probably in bed. She asked me to send you in alone when you got here."

Then, Flint showed up.

"She'll kill you, Alex!"

My spine froze. "You're not coming?" I asked.

"She wanted to talk to you privately," he said, gently ushering me across the suite. "She thinks I'll do everything I can to prove you're not her relative. But you can do that, right?"

I nodded. Not much, but enough, I hoped.

He stopped and gently placed his hands on my shoulders. "You okay?"

"She'll kill you, Alex!"

I half-nodded again. "For twenty-five thousand? Yeah."

Burke smiled, grasped a handle, opened one of the doors, let me in, and closed it behind me.

The bedroom looked as big as the main room I left behind. The furnishings were just as old-looking, but elegant, even in the dimmed light of the lamps on the nightstands to either side of the king size bed. It was one of those luxury models, the kind with a base that's three feet off the floor with a mattress and box spring that add another three feet. It reminded me of a fairytale my mom used to act out for me when I was little and she was sober, the one about the princess and the pea. You've heard it: the princess who was able to feel a tiny pea through a bed stacked with mattresses was considered sensitive enough to marry a prince, or something like that.

The princess here was older than the one I imagined when I heard that story, but she definitely looked like royalty. Her body lay under the bed's thick covers and her head rested on one of many thick, white pillows at the head of the bed. Her silver and red hair was only slightly mussed; I was surprised that it wasn't sitting on a bust across the room.

Her hands were at her sides, palms down.

Her face had no makeup. She looked older than she had in the ballroom, but still not bad for someone of her years. Her eyes were closed.

She didn't make a sound.

Magnolia Fallston, who wanted to see me, and possibly kill me, was asleep.

I stepped toward the bed and whispered, "Miss Fallston?"

Nothing.

"She'll kill you, Alex!"

I inched closer. "Miss Fallston?"

I moved deeper into the room, watching the old girl's chest as she breathed. Short breaths. Shallow. Just what you'd expect.

If she stopped breathing now, no one would be suspicious.

I stopped at the left side of her bed and placed my hand on the nearest pillow.

"Grandma?"

Nothing.

Slowly, I pulled the pillow off her bed and held it with both hands.

"She'll kill you, Alex!"

No, she won't.

I gently started to place the pillow across her face. That's when the old bat snapped her head in my direction, raised her right hand— which I couldn't see because her body blocked it—and fired a concealed snub-nosed revolver at me.

The bullet tore through the shoulder of my dress, taking a small chunk of my own shoulder with it. I screamed, grabbed the bleeding gash, and fell to the floor; the pillow fell on top of me.

Burke burst into the room. "Magnolia! What the—what the hell?"

At the same time, she and I yelled the same thing: "She tried to kill me!"

"One at a time!" Burke said.

"She shot at me!" I cried. "She was sleeping when I came in, I—I walked up to introduce myself, and bang!"

"She tried to smother me with that pillow," Magnolia said. "I told you that Francesca's girl would try to kill me if I gave her the chance, Bryan, and she walked right into my trap!"

"But she's not your granddaughter," Burke said.

"She called me 'grandma,'" Magnolia said.

Burke looked at me. "I thought so."

"What?" I asked.

"I suspected after I checked you out but I didn't say anything to Miss Fallston because I didn't want to get her hopes up," Burke said. "When she saw you in person and told me she wanted to see you, I went along with it. I mean, your mother was an actress, or tried to be. Women like that are all over L.A., but I rolled the dice. I figured that, whether you were related or not, the matter would be settled and she would finally let me draw up a proper will for her."

Loud banging on the door, followed by, "Hotel security!"

"Coming," Burke yelled. He walked up to the foot of the bed and held out his hand to Magnolia.

With a flourish, Magnolia bent her old body forward and placed the gun in his hand. "I don't need it anymore. She knows not to mess with me."

"Do not move," he said as he backed out. "Either of you." He left the door to the main room open, so we were able to hear him admitting two hotel security guys in dark suits, as well as Ogden, still in his tuxedo from the banquet. The security bulls said something about "this gentleman" being on his way to the suite to see Miss Fallston when he heard what sounded like a gunshot, so he called security from a house phone.

Magnolia and I looked at each other again. This time, neither of us looked away.

"You have Francesca's eyes," she whispered.

"I'm surprised you remember. You haven't seen her eyes since you threw her out of your life, bitch."

"I didn't throw her out," she snapped. "She left me. She left to become an actress on television, just like her father left me to become a movie actor. Neither of them wanted to be seen around an old radio drama queen who was dubbed 'too plain-looking' by casting agents. Your grandfather was just jealous because I always got top billing in our broadcasts."

"Grandfather," I said. "Randall Meriwether."

"He wanted his own spotlight," Magnolia went on. "Then, Francesca said I was jealous, that I was afraid she'd succeed where I failed, but that wasn't it at all. I...I just didn't want to be left alone. They couldn't stand being surrounded by dusty boxes of scratchy transcription discs, and old photographs of other 'plain' people from a dead art form. But I can't understand why he tried to warn me about you."

"He warned you? Randall?"

She nodded. "As clearly as if he were in the room with us right now. 'She's just waiting for the right moment.'"

"'Don't give it to her,'" I said.

"'If you do,'" Magnolia said, "'I swear, she'll kill you!'"

Then we both said, "'She'll kill *you*.'"

I finished my sentence with "Alex."

She finished hers with "Magnolia."

We couldn't believe it.

From the looks on the faces of Burke, Ogden, and the security guys—all of whom had been listening to us—neither could they.

Ogden whipped his pocket square out of his jacket and trundled over to me. "Jesus Christ, Alex." He pressed the handkerchief against my wound so hard that it hurt worse. I took it out of his hand and did it myself.

"Ambulance will be here soon," Burke said.

'With the police," one of the security guys said. "Let them sort this out."

"Why didn't you ever tell me she was your grandmother?" Ogden said, eyeing Magnolia like she was the Lost Ark.

"You would have just used me to get to her, to get her fucking *Intensity*, and to get her to sign your fucking photos —"

"Oh, and you weren't using me and the channel to get to her?" he asked, sounding almost like a private eye, and pissing me off more and more as he unraveled my plan. "You knew she was an old radio star, you heard the channel on the radio, and you figured I might get you access. But why were you trying to kill her?"

"Because I hated her fucking guts!" I yelled.

In a room full of fucking witnesses. Dumb.

As Flint said, the waterworks came on full blast. Could you blame me? "Because she turned her back on my...I mean, I thought she turned... she says she didn't, but my mom said..."

I looked at Magnolia, shook my head, and whispered, "Goddamnit."

"Alex." It was Burke. He looked disappointed. "As I mentioned before, Miss Fallston has no will. Under California law, her entire estate would have gone to her next of kin. If you'd simply come forward with proof of your identity tonight, you might have been a rich woman."

"With the rights to *Intensity*," Ogden whispered.

"*Intensity*," I whispered. "I get it now. Randall was telling me a story to scare me away from her."

"And to warn me that you were coming," Magnolia said. "Even after leaving me behind all those years ago, Randall still loves me." She sat back against her pillows, looking like she'd been shot in the face by Cupid. "I wish I could see him, thank him. It almost makes me want to go to my rest now."

"'The Widow's Rest,'" I grumbled.

"I knew there had to be a reason why someone like you would work for someone like me," Ogden said quietly. "Even prison doesn't make a girl that desperate—and I've been a pen pal, so I know!"

Magnolia turned to Ogden. "She works for you? Are you part of this?"

"Yes, ma'am," Ogden said. "I mean, no, ma'am, I'm not part of anything. I just hired her for the sex."

Everyone in the room looked like they were going to throw up right along with me.

"What?" Ogden asked. "A guy can hope. Geez, Alex, why do you think I told you that story about Casey on the drive up? Character development, establishing audience empathy. That's just good, basic storytelling, like the best radio shows.

"You should try listening to them once in a while, Alex."

———

As the paramedics wheeled my gurney out to the ambulance, I didn't pay attention to the conversations I'd left behind—Ogden talking to the police about me, Burke talking to Magnolia about her case for attempted murder, or his case for misrepresentation since I didn't tell him I was her granddaughter, Magnolia telling Burke that it may have all been due to years of misunderstanding, but I *did* try to kill her, so...

I ignored the crowds that had gathered in the Faulkner lobby, and on the street outside. I heard the buzz of radios from the police cars I passed, and the ambulance I was loaded into.

For only a moment, I thought that I might get away with it, that things might even work out between me and Magnolia down the line.

That is, once the police sorted everything out. Handcuffing me to the gurney was just a precaution. Sure.

As we pulled away, I should have heard the paramedics' dispatcher on their speakers.

Nope.

I heard Steven Flint.

Randall Meriwether.

Grandpa.

On the air, in my head.

He knew how the story ended. Karen's story, anyway. *Close enough.*

"Turned out that Karen wasn't the relative Aunt Bertie was looking for, just a desperate girl taking her shot at millions from a desperate old lady. Her inside man at Hollander Labs faked the blood work, but when he wanted more money, she plugged him. Plus, she'd cozied up to André the chauffeur in his favorite bar and promised him a big slice of the Whitfield money pie if he smuggled out books about the family from the mansion's library. That's how she faked the genealogy.

"After the trial, Aunt Bertie rewrote her will, leaving most of her money and property to charity—less a more-than-generous bonus for a more-than-grateful private investigator who gives her a call from time to time to make sure she's doing okay."

"And what became of Karen? Well, what else do you do with a killer librarian?

"You throw the book at her."

MUSIC: ORCHESTRA UP & OUT

THORN
by Michael Critzer

Justine touched the ear piece that was woven into the side of her domino mask and said, "Thorn to Scepter."

She was crouched in the shadows in a black body suit, and she imagined how her warm breath must look floating out into full moon's light. Finally, Ammon's gruff and disciplined voice replied, "Go ahead, Thorn."

"Klarios has been wandering around Old City since he left town hall. No sign of the governor's daughter. And now he's entered a warehouse on the docks—alone."

"Good work. Proceed with caution."

"I can't. He's focusing his gaze directly on what's in front of him. I can't take in his periphery."

"What about others in the vicinity or trace memories?"

"None. The nearest person is a prostitute down the street, and the warehouse has been vacant for a while. It's like he knows I'm watching through him—Ammon, could he know I'm blind?"

"No first names!"

"Sorry, sir, it's just that—is it possible that he's also a telepath?"

There was radio silence for a moment before Ammon responded. "He wouldn't have been able to hide any extensive ability. But it's possible that he has some limited perception. He may have led you around to get a better reading."

Justine pushed her unruly blond hair away from the infrared lenses Ammon had placed on her mask to appear as though she had sight to augment. It's important to shield weakness. His words echoed in her memory, and she felt like an amateur for forgetting them.

"Stay put," Ammon said. "I'm sending reinforcement."

"Yes, sir." Justine hated the whiny adolescent tone of her voice, but she couldn't help it.

"Scepter out."

Time passed slowly as the cold began to seep through her body suit, but drawing the short cape around her only added to the feeling of ineptitude. The weight of the Kevlar grew uncomfortable. Justine wondered who Ammon was sending and how long it was going to take. She had closed her mind off from Klarios, just in case, but she began to wonder whether or not he really had been aware of her presence. What if his actions were just a coincidence? What if the governor's daughter was inside that warehouse and he was doing unspeakable things to her? She had been promised alive if her father dropped out of the election—but not untouched. And the heroic Thorn was simply sitting outside, waiting for more able-bodied help. The thought was so terrible that she let down her defenses in a reckless moment and made contact with Klarios once more.

Justine saw the back of her own head and a rapier poised for an attack. There was just enough time to spin around and knock the blade aside with the guard on her forearm. A roundhouse kick to his stomach left him splayed on the rooftop, gasping for air.

She was doing the same from shock and adrenaline. Luckily, the blow had shattered his concentration and she was able to take in her full surroundings through his wild, momentary glance. There was a roof access door behind him and the warehouse's skylight off to the side. Klarios was quick, though. He was already closing his periphery and picking himself up, still clutching the rapier. Justine tossed a bolas at his feet, but he handily jumped over the twirling tripwire and advanced with a swinging blade. She parried again with her other arm guard. He wasn't aiming for the armored parts of her suit, the ones highlighted in red to draw attacks. Klarios was well trained and dealt only blows that would kill or disable. He moved so quickly that it was all she could do to protect herself. She needed to gain the advantage and fast. When his next thrust came, Justine faked left, leaving his blade behind her, and pushed off of his shoulder to leap for the top of the roof access door. As she did so, a knife appeared from his other sleeve and he sliced into the air.

Justine felt the impact and touched the gash in the front of her bodysuit as she landed. Her skin was unharmed, but the vital organs of her abdomen were now unprotected. *Where was Ammon's help?* Klarios' vision broadened again as he began to laugh and she saw the worried look on her own face, crouching above him in her slashed suit.

She used the opportunity to take him off guard and leapt again. He sliced upwards once more, this time with the rapier, but a well-calculated bolas sent it flying from his hand, and she dropped a smoke pellet at his feet. *Let us both be blind,* she thought, focusing on her other senses.

He approached loudly from the right, and the wind from his coming knife rushed towards her face. She caught and twisted his arm until the blade fell clanging to the ground, but she didn't move fast enough to avoid his other fist. It slammed hard into her exposed stomach. He reached for her neck, but she swallowed the pain and spun away from his grasp. He used the momentum, though, and flipped her over his shoulder. She went flying through the air and crashed through the skylight.

Her only choice was to fire her grappling hook blindly, but on reaching for it, she caught a vision of herself falling and of a woman's arms reaching out to catch her. She felt their firm hold and saw herself being flown back up through the broken skylight to land on the roof of an adjacent building.

"Are you alright?" the woman asked, setting her down gently and looking her over.

Justine saw her rescuer's reflection in her infrared lenses and immediately recognized the statuesque figure in the scant, toga-like costume with long red curls and round polished shield. "You're a long way from home," Justine said, getting to her feet as quickly as she could. *Why did it have to be her?*

"And you're welcome," the woman said playfully.

"I had it under control!" Justine realized that by calling in a big gun, Ammon was acknowledging just how much she did not have it under control.

The woman pointed to the torn suit. "It doesn't look like it."

Justine drew her cape tightly around her. "Since when is Libaertus one of the Scepter's patrol? Aren't you sanctioned by the feds?"

"I'm no government whore, if that's what you're implying."

"Whatever," Justine sighed, as she walked to the edge of the roof and began scanning the warehouse for Klarios.

"Is the girl in there?"

"I don't know, but he's back inside." Justine centered herself with the breathing Ammon had taught her. A temper tantrum wasn't going to make her feel any more competent. "He's different from the usual riffraff," she said finally. "He's calm and calculating. It's like he's in *my* head. He anticipates every move I make."

"But you disarmed him. I saw that much from a distance."

"He was distracted, and I was off guard. I got lucky, but I need to focus. Ammon taught us to cover ourselves from every angle."

"There's more than one way to gain the upper hand. You wait here," Libaertus said in the recognizable tone of an order, and with a sudden gust of wind, she was gone.

Justine knew she was outranked. Libaertus was not part of the patrol but had a history with Ammon that predated it. Still, Justine could not get past the desire to prove herself. It was agony to sit and wait again. With a new pair of eyes on the scene, she would no longer be confined to Klarios' closed focus, and if Libaertus needed help, how would it look if Thorn had been standing nearby and doing nothing? After justifying it to herself, she jumped from the rooftop and used the trace memories of Libaertus to grapple her way back to the warehouse.

She landed near the broken skylight to get a fresh scan. Libaertus was just now preparing to confront Klarios. But there was someone else, a new presence, barely detectable. Justine wondered if it was someone else trying to cloak from her, but the random flashes of vision were too sporadic and incoherent. Could it be the governor's daughter, drugged, or unconscious? As Libaertus landed in front of a slowly pacing Klarios, Justine decided to investigate. She dropped through the broken skylight and worked her way down a pile of crates unnoticed.

Klarios did not seem surprised by Libaertus' sudden appearance. "All by yourself?" he sneered.

"Where is the girl?" Libaertus asked.

"The little thorn I had to pluck, but you—a federal agent with no evidence to hold me? You, I will simply leave to your impotence."

Libaertus forced her shield into his chest as he tried to pass and said, "I'm not asking for the feds."

Justine was impressed and held her breath as she saw the corner of Klarios' mouth contort into a sinister curl and say, "That's my girl."

But what happened next came in such a flurry that she had to break her connection to keep from getting overwhelmed. The clang of sword against shield echoed through the building, and she moved away from it until a trace memory from the fading presence came into focus. It was of a dark corner ahead of her.

She concentrated for more information, but the battle was approaching, and eventually she had to tap back in to be sure she remained hidden. Both opponents were now widely aware of their surroundings. Klarios watched Libaertus step in and out of her open sided toga, and his eyes lingered on her chest, which heaved with the breath of exertion. It made Justine draw her cape around her exposed midsection.

He managed to land his blade here and there, but his attacks did little damage, and most were rebuffed by Libaertus' shield as he in turn dodged the heavy blows of her fist. Yet as Justine watched, she realized that Klarios was learning his opponent's moves, drawing out attacks and countermoves over and over again to learn the patterns. Is that what he had been doing with her? Eventually, Libaertus swung her shield out to deflect a swipe of his blade, and he brought his sword around behind it with lightning speed to stab at her exposed shoulder. It did not fully penetrate her fortified skin, but it cut easily through the clasp that fastened the strap of her costume, which fell away to expose her right breast. His vision immediately focused in on it, and Libaertus' fist entered from the right, to close his eager eyes.

Justine was about to step forward to help finish him off, but another trace reached her from the elusive presence. It was the image of a rusted metal door, and a rogue trace memory from Klarios told her that it was only a few paces behind her.

They were old memories, so Justine moved with caution, truly blind to what may have changed in the area. Her outstretched hands found that the door was still cracked open, so she poured all of her focus into her working senses, took a deep breath, and stepped inside.

"Hello?" she whispered. It was cold and felt empty. The air did not move, but there was the smell of blood. She had to prepare herself for the possibility that something was waiting for her—something cloaked and biding its time. Slowly and quietly she stepped, her entire body on alert.

Something closed around her foot.

She jumped back as whatever it was let go of her. She caught a faint vision of herself, terrified and standing above a bloody outstretched arm. The hand was manicured—a woman's hand, and Justine knew she had found the governor's daughter. She knelt down to feel for a pulse, but it was gone.

———————

Justine walked back out into the warehouse and realized that it had been quiet for some time. Libaertus was standing beneath the skylight over a moaning and barely conscious Klarios, who lay helpless with each of his limbs broken. She didn't seem surprised when Justine approached.

"Find anything?" she asked, still looking down at Klarios.

"The girl is dead," Justine said. "She bled to death as he fought you."

Libaertus looked grim and after a moment said, "A bereaved governor wouldn't run anyway, and the dead can't testify. He was careful."

"Not careful enough," Justine said, admiring Libaertus' handiwork though the recent memories in the air. "Justice would be to execute him."

Libaertus shrugged, "I'll take him to Ammon."

"Are you okay?" Justine asked, pointing to the torn toga.

Libaertus looked down, and there was a faint smile in her voice as she refastened the strap. "Yes, it's rigged to fall apart—strategic distraction to gain the advantage." She looked up at Justine, who saw herself disheveled and covered in the young girl's blood. "You might consider keeping your own alteration," she said, pointing to the exposed midriff.

Justine thought about it for a moment. Ammon wouldn't approve, but as she called up the image of Libaertus fighting Klarios, exposed and dangerous, she liked the idea that there was more than one way to gain the upper hand.

WATER TO SHARE
by Phil Giunta

Beyond the impenetrable diamond casing of the sarcophagus, Hannah slept. Frozen in cryonic stasis, her frail body was clothed in a simple gray elastic material that prevented damage to her skin. Microscopic robots known as nanites had been programmed to protect her cells and vital organs, allowing them to remain perfectly preserved at 77.15 Kelvin. Never mind that nanites had been banned by the System government years ago.

Dr. Isaac Geary gazed into the transparent "tank," as they called it. At the time his wife's cancer had been diagnosed, he hadn't yet perfected the method for transferring human consciousness to a positronic brain. Even now, long-term memory still showed an unacceptable degenerative rate in stasis. Hannah had entered cryonic preservation three years ago. Were Geary to transfer her consciousness to the android now, he would doubtlessly save her mind, but would she still remember him?

He dared not leave it to chance. Rather, Geary continued to work feverishly, programming a new generation of nanites that would retain and enhance human memory until such time as Hannah's cancer could be cured.

Yet Geary's time was short. By now, the System had surely discovered his efforts. If arrested, he would be imprisoned for breaking the almighty

Moral Code. For if God had wished humans to be immortal, She would have created us so. It is not our place to undermine the Will of God. Yet if there were a God, would She not want mortals to use the intellect She had bestowed upon them?

As if sensing his thoughts, the perimeter alarm screeched from the far end of the computer console. System police were approaching, surrounding his laboratory from all sides. There was nowhere to run, but Geary did not fear them. He had always known the day would come when he would fail Hannah, but damn the System, he had to try.

They'll probably let you die, my love. If they do, I will follow. Otherwise, I'll come back for you and bring you back to life. Either way, we'll be together forever.

Geary imagined Hannah, her vivacious smile lighting up her hazel eyes. He wanted to run a finger playfully down the bridge of her nose, to kiss her full lips. All untouchable now beyond the frozen transparent shell.

The laboratory's perimeter alarm grew into a blaring klaxon. He turned away from his wife to silence the damn noise.

Three years later.

"Engines two and five are fried."

Zailyn's crisp, contralto voice was barely audible over the cacophony of alarms. Nearly every station in the patrol ship's cockpit was screeching a warning, all vying for immediate attention.

She turned in her seat at the diagnostics station. Behind her, in the captain's chair, Sandor craned his neck to look past her at the two red flashing lines on the monitor. "Can we shut off these damn alarms?"

"Trying!"

Zailyn worked the unfamiliar console, her hands frantically slapping buttons and flipping toggles. After nearly a minute, the cockpit fell silent save for the rhythmic humming of the three subspace engines that still functioned. She could feel Sandor's crystal eyes on her, but refused to acknowledge him.

"You should do something about that burn."

Zailyn ran a slim finger along the side of her head, tracing the length of scorched flesh from her left temple back to the top of her ear.

Or where the top of her ear had been.

She smoothed back a stray lock of raven black hair. The rest was tied in a tight braid that ran the length of her back. At its end, a decorative wooden clasp about twelve centimeters long concealed a short dagger.

Zailyn considered herself lucky. If it had struck a few centimeters to the left, the pulse from the Syssie's blaster would have drilled a hole through her head. Instead, the shot had merely burned a line through her hair. She could cover it with strategic styling but decided instead to wear it like a badge of honor.

Her only regret was helping Sandor steal this Syssie patrol ship in the first place. It had been the best option at the time, but hadn't made their escape any easier, considering that all government ships were traceable on a restricted frequency. *Note to self: Don't try to pawn precious gems after stealing them from the neighboring planet's royal family.*

Sandor's right hand man, that chrome-domed scumbag Chauzard, had tried to disable the tracking device, but there was no time. Captain Keylan had been on their asses right up to the edge of the system before breaking off. The relentless bitch had probably hauled it to the nearest precinct base, where she'd demand permission to continue pursuit outside her jurisdiction.

Saved by bureaucracy. Gotta love this galaxy.

"We ain't making it to Zhoreen." Sitting on the floor beside the starboard hatch, Nula shook her head.

Sandor whirled on her. "Speak only when spoken to. Is that clear?"

Nula met Sandor's gaze with equal ferocity but did as she was told. Zailyn ignored the exchange, focusing instead on her control panel. Nula wasn't even supposed to be here. She had tagged along looking for some excitement instead of sitting in class where she belonged.

Nevertheless, Nula was right. They'd never reach the Zhoreen system in this piece of flotsam.

That narrowed it down to one option. The only oasis in this black desert was a binary star system known as Thairn. Five planets orbited twin suns that, in turn, circled one another in a billion-year dance of death. A red giant, Thairn Secunde was a cannibal star leeching hydrogen from what had once been its larger brother, Thairn Prime. In another million years, the red giant would likely go nova.

Just as long as it isn't today.

Sandor looked at Chauzard, his partner and friend since their teen years, when they'd sold drugs and weapons to both sides in a civil war between their respective worlds. The pair had made a fortune both during the five-year conflict and after, while the Syssies had had their hands full with racial crimes, riots, and political assassinations.

Yet these two men could not have been more different. Chauzard was tall, stocky, and brutish, while Sandor's height and build were the only average characteristics about him. His short platinum hair and fierce blue eyes caused many a head to turn his way, and, like any practiced con man, Sandor used that to his advantage. No one ever saw the cunning behind those innocent eyes until it was too late.

When the situation called for it, he conducted himself with all the maturity and eloquence of a leader. Where Chauzard was the rough, Sandor was the impenetrable diamond.

"Zard, is there anything in Thairn that can help us?"

His friend was leaning forward, peering at a computer screen that added an eerie blue tint to his gray eyes. He pressed a few buttons on the console and shrugged his broad shoulders.

"The last planet, Orellan. Got an oxygen-rich atmosphere, though most of the terrain's a wasteland. Kilometers of arid, cracked plateaus and sand dunes. Could touch down and try to repair this bucket. Course, with two engines down, it'll be almost a month in the Empty Quarter."

The Empty Quarter was a region of unclaimed space between the Noltaq system, from which they had just escaped, and the Zhoreen Alliance. An expanse stretching about fifty light years, it contained few planets, most of them uninhabitable.

Sandor ignored the moans and sighs from his crew—except Neff, the zit-faced mute with the mop of saffron hair. Neff was from Lavoy, the smallest of Cadron's moons and dedicated to housing their society's "defectives" in an effort to keep the planet of Cadron itself "pure." Zailyn found the politics of her home planet repugnant, which was why she still hoped to take her mother away from there before she became too old for a society that discarded its elderly like so much garbage.

Once, while on the run, she and Sandor had hidden away on Lavoy where Neff provided refuge, food, and medical supplies. In return, Sandor had offered him a chance at freedom from oppression and humiliation at the hands of his own people.

Since then, Neff had proven himself a skilled pilot, learning almost any navigational and helm system with astounding speed and aptitude. Most importantly, having a silent partner who could tell no tales was an obvious benefit in their line of business.

Sandor sat back in the center seat and stroked the blonde stubble covering his chin. "Neff, get us to Orellan. Best speed. Zard, see what you can do about disabling that transmitter. Once we're planetside, I want to make sure we're left alone."

―――――――

Geary awoke and rolled onto his side, running a hand through his graying chestnut hair. He had awakened from yet another nightmare of his trial and exile from Noltaq. He curled into a ball and fought to control his breathing against the sickening dread of never seeing Hannah again. Panic attacks such as this had become a daily routine.

Across his cabin, a wall of computer monitors stared back. Many of them were dark and silent, either from irreparable damage or the simple fact that they were no longer relevant. It was for the latter reason that Geary was surprised to see movement on the center monitor in the second row. Long range sensors. Someone was coming. *Dammit!*

Geary didn't bother to shower first, or even dress before padding down the hall to the main computer center. The long-range sensors indicated that a police cruiser was headed straight for Orellan and would make planetfall in twelve hours. After three years, it was a good bet that sensor technology had advanced enough to detect a planet's climate and terrain from far beyond orbital space.

Doubtlessly, the System police were already puzzled at data that told them of lush forests and abundant bodies of water on this quadrant of the planet. Geary leaned over the center console, stretching his arm to touch the screen. The entire complex had been built by an advanced and long-dead civilization of beings that had evidently been taller than humans. It had taken him nearly four months to learn the systems after he stumbled upon them, and another year to fully interpret their language and numeric system. They had not called their planet Orellan. It was Rentassa.

Geary tapped the screen and expanded a menu of options. He chose the third one on the list. The display changed to a series of virtual bar gauges. Touching each one, he slid indicators into various positions and stepped back.

And slowly, Rentassa changed.

"Something ain't right here."

Chauzard pressed buttons and slid levers up and down the touch screen in front of him. He shook his bald head and muttered under his breath.

Sandor stood beside him, feet spread apart, hands gripping the back of his friend's chair as the police cruiser shook and groaned in its descent through the atmosphere of Orellan. "What now?"

"One minute, sensors show a lush forest with freshwater lakes and streams. Now, ain't nothing but dry desert."

"Which is exactly how you described it earlier."

"Right, but I'm telling you what I saw on the sensor images."

"Sensors are probably fried," Zailyn chimed in. "We stole this crate from the maintenance bay, remember. Who knows what the hell's wrong with it. Not like I had time to stop and ask while I was hacking the helm codes."

"Shoulda had Neff ask," Chauzard smirked.

The mute snapped his head to the side and glared at him, but Chauzard didn't acknowledge as he peered at the sensor screen. It finally settled in a consistent series of scrolling data and images.

"We'll be on the surface in seven minutes," Zailyn announced. "Strap in or hold on, this won't be a soft landing. Half the braking thrusters are shot."

"You couldn't have stole something better?" Nula snarked.

Sandor didn't bother to look at her as he buckled himself into the center seat. "Thought I told you to shut it."

"You keep talking to me like that and—"

"And what? I'll pitch your ass out the airlock right now, little bitch. You're not part of my crew. No one wants you here. For your own sake, don't speak unless spoken to."

Nula looked from Sandor to her half-sister, probably hoping for some familial support. She found none. Zailyn was focused on her job.

The vessel trembled and bucked, but there was no concern for the ship's stability. All police cruisers are built for atmospheric travel—of course, it was a much smoother ride when all maneuvering systems actually worked.

Still, Zailyn had full faith in Neff. She also thought that a brief talk with Chauzard was long overdue. It would be best coming from Sandor. The look in Neff's eyes told her that he didn't take well to ridicule.

You know what they say about the quiet ones…

"I think you're right, Zai, these sensors are hosed," Chauzard grumbled. "Getting traces of some crazy energy pattern down there I ain't never seen before. Dissipating fast."

"Weapon?" Sandor asked.

"Don't think so. Wasn't directed at anything, just dispersed over a large area. Gone now."

At the helm, Neff suddenly reached out and tapped Zailyn on her arm. Eyes wide with fear, he held up three fingers then slammed his right fist into his open left palm.

"We're gonna crash in three minutes!"

Chauzard spun. "I thought you said seven."

Zailyn ignored him, hands working her console frantically. "I don't have enough thruster power to slow this piece of—"

───────────

The others were shouting in panic—all but Neff, of course. Even Zailyn, for all her usual poise and composure, was now frantically trying to save their collective asses. She was sweating. They all were, drops floating away from their faces.

Floating?

Nula was the only one without a seat. Unable to strap herself down, she gripped a handrail beside the hatch and held on for dear life. She was suddenly weightless, the sides of her boots brushing against the cockpit's ceiling. Nula regretted tagging along. She should have listened to her sister. Too late now.

She gazed through the front viewports. Sand as far as the eye could see, even at this altitude. A gleaming bronze object caught her eye. It grew larger as the beige and pink expanse rushed to greet them.

Is that a building?

Nula would never know.

They had agreed to bury her near the ship.

Using the cruiser's port guns, the only ones that still worked, Zailyn blasted a hole in the sand about ten meters away. Beside her, Neff pressed a freeze pack against the right side of his swollen face. He did not look at her, but fixed his gaze through the viewport at what was about become Nula's grave.

Wordlessly, Zailyn limped aft where Nula's body lay, her neck broken. With no way to secure herself, she had been flung across the cockpit into the diagnostic console when the ship had plowed into the sand. The force caused the monitor to snap from its swivel arm and smash into Neff's face.

Police cruisers came equipped with nearly all of the medical equipment and supplies of an ambulance ship—including body bags. Chauzard assisted. He carried Nula's body from the ship, moving slowly to allow Zailyn to keep up. Sandor was already outside, watching but keeping his distance.

Probably a good idea right now, Zailyn thought darkly.

Finally, they reached the site. Chauzard knelt and placed his burden beside the hole. He repositioned himself so that he could gently slide her down into it, but as Chauzard moved, so did the ground. The sand shifted and poured into the hole, taking Nula with it. Her body tumbled over clumsily and disappeared, consumed by the desert.

"Dammit, Zai, I'm sorry."

Zailyn merely stared at the grave, now just a shallow depression of pink and beige. Her half-sister was gone. She'd gone out the way she came in—the hard way. "Don't worry about it. Not like she felt anything."

Sandor approached, standing respectfully behind and to Zailyn's right. "Should we say something? A prayer?"

"What the hell do you care? Thought you'd be glad she's dead."

"I'm a lot of things, Zai, but I'm no monster."

She didn't bother to respond, though a half dozen retorts came to mind. After a moment, Sandor nodded for Chauzard to follow him and placed a consoling hand on her shoulder.

"Whatever you think of me, I really am sorry."

The man she loved, a thief and killer. She could handle all that, but she hated his lies. Zailyn wanted to shrug him off, to take the dagger from the end of her braided hair and plunge it into his hand. She was a fool to stay with him.

Ignoring Sandor, she whispered, "Thanks for your help, Zard."

Chauzard nodded solemnly as he departed. After a moment, Zailyn was alone and wishing that she could jump into a hole in the sand.

How the hell am I going to tell Mom? Zailyn's parents had been divorced for a decade and a half. While her own mother was still alive, Nula had lost hers during a police raid at Ghanzing Belt six years ago—along with their alcoholic father. Zailyn and Nula had agreed it was no great loss. He'd been an abusive bastard who deserved what he got.

After that, Nula had been passed from one family member to another, one planet or moon to the next. No one could handle her. She'd been suspended for fighting so often, she started cutting school entirely. It hadn't taken long for even the toughest boys to steer clear of her.

Unlike Zailyn, such things as perfume and jewelry had been an anathema to Nula. She'd been as feminine as a slab of granite, with all the refinement of a veteran astro-hauler. Truly, there had been almost no family resemblance between the two. While Zailyn was built for speed, Nula had sculpted her body for strength, spending most of her free time lifting weights. Her fiery red hair had been perpetually trimmed nearly to her scalp.

Though separated by light years, the half-sisters had managed to stay in touch after their father's death. Zailyn, who had been living on Cadron when he was killed, pleaded with her mother to take Nula in. It had taken years, but eventually, her mother relented.

Zailyn had hoped that a stable home and family would change Nula. On Cadron, the two had grown closer to the point where the delineation "half-sister" had quickly melted away. They'd become true sisters and Nula had finally begun to mature, though still possessed by that restlessness.

Got that from Dad. We both did. And now it's gotten you killed.

"You don't look too good, Neff. Tell me where it hurts."

In the cruiser's cockpit, Chauzard's smile faded as Neff lowered the freeze pack. The left side of the mute's face was a swollen patchwork of purple, black, and pale yellow. Blood hemorrhaged in the white of his left eye, surrounding an iris of emerald.

"Seen worse. At least you're still alive. Just don't tell Zai I said that, OK? Might hurt her feelings, or she might pull that dagger out of her braid and slit my throat. Bet you'd like to see that, eh, boy?"

Chauzard slid a tool crate out from beneath the diagnostic station and flipped a red switch on its gray metal side. It began to hum and vibrate as a half dozen micro thrusters set into the bottom of the crate fired. Gently, the box levitated from the deck. When it was chest high, Chauzard reached out to stop it. "Finally, something that works in this dump."

As he maneuvered the crate toward the hatch, Chauzard threw up his hand in a desultory wave to Neff. "You just take it easy. Three of us can handle repairs for now. If you need anything, just yell."

This time, he immediately regretted the crack—especially when the freezepack smashed into the back of his head. Chauzard stumbled forward, sending the tool crate spinning out of control until it crashed into the first aid cabinet at the rear of the cockpit.

As he regained his balance, Chauzard pulled his blaster from its belt holster and spun to face Neff—who was already taking aim at his head. The bloodlust in Neff's eyes required no words. The two men stared each other down along the muzzles of their weapons.

"What's the matter, boy? Tired of taking shit from old Zard? All you gotta do is say so."

"Zard!" Sandor appeared in the open hatch. Without hesitation, he stepped between the combatants and approached Neff. The mute did not lower his weapon.

"Neff, I meant to have a talk with him a long time ago about fucking with you. Sorry I haven't done that yet, but it's going to happen right now. Put the gun away and when you've cooled off, I need you to run diagnostics on the thrusters, engines, and fuel while the rest of us assess the damage outside. Can you do that?"

Neff held Sandor's gaze for a moment before nodding. He gazed over the gang leader's shoulder at Chauzard one last time before stalking back to the front of the cockpit.

"You need to shut your damn mouth."

"That any way to talk to your oldest friend?"

"It's because we're friends that I'm telling you to stand down with Neff. Next time it won't be a bag of ice in the back of your head. You think you're the first smartass to pick on him because he's a mute? He's had a lifetime of that shit."

"I'm sure he has."

"You weren't there on Lavoy. I watched him deal with people who bully him. They don't stay breathing for very long. You're only alive because of your status with me, but even that will only go so far. Consider this a friendly warning. Keep pushing him and the next hole in the sand might be for you."

"So how screwed are we?"

The men backed away from each other as Zailyn approached. She was glad to hear Chauzard chastened. While she was grateful for his help with Nula, he could otherwise be a bastard.

Sandor sighed. "Neff's running diagnostics inside. We were just about to check the damage out here. Could use another set of eyes."

"How about another set of hands?"

All three drew their blasters on the newcomer strolling toward them from the cruiser's aft. He was taller than Chauzard, helped by his ramrod-straight posture. A one-piece tan jumpsuit hung from his gaunt frame. His head was wrapped in a white cloth that covered the back of his neck and revealed only his face. Even that was mostly concealed behind enormous sun goggles.

The man held up both hands, palms out. "I'm unarmed."

"Who are you?" Sandor asked. "Where did you come from?"

"Name's Isaac, and I come from the other side of those sand dunes in the West, where I've lived for the last three years."

Zailyn was astonished. "Three years?"

"How come we ain't see you approach?" Chauzard holstered his blaster.

"You seemed preoccupied, whoever you are."

"Maintenance crew with the Noltaq Police," Sandor said. After introductions were made, he continued. "We were taking this cruiser out for a test run, but we had engine problems. We hoped to set down here for repairs, but the landing was a little rough."

"So now matters are worse."

"Afraid so. We didn't know anyone lived on this rock."

Isaac smiled thinly. "I wouldn't call this rock home had I not crashed here. Like you, I had engine failure, and my communications system was destroyed on impact. I didn't have the parts to repair it. I barely had a ship left, in fact."

"No one tried to rescue you?" Zailyn asked. "Family? Friends?"

"None of the above, my dear, because I have none of the above. May I ask, are you from Cadron?"

"I am."

"I thought as much from your violet eyes. They're most intense. Legend has it that the eyes of a Cadronian woman have the uncanny ability to detect even the smallest lie."

Zailyn shot a sidelong glance at Sandor. "If that were the case, I wouldn't be here." *And my sister wouldn't be dead.*

Isaac smiled. "Everyone ends up exactly where they belong in the end. As for me, I probably have no life to return to, but surely you can contact the closest precinct for help."

Zailyn thought of Captain Keylan. By now, she had probably obtained permission to breach her jurisdiction. She and her crew were probably—

"Already on their way," Sandor said. "Of course, that's a week out at best speed. We only have enough food and water aboard to sustain four people for a few days. I have another crewmember inside."

Isaac nodded. "No worries. I have enough to share. Well, Thairn Prime will be setting in less than hour. It's too late to start repairs now. Thairn Secunde rises at a little after ten o'clock. Remarkable sight, everything bathed in red, but the light isn't worth a damn to work by. You're all welcome back to my hovel for dinner and conversation. As you imagine, I don't get the chance to entertain much."

As they rounded the pastel dunes, following the sun as it melted into the rippling horizon, Sandor and crew halted in the shadow of Isaac's towering ship—all except Neff who had agreed to stay with the cruiser. He had forwarded the results of the diagnostics to Sandor's commphone, along with a list of parts needed to get the cruiser space borne.

The wreckage that protruded from the sand loomed over them nearly one hundred meters high by Sandor's estimate. Its bronze-plated titanium hull, tarnished and pitted, widened into a massive trapezoid toward aft. Each of the four engines could swallow a pair of police cruisers.

"That's an antique capital ship," Sandor said. "Retired from government service over a decade ago. The old man must have bought it at auction after the Syssies stripped it down, which means he had money."

"Maybe he still does," Chauzard said.

Sandor nodded. "The rest of the ship must be buried, or scattered in pieces, depending on the impact."

A short distance ahead of them, Isaac turned and waved his arms. In unison, the trio started toward him.

"Why did you tell him another vessel would be coming to assist?" Zailyn asked.

"Because I have no doubt that Keylan will show up sooner rather than later. I needed to make us sound legitimate. Our new friend may have parts aboard his ship we can use to fix the cruiser. Then we can get the hell out of here before the good captain arrives."

"But you told him our real names."

Sandor shrugged and flashed a lopsided grin. "Not like we're taking him with us. Who's he going to tell?"

"Keylan."

"You know me, Zai. I don't leave witnesses."

———

Once they caught up with Isaac, he led them down a long, shallow slope. It wasn't until they reached the bottom and saw the airlock door jutting from the incline that Sandor realized they'd been walking atop the ship.

"When I crashed," Isaac began, "the ship plowed into the sand like a shovel, but over the past four years she's been steadily sinking and sandstorms have covered most of her. I've had to dig out this hatch a hundred times at least."

Zailyn pointed to a small, gurgling pond about twenty meters away. "Is that your water source?"

"My little oasis, yes. The product of an underground spring. It appeared the day after I crashed. I think my ship gouged out a channel somewhere down there and released enough pressure to push the water to the surface. A lucky accident. Nevertheless, I recommend boiling before drinking."

Isaac pulled a lever beside the hatch and turned it to the right. The door slid to the left but stopped about midway. Isaac leaned into it and pushed it open with a grunt.

"Sand gets into every damn thing. This way."

The sun had faded beyond the horizon, and in the east, past the bronze landmark that had been Isaac's ship, the stars were just becoming visible in the darkening sky.

Once inside, Isaac punched in a code on a nearby wall console and the door slid closed smoothly. Just then, an inner hatch opened to reveal a dimly lit corridor.

"Let me give you the nickel-plated tour."

———

Geary knew these people were dangerous. He'd heard everything they'd said since their arrival and had watched as they'd clumsily buried their dead comrade. The woman with the braid, Zailyn, seemed most affected by the loss. She was also clearly disturbed by Sandor's threat to murder Isaac. He filed these observations in the back of his mind.

Though he seemed clever, Sandor's "maintenance crew" story had been ludicrously transparent. They certainly didn't dress like space greasers, and, unless society had degraded drastically in the last three years, they were too quick to draw weapons on a lone stranger—and each other. It was more plausible that they had hijacked the cruiser.

Still, Geary was well protected. If they should move against him, he knew precisely how to handle them.

———

Isaac led them into a dimly lit maintenance shop with workbenches and tables filled with circuit boards, mechanical parts, and tools of every kind. It was all he could salvage from the ship's aft section.

The place reeked of lubricant and the floor was gritty with sand, some of which had been intentionally used to soak up spilled oil and other mechanical fluids. It made Zailyn feel even filthier than she already was.

"I've no doubt the parts you need for your cruiser's engines and thrusters can be found among this clutter, or at the very least we can rig something suitable. Plenty of time for that after dinner."

"I don't want to impose, but is there a place we could clean up first?" Zailyn asked.

"My dear, I can do one better. Follow me."

"A few of the crew cabins still have working showers. They run through the water filtration system."

"Recycled water," Sandor surmised.

"Purified and bacteria-free. You're more than welcome to them. You all look like you could use a change of clothes, too. There's a selection of various styles and sizes in the closets. All of them clean, some never worn at all. If it fits, it's yours."

"How do you power all of this?" Zailyn asked.

"Solar panels embedded throughout the entire hull. The engineering section that you were admiring on the way here harnesses the sun's energy and provides power to the rest of the ship buried under the sand. Of course, I keep most of the systems and lights powered off. Some parts of the ship are dark, so don't go wandering. This vessel still carries ghosts."

Zailyn looked from Sandor to Chauzard. The men seemed amused by the old man's warning. She was not. "Ghosts?"

"This was a warship in its prime, young lady, before it was stripped down and used as a cruise ship and then finally sold off at auction. People died aboard her."

"What's her name?" Sandor asked.

"Originally, it was *Jezebel*, sister ship to the *Ahab* destroyed in battle. I didn't have time to rechristen her before departing. That's a story for another time." Isaac pointed to a cabin at the far end of the corridor. "Knock when you're ready and we'll go to dinner. My treat."

———————

It took three minutes for Sandor to decide. Three minutes and a dozen Syssie police uniforms tucked away in the closet of one of the larger cabins.

"We have to kill him."

Chauzard frowned as he rifled through the familiar dark-green jackets. "No badges, no nameplates, but every rank is here from Corporal to Sector Captain."

Zailyn shrugged. "So he climbed the ranks."

"That would take decades for a career cop. Syssie uniforms changed at least twice in the last twelve years. These are all the same style—the latest one."

"Plus not every rank gets a new uniform," Sandor added. "That's reserved for Commander and above. Below that you get a new rank insignia, that's it. So why would he have so many uniforms?"

Chauzard dropped the jackets back into the clear tub. "They're all the same size. Average build. Ever seen a Sector Captain that wasn't a lard ass after years behind a desk? These can't all belong to one guy."

"Why don't we just ask him?" Zailyn said.

Sandor ignored the question. He stared silently at the uniforms for several seconds. *Could it be? Isaac is certainly the right age...*

"We're waiting."

"Androids."

Zailyn and Chauzard exchanged skeptical glances.

"It would explain why all of the uniforms are the same size throughout the span of ranks. It might also explain how Isaac has managed to survive here for this long. There was a brief experiment six years ago that introduced androids into law enforcement."

Zailyn nodded solemnly. "I remember."

"But it was terminated when the religious zealots took over the government. The androids were pulled from service, presumably destroyed."

"Except for the one that got away?"

———————

"Most of the food replicators work, although I've had some corruption in the database so the menu's a bit limited. Don't order anything with red meat. It locks up the terminal and we'll have to reboot it. Everything else is good."

Isaac had escorted them to a crew lounge complete with rows of tables each with a plush chair on either side. All of the furniture was bolted to the deck. Scattered books, holo games, circuit boards, and mechanical parts filled some of the tables. The rest, while scratched and chipped, were spotless. The air was redolent of cleaning chemicals.

The green-and-blue upholstery on the chairs was hardly frayed, with one exception. While waiting for Sandor and his crew to order their meals, Isaac sat and played a holo word game until it was his turn.

"I wonder if I might ask a favor of your crew member still aboard the patrol ship," Isaac began when they were finally all seated.

Sandor swallowed a bit of bread. "Anything."

"When I was forced to leave my world, I left behind my wife, Hannah. She was terminally ill with one of the few types of cancer that hadn't been cured."

Isaac's eyes glistened as he paused briefly. "She was in cryonic stasis when I left her."

"You want us to look up your wife on the grid."

"Yes, sir."

"Why were you forced to leave?" Zailyn asked.

Isaac drew in a long breath. It returned as a sigh heavy with regret. He wiped his eyes as he replied. "I was experimenting with nanites for use in repairing and regenerating human organs and tissue. As you well know, the current regime of religious barbarians outlawed any form of artificial life and life-preserving technology."

"Including androids," Sandor said.

Isaac nodded. "That was my first project before I turned my attention to nanotech. I had created a series of prototype androids to serve as cops and other hazardous jobs. We piloted them successfully in the Ghanzing Belt. An entire drug trafficking operation was shut down with minimal casualties. Well, human casualties."

Sandor slid his plate onto the table beside him. "Yes, I remember it."

"System police were on the verge of signing on to expand the use of my androids until the government was overthrown and I was exiled."

"I see." Sandor relaxed in his chair and muttered. "Minimal human casualties."

Everyone looked at him just as he pulled his blaster and shot Isaac in the head. The scientist's body slumped, his plate crashed to the deck.

Zailyn screamed.

Sandor holstered his weapon. "My family was killed on Ghanzing Belt by your fucking androids."

Hours later, Zailyn still refused to speak to him. She had just started to grow fond of Isaac. He reminded her of the better side of her—*no, he's long gone and good riddance.* The loss of Nula had obviously softened her. In their chosen lifestyle, attachments were fleeting. Life was cheap and liable to end without notice.

Including hers.

Yet she also feared being alone. It's what kept her from leaving Sandor, and he took advantage of that whenever it suited him.

Chauzard emerged from the maintenance shop, hands and arms streaked with grease and a few minor cuts. "It's all there. Everything we need, even anti-grav carts to haul it back to the cruiser."

"How convenient," Sandor said. "Tonight, we'll sleep in the cabins. At first light, we'll move out. Take some of the clothing with us."

Zailyn shook her head. "I'm not sleeping in this ship. Isaac said she has ghosts, and you just added one more."

"He was speaking metaphorically. In the morning, I'll need you to find whatever you can to collect water from that spring outside. Ship's reserves are low, but if you want to leave tonight, feel free. Don't get lost in the dark."

Zai held his gaze long enough to realize she would relent yet again, though that's all she would give him tonight.

The following morning, Isaac's body was gone—along with the plates, cups, silverware and other clutter. Aside from the tables and chairs, the crew lounge was entirely empty, as if it had never seen a human soul. The faint aroma of cleanser remained, however.

The tattered chair that Isaac had occupied the night before had either been completely reupholstered or simply replaced.

Sandor clenched his jaw, shot a sidelong glance at Zailyn. *This vessel still carries ghosts.*

"Maybe this is a different crew lounge."

"No."

"We don't know this ship, Zai. We could've taken a wrong turn."

She shook her head. "No."

"Where's Zard?"

"I don't know. Gathering spare parts?"

"I'll help him. We still need a supply of water."

Zailyn held up two empty plastic jugs. "All I could find. I'll fill them and wait for you outside. I'm not stepping foot back in this ship."

Sandor stood in the doorway of the maintenance shop, staring at the empty anti-grav cart that should have been filled with spare parts by now. "Dammit, Zard, where the hell are—"

Zailyn's scream answered his unfinished question. Sandor emerged into the blistering heat, squinting against the unforgiving glare of a binary-star morning. To his left, Zailyn stared into the crimson water of the oasis, where Chauzard's lifeless body lay prone, bleeding out.

She dropped the jugs and trudged off wordlessly, avoiding Sandor's gaze. She scaled the slight incline that led to the top of the buried capital ship and disappeared from view.

He made no effort to stop her. Instead, he approached the edge of the oasis and lowered himself to one knee. He reached in with both hands and dragged the corpse of his oldest friend onto the dry, pink sand. The dagger fell out of Chauzard's throat, which was cut one from one side to the other.

Sandor recognized the weapon instantly. He hadn't even noticed it was missing from Zailyn's braid. Apparently, neither had she.

Or…

He pulled his commmphone from his belt and sent a text message to Neff.

[Zard is dead. Need your help hauling parts back to the cruiser.]

[Already here. Look behind you.]

Sandor glanced over his left shoulder. Neff stood at the airlock of Isaac's ship.

"Do you know who did this?"

Neff shook his head.

"Why did you come here?"

[I sent messages overnight to all of you. No one replied.]

"When did you get here?"

[Two hours ago. You were all still asleep. I didn't want to disturb. So I wandered the ship for awhile.]

More than enough time…

[I'm sorry about Zard.]

"How did you get in? The door's coded."

[You know I'm a hacker.]

"You were certainly quiet."

The mute merely stared at him, his expression deadpan. He seemed to know where Sandor was leading. As such, he moved his right hand closer to his blaster.

Sandor did the same.

"Stop!"

Zailyn stared down at them from atop the capital ship. "Stand down, boys."

"He killed Zard."

"You don't know that. You found him after I—"

Sandor held up her dagger. "With this."

Zailyn fell silent as she reached back and swung her ponytail over her shoulder. She unsheathed the…comb? A metal comb! How the hell—

"You lost this when we crash landed?"

Zailyn nodded. "Neff found and gave it back to me. He clipped it back onto my braid for me just before I blasted the hole for Nula's grave."

"And did you check it to make sure the blade was still in it?"

"No, I was distracted and upset, but it felt right. I mean, it had the same weight."

Sandor smiled thinly. "Many of these hair clasps are made with metal combs. They have about the same weight as the bladed ones. Remind me, where did you get the dagger?"

Zailyn shifted her gaze to Neff. "On Lavoy, around the time we met him."

"What a coincidence." Sandor twisted slightly, his arm whipping forward. Zailyn watched as her knife found its mark in Neff's forehead. He stumbled forward before collapsing.

Around his head, pink sand darkened to red.

"He saved our lives!" Zailyn shouted. "Took us in on Lavoy when we had nowhere to go. He was loyal!"

"He had motive. He had opportunity." Sandor lifted his gaze to Zailyn. "And he had help."

Zailyn started to speak, but he cut her off. "Even if Neff somehow managed to hack his way past the airlock, he would've had to find the crew quarters. He couldn't have done that on his own. This ship is a labyrinth."

"I had no motive to kill Zard."

"Except for the time he raped you."

Zailyn felt her mouth drop open.

"You didn't think I knew about that."

"And you never did a damn thing about it?"

"You could've left at anytime. In fact, you're free to go right now. Oh, but you won't leave me. You can't make it on your own because you're weak. So weak you let yourself get raped."

"You son of a bitch!" Zailyn went for her blaster.

It never left its holster. Instead, she stumbled backward before falling to her knees, gaping down at the smoldering hole in her thigh. Through gritted teeth, she snarled at the pain of scorched flesh.

"I, on the other hand, have no problem surviving on my own."

Sandor's second shot opened her chest. Zailyn toppled onto her side, the palm of her hand pressing into the soft pink grit. She thought of Nula, of their father. *Are you together now?* She would find out soon enough. Zailyn raised a fistful of sand toward the sky.

And watched it slip through her fingers until her time ran out.

———

Her entire body jolted.

"Myoclonic twitch. Perfectly normal at this stage."

Stage of—

"What?"

Zailyn opened her eyes with a gasp and squinted against the ceiling lights. Ceiling lights?

She tried to push herself onto her elbows, but her arms refused to move. It was an effort just to slide her hand along the satin sheet covering her. She raised it just enough to see that she was naked. She felt her chest quiver as dark possibilities raced through her mind. She dropped the sheet, then lifted it once more.

The hole in her chest was gone, not even a scar remained. The skin was merely red and slightly tender. Her eyes darted around the room. Across from her, a flat computer monitor filled the wall. Two empty beds flanked her on either side. A few steps beyond the one on her right, a corridor led to parts unknown. Naked or not, Zailyn had found her exit.

She flexed her other hand and reached for the dagger at the end of her braid, only to find her hair unbound and strewn across her pillow.

"Ah, the fair princess awakens at last."

A man moved into view from her left. An impossible man. A dead man. Zailyn opened her mouth to speak but found her brain unable to conjure words.

"I don't believe we've met." Gently, he took her hand in his and raised it to his lips. After a brief peck on her knuckles, he smiled. "Doctor Isaac Geary."

"Isaac," she whispered. "We met yesterday, you showed us…around your ship before Sandor—"

"Not I, my dear. I was observing you from down here the entire time. You interacted with an android." He sighed and shook his head. "Last working unit I had left, in fact. Rather remarkable likeness, don't you think? Pity, it was a fantastic chess partner. Although I suspect it let me win more often than not, but I digress."

He pointed to her chest. "I should have a look at that."

With a glare intended to convey her indignation, Zailyn yanked the sheet up to her chin.

Isaac merely chuckled, which annoyed her all the more. "You realize your clothes did not remove themselves. At my age, I've seen it all, young lady. I merely wish to check your wound."

Zailyn's grip on the sheet remained firm.

"Zai. May I call you that? Zai, I know you're feeling disoriented and vulnerable, but I have an idea."

He reached for something behind her head. After a second, she found her hand once again in his as he wrapped her fingers around the grip of her blaster. "I'm giving this back to you. If I do anything untoward, you have my blessings to shoot. Of course, I would oblige you to keep in mind that I'm not an android. I stand before you the last of me."

The resemblance between this man and his android was uncanny, right down to the sorrow in the eyes and congenial smile that engendered her trust. With a sigh, she lowered the sheet to her navel.

Isaac leaned in. Zailyn turned her gaze to the ceiling as he gingerly pressed and rubbed the skin between her breasts. "Beautiful," he said wistfully.

Zailyn waved the blaster next to his head.

"And when I say that, I refer to the perfect healing of what would otherwise have been a fatal wound...as well as your most ample bosom."

Though she twisted her lips and sneered at him, she found his honesty amusing and didn't mind the compliment either. She cleared her throat. "How?"

Isaac retrieved a glass of water from what she surmised was a counter behind her bed. "Drink this."

He helped her sit up and supported her back as she tentatively brought the glass to her lips.

"It isn't poison. If I'd wanted to kill you, the past two days provided ample opportunity."

"Two days?"

"That's how long you've been comatose. Now drink."

She did as ordered and quickly learned that it was not water. Rancid prune juice mixed with engine coolant came to mind. She launched into a coughing fit that damn near made her vomit. Isaac patted her back.

"What was that shit?"

"My own concoction to clear away the cobwebs."

He began massaging her shoulders. His touch was firm yet soothing. She allowed her head to roll back. "How did you heal me?

"Nanites."

Zailyn jerked away and leveled the blaster at him. "You put those things in my body?"

Isaac raised his hands but did not back away. "I assure you, they healed your wounds, including that nasty burn on the side of your head, and then deactivated."

"They're not natural. They're against the—"

"Laws of God. Yes, so I've heard. So is a life of crime, said the doctor to the gang member leveling a gun at him."

"You gave it to me."

"And does it make you stronger? Does it feel good to have the power of life and death right now, this minute? Are you going to kill me?"

After a few moments of deliberation, Zailyn tossed the weapon onto a neighboring bed. "There's been enough killing since I got here."

"True enough. You should be more discriminating with the company you keep."

Zailyn's eyes widened. How could she forget? "Sandor. Where is he?"

"After a day of wandering the desert in search of your stolen cruiser, he returned to my ship. Since then, I think he's been plotting his next move. Though I dare say his emotional state is clearly deteriorating. As far as he's concerned, he's very much alone."

"Why couldn't he find the cruiser? It wasn't that far away."

"I'll explain later. Just know that you're safe. He'll never find you down here."

"Where is 'down here?'"

"Infirmary, of course. Look around you."

"Were you able to save Zard and Neff?"

"Able to, yes. Inclined to, no."

"Why not?"

"Sandor was correct. Your mute friend killed Zard with your dagger. I don't save murderers, or rapists for that matter. Besides, my resources are limited."

Zailyn squared her shoulders. "Does it feel good to have the power of life and death?"

"Feelings have nothing to do with it, child. Merely a matter of self-preservation."

"But you saved me. Why?"

"I saw something more in you. I saw how you genuinely mourned your sister at her graveside. I saw the way you behaved after Sandor shot my android. You thought he'd killed me and it upset you. You're not one of them."

Zailyn looked away. "I thought I was. Of course, I thought I was in love with Sandor, too."

"Then why are you with him?"

"We've known each other since school. He was always getting into trouble, but he was attractive, charming. All the women wanted to be with him. We saw each other sometimes, had some mutual friends, but after we learned that we'd both lost family at Ghanzing, we grew closer.

"Sandor was always looking for excitement, a piece of the action wherever he could get it, legal or not. I saw the money he was making and I realized that if I could get in on that, I could finally get the hell off Cadron and maybe take my mother somewhere better. She has nothing to look forward to there. The government abandons our sick and elderly to rot."

"I see," Isaac nodded. "So you also lost someone as a result of my androids, yet you don't share Sandor's desire for revenge?"

"For Ghanzing? No. For the nanites, on the other hand..."

Isaac grinned. "And I gave you a weapon. You had your chance to use it, yet here I stand. I think I made the right choice. And speaking of weapons..."

Isaac produced a small rolled towel from his pocket. He unraveled it to reveal her dagger. "Cleaned and polished."

She took it, turned it over in her hands. "Well, it's all over now..." she whispered. Finally, she gazed around the room. "So why didn't you show us this infirmary during the tour of the ship?"

"We're not in the ship, my dear."

"Then where?"

"Questions, questions. You know, there is someone else here who is anxious to see you. Now, don't get nervous and reach for the blaster. I said you're safe here."

"I'd feel safer if I had some clothes on."

"Oh, come on, Zai, it's only me."

Zailyn spun to see Nula strolling over from the other side of the infirmary. She felt her mouth drop open as she jumped to her feet, letting the sheet fall to the floor. She stumbled into her sister's arms just as her knees gave out.

Nula chuckled. "Take it slow, girl."

"How long have you been here?"

"About four days."

Zailyn looked at Isaac. "How did you get to her after we...after we buried her?"

"Nula ended up falling into a tunnel that collapsed when you blasted a hole for her, uh, grave. I sent my android in to retrieve her body and determined that there was still time to save her the same way I did you. Nula, what do you remember before waking up here?"

"The ship was crashing. I was holding onto a rail. I was weightless for a few seconds before I lost my grip and then blacked out."

"You had severe brain hemorrhaging. The hippocampus region was swollen. I think I finally..." Geary thought of Hannah. *Could I save her now and preserve her memories? Maybe if I brought her here...*

"What?" Nula asked.

Geary waved dismissively. "Not important right now. Thank you, Nula. Before we go any further, as much as I enjoy ogling your sister's perfectly round posterior, would you mind getting her some clothes? I need to deal with our new visitors."

"Who?"

"Yet another police cruiser landed a few clicks south of here about two hours ago. The crew is headed this way on foot. I presume they're looking for you."

"Captain Keylan," Zailyn surmised. "This just gets worse by the minute."

"Worry not, my dear, I have no intention of turning either of you in. However, I have to give them someone. It occurs to me that I can't have an armed madman running amok aboard my ship."

"I won't miss that bastard," Nula said. Zailyn nodded.

"Good. In that case, ladies, I have a plan."

From his position behind the crescent sand dunes just east of the *Jezebel*, Geary observed the approaching contingent of Syssies. Despite the derogatory sobriquet, Noltaq system police were anything but cowardly. They had a well-earned reputation for relentless brutality against the criminal elements no matter what the offense—a fact that Geary was counting on.

With a deep breath, he stepped out into view. He allowed himself to tumble down the side of the dune before charging toward the officers trudging toward his ship.

"Thank the Maker!" Geary waved his arms above his head. "Help me, please!"

Two of the officers drew their blasters but the leader, larger in every direction, held up a hand signaling for them to stand down. As he closed the remaining few meters, Geary lost his footing and fell face first into the sand. *Well, this should enhance the effect. Hannah always said I was quite the actor.* He lay still for a moment before crawling toward them. The officers met him halfway.

Geary rolled onto his back. "He's insane! He killed his own people! He tried to kill me, but I escaped."

The leader leaned over, momentarily obscuring both suns, and lifted Geary to his feet with one hand. "Identify yourself."

The woman's badge read "Keylan." She was a head taller than everyone else around her and about twenty kilos heavier. While her olive complexion was smooth and flawless, the captain's eyes were black, such that Geary could not discern iris from pupil. Not even the heat from binary stars could remove the chill inflicted by her gaze. She could doubtlessly halt a riot without need of words or weapons.

"Isaac, ma'am," Geary panted. "Isaac Geary. I live here."

"No one lives here."

"Not until I crashed here three years ago. I was exiled from Noltaq. Look, I don't have time to explain, he just showed up a few days ago."

"Who?"

"He calls himself Sandor. I think he stole a police cruiser. He put down here for repairs. He said they—"

Keylan exchanged glances with her men. "Where is he and how many are there?"

"Just him. He killed the other two. He's hiding in my ship. I think he's lost his mind."

"Take us to him."

Geary stopped before two mounds in the sand, each marked with a holster belt minus the blasters. Presumably, Sandor had confiscated those.

"His comrades. He called them Chauzard and Neff."

"What did they look like?"

"The older one was bald, about my height. The other was a mute, young with ginger hair."

"Definitely fits the description of Sandor's gang. Was there a woman with them?"

"Died on impact. They had a violent landing. She was buried near the stolen cruiser a few clicks north of here."

"Damn. I suppose we'll never be able to ID her. Never really got a good look at her. She only traveled with them occasionally." Keylan nodded toward the *Jezebel's* enormous bronze aft section jutting out of the sand. "Yours?"

"Yes, ma'am."

One of the officers, Sergeant Ellimov according to his badge, let out a short whistle. "That's an old ship."

"I'm an old man. This way."

Once inside the airlock, Geary led them down the corridor to the crew lounge. "He's been in there for two days," he whispered. "As far as he's concerned, everyone else is dead and he's alone."

"He is about to suffer a rude awakening. Remain here."

"Yes, ma'am."

Keylan nodded to her men and all three drew their blasters. The captain raised her hand and counted down from three. Geary leaned against the far wall as Noltaq's finest stormed the lounge, followed by unintelligible shouting interspersed with profanities and a surprisingly lengthy firefight. Apparently, Sandor would not go down easily.

All the while, Geary stifled a yawn, brushed sand from his clothes, and checked the time on an antique pocket watch given to him by Hannah as a birthday gift. *Soon, gorgeous. Very soon now. You're practically in my arms already.*

After a second round of colorful expletives, and a short salvo of weapons fire, all was silent in the lounge. After twenty seconds, Geary craned his neck to risk a peek into the room.

Sandor was most definitely dead. He lay in a crumpled heap on the floor against the far wall just below the food replicator—what was left of it. The touch screen was riddled with smoking blast holes.

Geary tossed up his hands. "Dammit, that was the last working food replicator."

"Sir, don't you think you've had your last meal on this rock? We plan to take you with us, of course."

"That might be complicated. However, there's something I'd like to show you."

"When my ship crashed, it broke through several sections of tunnels like this one. I didn't realize it right away, of course, but when I stumbled upon them I decided to explore."

Pale orange light strips activated as they advanced through a wide passage lined on either side with pipes and conduits.

"Where are you taking us?" Keylan asked. Her hand hovered over her holster.

"To one of the greatest scientific discoveries of the century, perhaps of all time."

Sargeant Ellimov and the other one, Bradova, were on high alert. Their expressions were a mélange of curiosity and wariness as the group reached a set of double doors at the end of the tunnel.

"Relax, everyone." Geary punched in the code and the door parted. He stepped aside and gestured for Keylan and her men to precede him. "What you are about to see is a thing of beauty."

One of the men whistled as he entered. "I'd have to agree."

Geary stepped around the officers. "What you are looking at here—"

The women looked up from a computer console along the right wall. Zailyn's hair remained loose and somewhat unkempt. Her dagger was nowhere to be seen. She had chosen an outfit similar to her sister's, short sleeved pastel shirt and form fitting khakis.

"—doesn't need an explanation, Doc." Bradova grinned.

Geary held out both arms and embraced the women. "Girls, we have guests. Captain Keylan, these are my granddaughters Senia and Valese. I took them under my wing when their parents died unexpectedly."

Geary observed Zailyn's deadpan expression as she met Keylan's gaze. If the captain recognized her, there was no outward indication.

"What about Sandor?" Nula asked.

Keylan drew her shoulders back and inflated her chest. She spoke in a crisp, intimidating tone. "That threat has been eliminated…permanently." Was there a slight grin of satisfaction tugging at the corners of her mouth?

Zailyn closed her eyes and let out a long breath.

Geary gave her shoulder a fatherly squeeze. "I cannot imagine the kind of woman that would travel with such vermin. I was forced to hide my girls away from the whole lascivious lot."

"I can see why." Keylan gazed at Nula and yes, this time the grin was unmistakable.

Nula's eyebrows shot up as her face reddened.

Geary snapped his fingers. "Where are my manners? Might I offer you and your men some water, Captain?"

"That would be appreciated."

Geary stepped over to the control panel and activated a line of small touch panels lined up below a massive viewscreen that consumed the entire width of the wall. Finally, an exterior image of the desert appeared, bathing the entire room in a vivid pink hue.

"Would it surprise you to learn, Captain, that Rentassa is actually forty percent water?"

"Beg pardon?"

Geary raised a hand toward the viewscreen. "This planet is called Rentassa."

"I think you've been out in the binary suns for too long, Doctor. This planet is Orellan, and it's very dry and very dead."

It was Geary's turn to grin. "Not to the civilization that built this." He pressed two icons on one of the small monitors then slid a finger across the one beside it.

An audible hum from somewhere beyond the walls grew steadily into a high-pitched whine. Geary turned away from the viewscreen and clasped his hands behind him. Nearly in unison, all three officers moved their hands above their holsters. His "granddaughters" merely looked at him expectantly until their eyes were drawn to the viewscreen.

As Geary regarded their expressions, the illumination dimmed, casting their faces in deep green. He took satisfaction in their awe. He'd felt it himself the first dozen times.

Finally, the room fell silent. Geary waited.

"What the hell just happened?" Keylan asked finally.

"So that's what Zard saw."

All eyes turned to Zailyn.

"Who?"

"Uh, the bald guy. That was his name, right? Zard? I overheard him say something about their ship's sensors reading a forest one minute and a desert the next."

"I thought your father kept you tucked away from them."

"Surveillance camera throughout the *Jezebel*, Captain," Geary informed her. "Once I translated this ancient language, I was able to link up some of my equipment to the computers here. We were able to monitor everything Sandor and his crew did and said. We don't even live on the ship anymore. No need to. You asked what happened. Come with me."

He led them through a different passage, this one angled up toward the surface. After a few minutes, smooth metal walls and artificial light gave way to jagged rock on all sides. Sunlight shone in from an opening ahead.

They emerged on a hillside covered with lush trees and shrubs. Directly ahead, a stone path led to a clear freshwater lake that stretched to the horizon.

"Did I say forty percent water, Captain?" Geary smiled. "Why not fifty or seventy? I have plenty of it to share. Enough for the entire galaxy."

"I don't understand. Where are we?"

"Not too far from where you landed. Your vessel is on the other side of this hill. What you're seeing is instant terraforming. According to what

I've learned from the ancient database, there are dozens of these machines spread out across this dry, dead world. Each one can alter the molecular structure of the landscape for a thousand kilometers or more. Imagine duplicating this technology."

"Starvation, poverty, even war would become obsolete." Keylan shook her head in amazement. "You could write your own ticket."

"My needs are small, Captain. In fact, I'd prefer to write a ticket for someone else."

Six months later

"This is gorgeous, Isaac."

"No more so than you."

Hannah laid her head on his shoulder and he ran a finger gently down the bridge of her nose. They sat on a giant palm taken from a tree that, until now, had only existed on one planet in the known galaxy.

Tame waves caressed the beach, occasionally reaching as far their toes. This time, the sand was powder blue. Geary had grown tired of pink.

"As far as the eye can see is yours, love. From the moment I discovered the power of this technology, I knew it would bring us together again. Of course, I had no idea that it would inspire a rebellion on Noltaq that would overthrow the religious zealots."

Hannah lifted her head and kissed him. Their years apart melted away, forgotten. He turned to her, pulled her on top of him as he lay back onto the sand.

Someone cleared their throat.

Geary opened his eyes. Hannah glanced up.

Nula was grinning. Zailyn folded her arms. "Get a room."

Geary sighed. "Children never give you a minute's peace. So, Zai, how goes the business of ferrying curious scientists and politicians from every surrounding system to and from our little world?"

"Lucrative."

"Boring," Nula added.

"It may lack adventure, young lady, but your current shipmates are far less hazardous to your health. So, have you come for a dip in our ocean? The water's fine."

"We didn't bring swimwear," Zailyn said.

Hannah shrugged. "It's a private beach, just the four of us."

"And considering I've seen you both in the buff, what's the harm?"

Hannah raised an eyebrow. "Just what have you been up to while I slept, husband?"

"The nanites made me do it."

Zailyn glanced at Nula. "Shall we?"

"I will if you will."

Hannah stood and began shucking her swimsuit. "I think I'll join you. Coming, Isaac?"

Geary stretched out on the palm leaf and enjoyed the view. "As a scientist, I'll just observe."

"Dirty old man," Zailyn said. "By the way, I've been thinking more about getting my mother off Cadron. I was hoping to bring her here. I think she'd be happy. If that's OK?"

"You don't need my permission. This is not my world. It belongs to the galaxy."

"That reminds me. I keep forgetting to ask. What does Rentassa mean?"

"It means 'new life', my dear. Rather appropriate for the four of us, wouldn't you agree?"

DELUGE
by Stuart S. Roth

Doctor Jahn Calvert watched the darmat through the durma-plex portal. It was a tan-skinned, graceful creature; one of the quadruped predator offshoots of the "mother originator." It resembled an Earth lion, except that it had no fur and its body was taller and thinner in adaptation to Proxima's lower gravity and atmospheric pressure. The creature paced back and forth next to the cliff edge. Calvert finally gave up watching and returned to his study of the Sky-tel data.

Sky-tel had been the first earth visitor to Proxima. That was ten years ago. Since that time, the satellite had sent back detailed maps of the surface, geological probe data, atmospheric composition stats and the usual pre-colonization goodies.

Calvert kicked back in the chair and scratched his salt-and-pepper beard. This was a long way from the sterile environment of the Valles Maranaris Zoo on Mars, but this is how he liked his xenobiology.

Occasionally, the young bridge officer would disrupt him in order to reach a control or adjust some display. Unlike most scientific observers, "Yawn", as the crew had paternally dubbed him, had tried to remain unobtrusive. The military was here to do a job and the last thing he wanted to do was interfere with it.

Calvert studied the Sky-tel photos. Their high-resolution images showed the base camp ship sitting on the edge of the continental plateau,

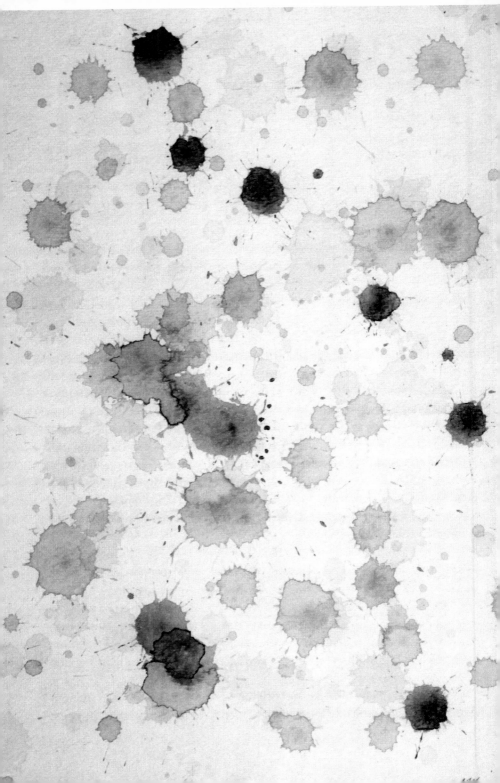

with the coastline dropping off as a sheer cliff to the sea. The cliffs were tall enough to prevent moisture from reaching too far inland. The coastal plateau was lush and green, while only a few miles inland the land turned to a desert. That suited both the colony planners and environmentalists. The colony could be placed in the arid fringe, and draw water from irrigation channels.

What interested Calvert more about this region was the way the sea jutted inward to form a round, deep-walled gorge—the "Proxima Punchbowl." Base camp rested on the edge of the bowl and a thick cloud layer always obscured the bottom of it. The puzzle was that the bowl had smooth-as-glass walls. Sky-tel data showed it would have been perfectly circular if not for the entrance to the sea. It looked artificial, but ten years of data showed no intelligent life here. Wind and rain could do amazing things. Probes sent to the bottom showed a tropical sub-biosphere had developed there. Amazing.

"Jesus!" the young deck officer shouted.

"What happened?" Calvert nearly jumped out of his skin.

"That darmat out there. I was watching it and—well, then it just jumped off the edge."

Calvert passed him a side-long glance. "Must have got too close and—"

"No, sir. I saw it. The cat just leaped into thin air."

An army of robot bulldozers, graters and pre-fabricators busily carved out the foundations for what would become a human colony of thirty thousand. Most of the ship's surveyors were two miles north, puzzling over how to make the irrigation system work. Proxima was mostly land, with the land surrounding a single, large sea. At some time in its history, the ocean had been level with the land, but a great volcanic event had collapsed a substructure beneath the water and caused the entire body to fall rapidly. Some cliffs were five miles high.

Moisture brought up from the sea never reached very far beyond the high cliffs. Rain-rich air would be forced to give up its moisture only on the narrow edge of the plateau, creating great torrential rivers that were only fifty miles long, but nearly as wide. At other times of the year, waterfall would be so scarce that the rivers would dry to mere trickles. This was the problem facing the irrigators.

"Yawn, I can't give you Sky-tel," Major Larson cut off the rambling professor.

"I need to know more about the Punchbowl. Do you know how frustrating it is, looking at the same cloud layer?" He slapped the printouts on the ward room table.

"The satellite is in use by the survey team, be reasonable about this."

"A monkey could tell them what to do! Blast a damn collection pool and run pipes. There, problem solved."

"That's what a Big Val degree buys these days?" Larson jabbed. The zoo at Valles Maranaris had produced a number of scientific observers who had been real pricks to Larson on prior missions. In the past three months he and Yawn had never argued about anything. "Why the sudden hurry?"

"One of his cats fell off the cliff yesterday," First Officer Winslow piped in. "He wants to climb down and fix its leg."

"First of all, it isn't a cat, secondly..." Calvert cursed himself for being dragged down to Winslow's level. "The Proxima gorge is a unique geological and xeno-life reserve. It should be studied to see what effects there will be to putting a colony next to it. I'll go down myself, all I need is use of the space platform long enough to plot a landing course."

"This list of data is more than just a landing. It's a shopping list."

"I need to know what plant life is down there. You try landing the skiff in a tree."

"Priorities of the mission, Yawn," Larson concluded. "You know the drill."

Calvert lowered his gaze to the ground as he spoke. "Then you leave me no choice but to call in a potential biological hazard alert."

Larson and Winslow exchanged a bad look between them.

"Regulations state that all personnel will be subject to quarantine and must use protective gear until full determination of the danger is reached," Calvert added.

"Shit! Do what you want, I'm not following this crap," Winslow shouted, but Larson knew better. Regs said the scientific observer could make a hazard call at his discretion—even if everyone knew it was only to get his own damn way.

A faint alarm sounded from one of the instrument panels. "Proximity alert," the crew boss explained. "Always goes off if one of the local critters lingers too close to a sensor."

A second proximity alarm sounded. "Two at one time." The boss got out of his chair to check it out.

Suddenly the room was engulfed in noise. Louder, more urgent klaxons told them that money was in danger. "Robot command shutoff!" Winslow said. "Something has overturned one of the drones."

"Camera three online," the crew boss added. "I'm pumping it down to the ward room. Doctor Calvert, you might want to see this."

Onscreen, almost indistinguishable amidst the clouds of sand and dust being kicked up, were herds of animals. Darmats, along with sand feeders, prairie herbivores and other multi-legged creatures he had never seen before, filled the screen. "Are they heading for us?"

Larson tapped Winslow. "Sound the alarm. Get our people inside and advise the survey crew what's going on."

The storm of animals passed by like a wind. Everyone assumed they would reach the cliffs and stop. Calvert, Larson and the bridge crew watched as the mass of creatures swarmed around the landing struts of the baseship, overturning equipment and pre-fabs before reaching the Punchbowl.

They didn't stop at the edge. It was a thing of awesome horror to watch. Hundreds and hundreds of the beasts just ran blindly to their doom.

The crew boss heard Sky-tel chime for more data. He pulled himself from the spectacle and loaded the prepared uplink package. When the computer accepted it, he hit the transmit sequencer.

Instantly there was a change in the herd's behavior. Those that could stop themselves in time veered away from the cliff and attacked the ship. They leaped onto the nose and airfoils. It sounded like war drums pounding out on the hull.

"This is insane," Winslow flinched back.

"Doctor? Do you have any ideas?" Larson asked.

Calvert noticed the crew boss completing his transmission. He'd become familiar with the uplink system from his many reports broadcast via Sky-tel to science command. Once the transmission signal had completed, the sound of the beasts against the hull subsided. They peacefully returned to jumping into the Punchbowl.

"Darmat species and sub-species make up over one-third of all animal life on this planet," Calvert explained to the crowded wardroom. "Unlike on Earth, evolution here on Proxima has allowed one branch of creatures to retain its genetic uniqueness, despite the vast variety of physical forms it may take."

A holographic display illustrated his point. "The six-legged herbivore eserophin, the four-legged darmat predator, the winged sauron, from a micro-biological level they are all the same type of creature. All come from the same 'mother originator.'

"Darmats make up one-third of all species on this planet. They may be the most adaptive creatures in the universe. Their diet consists of the other two-thirds of the animal life and most of the plants. In short, they are the linchpin for this entire ecosystem. If humans coming here is going to disrupt their patterns, we have to know now."

"But they are jumping into the gorge, not at the ship," Larson said.

"Hardly a natural phenomenon—"

"How the hell do you know what is natural for them?" Winslow barked from the back of the room.

"Our ship is conspicuously close to the gorge. Its functions could be inciting them, as we already know the transmitter to Sky-tel does."

"Lemmings!" Winslow added. "Stupid buggers run into the sea on Earth."

"This is the only recorded incident of this type of behavior in ten years of study. Gentlemen, the order comes from science command, not me. We need to halt terraforming operations until more is known about what is going on."

The meeting ended in grumbling discord. Officers and men knew this could well affect their bonuses.

"Hey, Major Larson," Calvert caught up with him in the corridor. "I'm really sorry about all this."

Larson jabbed at him with his finger. "Listen, Professor, I don't care if a bunch of these things jump into a gorge. I don't even care about the delay and bonus. When a colonization job stops, all of the plans, all of the time-tables go to hell."

Calvert tried a disarming smile. "Technically, from what you just said, you do care about the delay." His attempt at humor failed completely.

"The plans get all screwed up. I like everything in its place. Its proper place."

Calvert took a step back. "I suppose now would be a bad time to ask for two men to help me catch one—"

Larson threw up a fist in a gesture that was half warning, half wave away, then he left for the bridge. Calvert followed. "I'll give you your men," Larson called over his shoulder in a moment of weakness. "Anything to hurry this thing along!"

"Sir," the crew boss handed him a printout. "Sky-tel reports a hurricane moving in. Landfall to the south in two days, with a chance of it moving up the coast."

"Thank you." The major turned to Calvert. "The perfect end to a perfect day."

———

Catching a darmat proved more difficult than Calvert had imagined. They were agile and graceful creatures, capable of great bursts of speed. As they trickled to the edge of the precipice, their movements were slow and lumbering, but as he and his two assistants moved in with nets and stun guns, they would wake in a blur and disappear off the cliffs.

Calvert walked to the edge. He stood so close that his toes hung over the abyss. The rim ran in a wide arc, disappearing to his left and right. Below was a thick layer of clouds, up from which came a howl of wind and the mystic call of great heights. It was hypnotic. What could be down there? He stood there, feeling the wind blowing against his jacket. It was a cool, dry air. All the moisture had been wrung out as condensation in the clouds below. Beyond the horizon was an approaching hurricane. Perhaps its winds were strong enough to reach from the great sea up to the top of the bowl.

"The transmitter," Calvert said. "We can use it to lure one of them. Then we circle it and hit it with stun guns."

The crewmen, joined by two off-duty officers, formed a semicircle around a pole driven into the ground. At the top was a weak transmitter. They waited eagerly, knowing that the next preoccupied "cat" would be no match for them this time. As time passed, they had to take turns sitting, and the two volunteers left them.

Calvert resorted to desperate, silent prayers, but no new victims dribbled into the camp. Then the rains began. Winslow delivered some rain gear, not out of concern, but as a chance to deliver some ridicule. Calvert ignored him.

The hard-packed earth turned to mud. Calvert looked up from the little rivulets forming at his feet just in time to see the darmat enter the camp. It trotted beneath the baseship and passed the transmitter. Then it moved to the diminished circle of men. Dark red eyes scanned the humans and the muscles of its back legs began to ripple. Just before it leaped clear, Calvert turned on the transmitter.

The darmat turned and snarled. A mouth with rows of curved razor teeth tried to bite back at the unseen transmissions. When this failed to stop the fever in its brain, the creature leaped at the transmitter.

Slipping and sliding, the men descended on the biting, growling creature. Stun guns made its rage more intense, but slowly managed to sap its energy. Calvert and crewman Hanley moved in with the net. Stun blasts flashed. Winslow even joined the fight. The creature raised a final, tired paw, then collapsed. The net was thrown over it and a round of cheers went up from the crewmen who had assembled under the baseship.

Calvert shook hands with each of the men. Hanley began tying down the rope, but realized he had left the magnetic hoist by the precipice. "Save it 'till I get this fellow buttoned up, Doctor. If it gets up now we'll feel pretty stupid." He ran to the edge and reached for the mag-lock.

Dots appeared in the sky. They soared gracefully. Calvert followed Hanley's gaze and saw them now. Half a dozen at first, but as the eye adjusted to the light, one could see many more, higher up.

Shadows passed over the camp. Saurons with fifteen-foot wingspans glided overhead. More and more came. Calvert ducked as one nearly clipped his head. The others dived to the ground as things became tense. Hanley squatted, mesmerized. He turned this way and that to get a good look at the birds. Then one dived out of the formation.

Calvert saw the swift-moving shadow. "Hanley! Get down!" No time. The bird reared back too late. Hanley raised his arms to stop the approaching claws and wings. He let out a scream and tumbled backward over the precipice.

Everyone watched in icy silence. Calvert felt the eyes of the others fall on him.

"Another change in the storm track." The crew boss handed Larson the report. "Should make landfall in our area within nine hours. Shall I alert the survey crew?"

"Get them back and dedicate Sky-tel to tracking its progress. We should be safe on the plateau. Heavy rains, tolerable winds. Where is Doctor Calvert?"

"In the science center, I think, sir."

Since the death of Hanley, a somber tone had filled the ship. Larson had never lost a man before. It bothered him, bothered him badly, but not in the way he thought it would. For every mission, he had to prepare a budget. That budget included a contingency for a death or two. That, of course, did nothing to diminish the feelings of guilt and responsibility that would plague a commander later, but it was meant to help him get on with the present. Losses were expected and were accrued for. What bothered Larson was that the man had died for something stupid.

He watched Calvert through the observation window. The professor was monitoring the sleeping darmat with a scanner.

Larson slid open the door. "Yawn, the storm is moving in. It will be here in nine hours."

Calvert looked like a man who had already been through a hurricane. He looked tired and strung out. "These brain waves are different from the recorded patterns."

Larson felt his anger well up. It was clear the doctor felt some remorse for Hanley's death, and damn it, he should. He wanted to wring an apology from the man, but what good would that do?

"They react to our transmitter. However, I don't know why. Their whole nervous system is acting on a hyper-intensive energy, some type of adrenaline perhaps."

Larson watched him for a moment. "The hurricane is on its way. I'm retracting the scientific equipment."

"No. I need to see what is down that hole," Calvert demanded. "Sky-tel—"

"Is monitoring the storm!"

"Whatever is doing this to these creatures is down in that gorge. It may be gone after the storm."

"There's nothing down there. Preliminary scans show nothing but a jungle. I thought you said it was us causing this. Which is it then?"

"Maybe we are; I don't really know. The crew boss told me he was getting feedback on the uplink signal." Calvert pointed to the darmat. "That signal is washing back over this entire region. Are the saurons still outside?"

"Most of them have flown into the gorge," Larson answered.

"Give me a skiff then!" Calvert paced the room in frustration. Larson guessed that maybe his own adrenaline was elevated.

"Doctor, I think you should gain some perspective here. We have a very dangerous storm coming in. I'm not giving you a skiff."

———————

"Gain some perspective." Those were the words Calvert repeated as he clubbed crewman Bartello over the head and climbed into the jump skiff.

Larson had assigned a reluctant Winslow to performing a frequency scan of the area, as a sop to the professor's needs. He was on the bridge when the two-man aerolite-like device glided across the viewport. Everyone liked to see the tightly wound first officer spin out of control at one incident or another, and they weren't to be disappointed now.

Winslow's parents had always cursed up a storm when things went wrong, and he was the apple that hadn't fallen far from the tree. After a flurry of obscenities turned his face red, he tried to calm down. "Calvert, you dumbass! Mars egghead! Get the hell back here!"

Calvert didn't bother to respond. Through the transparent walls of the skiff, his face and body looked tense. He fought the updraft from the Punchbowl and guided the craft over the cliff.

———————

Larson studied the Sky-tel charts of the storm and noticed a particularly high level of electromagnetic energy in its wake. It wasn't particularly uncommon in a storm, but it did catch his eye.

Looking over Calvert's equipment, he noticed it was capable of simulating any type of transmission, from high-gain to low-wave, even the electromagnetic backwash from the ship's drive units. He looked at the chart a second time, then set the dial on the simulator to the frequency reported by the satellite. The machine sent a burst through the room. The darmat reacted instantly with a frantic twitching of the muscles. Another machine showed a spike in brain wave activity.

Larson skimmed through his data sheets. These electromagnetic bursts were quite common in storms monitored since their arrival. They were centered in the heart of the storms, but dispersed in a wide, circular pattern over hundreds of miles.

His communicator chimed and Winslow's voice sounded. "Calvert's taken off into that pit of his."

"I'll be right there."

———————

Calvert had to fight the controls every inch of the flight. The fierce updrafts threatened to push him into the cliff wall. The aerolite was equipped with a proximity sensor that pinged out the danger. Each time the pings became frantic he pulled back on the instrument controls.

He ignored the calls from the base camp. His recent actions seemed like a blur of distant memories. Somehow they seemed justifiable, despite the little voice in his head that warned otherwise. Then, as if in an attempt to silence his rational mind, his brain wondered what would happen if one of the suicidal darmats should choose to jump off the cliff while he was descending. Wouldn't it be ironic, killed by one of the very creatures he was trying to save?

The craft descended into the thick, billowy layers of clouds. The aero-skiff's lights created a rainbow aura in the moisture outside. Turbulence was even worse here. A couple of times he almost lost control. The ping of the proximity sensor stabilized, and he broke free of the cloud cover.

Beneath was a wide rainforest of red, blue and green vegetation. The walls of the Punchbowl were smoother here. The skiff's lights reflected off them as if they were mirrored.

Everything was murky. Light rays filtered in through occasional breaks in the clouds and were fractured into prismatic spectrums as they reached the forest growth. Moss and fungus grew on the walls as they continued below the tree line. Here, the winds had stabilized, and he found it easy to glide the skiff away from the cliffs.

Through the observation port at his feet, Calvert could see the resting-place of the suicidal animals. Thousands of their inert bodies lay in broken heaps. Sauron carrion-eaters fed on their remains.

Calvert located a clearing and set the craft down with relative ease. "Calvert! Calvert, answer me." Larson's voice replaced Winslow's on the communicator.

Feeling that some explanation was necessary, Calvert replied, "Major, I wanted to let you know that I am down and safe. I have to see what I can find here."

"The hurricane is due in less than two hours."

Calvert cut off the communicator and popped open the skiff door. Warm, moist air leaked in. It was heavier than the air on the plateau. He found himself choking on it at first. His body soon adapted, however, and he ventured outside.

Evidence was everywhere if he had had the presence of mind to realize it.

Layers of bones, picked clean with age and covered by moss and parasites, crunched underneath his feet. He selected a couple and dropped them into a specimen basket. The skiff had landed close to the coast.

Jungle sounds assaulted his hearing. Most of what was heard were the calls and mockings of the saurons. They made otherworldly, guttural cackles. Insects were another source of noise. They flocked and swarmed around him. What equivalent to malaria did this world possess? Was he insane for coming here? Perhaps this was as suicidal a gesture as the darmats leaping into the Bowl.

Turquoise water lapped ashore in powerful waves. Dark storm clouds loomed on the horizon. Ahead of these clouds were white specks on the water. As Calvert focused, he became conscious of movement to his left and right. The coast was alive with giant, seal-like creatures. Aquatic cousins of the darmats, perhaps. They were nearly silent against the loud crashing of the waves. The white specks in the water were more of their numbers coming ashore.

Sense finally took hold of him and he backed away. These beasts might appear docile, but in great numbers they could easily crush him underfoot. As he stepped backward, his feet caught on a root or stump and he tumbled over. Catching himself on a branch, he righted himself and heard the gnashing or sloshing claps of something. Behind him was a tubular hole leading into the mud. It had appeared from nowhere, and seemed to be the gullet of some sort of carnivorous plant. It slapped its mudflaps, trying to feel for the prey that had tripped one of its appendages. Satisfied that the meal had escaped, it submerged back into the mud. Calvert noticed its shiny exterior. The thing looked to be resistant to heat and other strong elements. In fact, it resembled the sides of the Punchbowl.

A rustling sound from behind told him the aquatics were moving. He ran for the skiff. All he could do was pray that there were no more tubes waiting to open at his feet.

The skiff offered no protection. Aquatics stampeded across the jungle in furious clouds. They buffeted the tiny craft, destroying its lift stabilizers and tossing Calvert about. When the herd settled, he found himself surrounded by a sea of them.

Calvert switched on the transmitter. "Larson, can you hear me?" He realized something: *The bones scattered about. This suicide ritual has happened before. The tube plant was probably adapted to take advantage of these events. Can it be some sort of spawning instinct?*

"We've been trying to reach you for the last hour. Yawn, get out of there." Larson's tone begged no argument. Calvert felt sure he would have obeyed, had the ship's systems been working.

"I can't. I'm going to have to weather it out."

"Negative. There is something coming." Calvert knew he wasn't just talking about the storm. "Something is in that hurricane. Maybe it's alive, I don't know."

Wind and rain began to blow through the jungle. The animals stirred and fought with each other as it whipped them into a fury. Rain began to splatter on the windshield.

"What do you mean?"

"Our transmissions, they're similar to something being emitted in the eye of that storm. It's attracting them to the gorge."

"Oh my God! A charnel pit." Calvert could see it now. "Something out there has evolved a very large telepathic net."

"Get out of there," Larson repeated.

Damn the safety systems. Calvert strapped in and engaged the engine. It wouldn't start. Rain began pouring down on the roof.

Out at sea, the storm grew into a swirling mass of dark clouds. Larson concentrated all of Sky-tel's analyticals on it.

"My gut tells me something is there," Larson interrupted as Winslow began diagnostic telemetry on the skiff. Calvert ran through the checks and finally did a re-route of some fiberoptic cabling.

"This is all we can do. Wish the bastard luck," Winslow said. "I've got his diag board mapped to this readout. Hit it, Doc."

Calvert could hear the winds of the hurricane touching the outer shoals. The sound was loud enough to penetrate the skiff bubble. Then, he heard the sound of trees snapping and undergrowth blowing about. He also noticed that the fighting and jostling of the aquatics had settled to an eerie calm.

Calvert pushed the ignition start button just as the strange quiescence of the aquatics spread to him. For a moment there was no response from the engines. This triggered a panic that shook him from lethargy. Suddenly, the control lights came on, red at first, then green. All go. It was impossible to hear the engine over the din outside.

"I've got it. I'm online and taking her up."

An ocean wave swept over the beach. It looked like a giant tongue lapping through the open jaws of the Punchbowl's narrow mouth. The storm struck the coast and lumbered into the gorge.

The skiff began to lift. It was a tranquil rise, considering the difficult landing. Calvert never considered how or why it was so easy. He felt peaceful and calm, confident he was almost home. The proximity alert pinged away, indicating he was a safe distance from the walls.

The deluge poured over the jungle canopy. It rained down on the saurons and aquatics and the bodies of the darmats. Steam began to rise, obscuring everything from view.

Calvert heard the buzzing in his head as blue sky opened. There was a loud crack and rain fell on him. It changed the color of his skin. Everything seemed dream-like, but his course was still steady.

Pain intruded!

The base camp waited on the plateau ahead. His calmness deepened. More pain!

He looked down at his arms.

Pain! Unbelievable pain!

He screamed and let go of the controls. Around him the canopy and the plasticine and metal of the skiff was dissolving. He looked down at his hands. They were already gone. Burning rain poured into the cockpit. It deluged everything.

"Yawn! Yawn, answer us," Larson barked into the communicator.

"He said he was airborne." Winslow tapped the status board. "The engine's offline." He turned to the major. "It was never *on*line. How could he think he was airborne?"

The diagnostic link to the skiff blinked out suddenly. The whole system had shut down.

For nearly two days the hurricane roared through the Punchbowl. On the plateau they experienced only minor storms. Larson placed the ship on two-minute takeoff alert, but nothing eventful happened to warrant an evacuation.

Sky-tel continued to report on the weather phenomenon. At the storm's eye was an unknown energy source. They recorded and gauged its strength, but could only guess at its nature. The conclusion was that it was some sort of creature, or group of creatures.

As the storm weakened, Larson took the crew down to standard alert. He began studying maps of the great inland ocean. The Punchbowl was unique because of its size. However, as one studied the maps more closely, it was possible to pick out similar geographic features. There were numerous smaller notches carved from the cliffs to the south and west. Whatever phenomenon was in the storm, it probably wasn't the only one of its kind.

On day three, the sky cleared, and Larson was able to walk to the edge of the cliff again. For the first time since their arrival it was possible to see the bottom of the gorge.

Winslow installed a binocular viewer. It showed scorched earth with brightly polished walls and floors. Rivers of brown and red ooze washed between piles of debris to make their way to a brown slick on the ocean. Bones, rocks and a few hard-shelled tubes of unknown origin were about all that were left.

"Found it, Sir." Winslow pointed into the gorge. "What's left of the skiff."

A probe was launched to the site. It raced into the Punchbowl and sank deep into one of the rivers of brown ooze. "Organic particles, amino acids, strong enzymes."

The pool in the ocean was growing smaller, despite the flow of new runoff. Whatever had been in the hurricane was still out there—absorbing its prey. Larson had a violent urge to throw up. Catching himself, he turned and walked toward the ship.

"Report the death of Doctor Calvert to Science Command. Advise the Terraform Council that I am authorizing a red flag."

PERCHANCE TO DREAM
by Susanna Reilly

"We're not going to make it, Sir!"

All eyes on the bridge turned to Captain Mark Forrester, awaiting the orders that would save them.

His eyes and throat burning from the smoking consoles around him, Forrester could only stare at each of them in turn, his eyes resting a little too long on Navigator Brianne Carlson, before shouting, "Brace for impact! Everyone brace for impact!"

The ship shuddered violently and another console exploded, showering the crew in a deadly burst of fireworks, illuminating the terrified looks on each of their faces as a shimmering red planet filled the viewscreen.

The screen went black.

Still not totally satisfied, Chief Renderer Alde Goord added a few notes to the list of final edits to be made. The final chapter of the space vessel *Intrepid's* saga would be transmitted to every holoscreen on the planet next week and it had to be perfect. Too much was riding on its success for there to be even the tiniest imperfection.

His holoscreen beeped a sunny melody, and he smiled as he hit the key to accept the vidcall.

"Oh, Alde." His wife's glowing eyes and gleaming smile always brightened his day. "We just watched today's episode. It's so brilliant! Please tell me Mark and Brianne end up together. They just have to end up together!"

Alde chuckled and smiled indulgently at the love of his life. "You know I can't tell you anything about the finale, so stop asking."

She flashed him a playful pout. "A girl's got to try. I'm so excited I just can't wait. And it's so much harder having a husband who knows all the answers and won't tell."

"You'd end up disappointed when you actually watch it if you already know what's going to happen."

"I suppose, but that doesn't make me want to know any less."

He laughed and shook his head.

"Okay, okay, I'll stop asking if you promise you're coming home soon. No more all-nighters, please."

"I still have a lot of work to do before the finale, but we're almost there. I think I can afford to spend one night at home."

Her smile lit up the room. "I'll have a very special dinner ready when you get here. Love you."

"Love you, too, darling. See you soon." Reluctantly, he broke the connection and switched back to the main screen to check for any messages from the production staff with notes for the final edits.

"Mr. Goord?"

Startled, Alde quickly cleared his screen and turned toward the unfamiliar voice.

"Who are you? How did you get in here?"

The man stepped out of the shadows and Alde winced. The media finding him had been inevitable, but why did it have to be Vander Warge? He had hoped the story would break through a legitimate news outlet, not this gossipmonger. But an agreement had been made among the senior staff. Whichever media outlet found its way to this facility first got the story—as long as they agreed to hold it until after the finale.

"I see you recognize me, Mr. Goord. Or should I say Dr. Goord. I understand you have quite a few degrees under your belt."

"Alde is fine," he responded.

"Then please call me Vander."

"What can I do for you, Vander?"

"Let's not be coy, Alde. I'm here about *Intrepid*. The end of its 14-cycle run is the only story of any import right now."

"You know I can't tell you how the show ends. Spoiling that would make you the most hated man in this part of the galaxy."

Warge chuckled. "Everyone knows how it's going to end. The same way it began 14 cycles ago, with the ship about to crash into a planet. There have been lots of whispers, though, about a surprise—a second segment dedicated entirely to what happened after the crash."

"That's an interesting rumor."

"If you like that one, you'll really like the others I've come up with."

"I'm sure they're fascinating, Vander, but I'm more interested in how you found your way here."

Warge chuckled. "Everybody else was focused on tracking down the big names—the producers, the financial backers. But you were this mysterious name buried in the titles—Chief Renderer. What exactly does that mean, Alde?"

"As has been explained many times, the show is completely computer-generated. I compile and render the images, making sure they're as crisp and clear as possible."

"I see. So why would you do that here instead of at the studio? What's the Chief Renderer of the hottest holocast on the planet doing working at a hospital?"

"It's not technically a hospital, Vander, it's a stasis center."

"What's the difference?"

Although no devices were evident, Alde assumed he was being recorded, so he chose his words carefully.

"All of the people here have been critically injured or have terminal, incurable diseases. They are kept in stasis until their bodies heal sufficiently or a cure is found for their disease."

"Which brings us back to the question of why you do your 'rendering' work here."

"It's out of the way," Alde responded with a thin smile, "and very quiet. Makes it much easier to concentrate not having all of the studio—and media—types hovering over my shoulder."

Warge chuckled. "I can see the appeal of that. But I have another theory about why you're here."

"Really, please share."

"According to the records I was able to dig up—and believe me, they were buried very deep—you spent a lot of years doing research on coma patients, specifically on the extent of their mental activity."

"Yes."

"It was a topic that hit close to home. Your sister was severely injured in a shuttle crash. She's still in a coma. Here."

Alde's throat constricted and he found it difficult to speak. "Yes."

"So it makes sense that you would do your work here to be near her. But then I had to ask myself, why is a doctor wasting his time doing rendering work for a holocast at all? So I decided to do what all good reporters do and follow the money. Imagine my surprise when, after a great many twists and turns, that trail also led me here."

"You're obviously very determined, Vander. I was assured the money was funneled through so many intermediaries, it could never be traced."

"It's a lot of money. I started out just following your salary, expecting you were using it to pay for the upkeep on your sister, but I was very surprised to find that a whole lot more than that ends up here. Why is that, Alde?"

"The only way you could have gotten into this building is if you agreed to the deal, but I have to hear it from you before we go any further."

Warge sighed. "I didn't like it, but I agreed."

"What did you agree to?"

"I agreed that in exchange for a candid chat with you and exclusive rights to the story, I will not share anything I learn or go public with any aspect of the story I had already figured out on my own until after the finale and wrap-up special air next week."

That agreement was sealed with an iron-clad confidentiality agreement. Warge might be a bottom feeder, but he wouldn't risk his career or his sizeable income by breaking the deal.

"Very well," Alde said. "Then follow me."

He led Warge out of his office and into the primary stasis chamber. As always, he stopped to look at the hundreds of stasis pods lining the room

232

in perfectly symmetrical rows. The sight always filled him with wonder and gratitude. So many people who needed his help to live again. The only sound was the barely audible whisper of the machinery that kept them alive.

The reporter stopped beside him, following his gaze. Each pod was in the center of a defined space, with a control console at its head and several chairs in a semicircle at its foot. The cavernous room was dimly lit, and the hum of the equipment maintaining the pods gave it an even more sinister feel. Warge coughed to break the uneasy silence.

Alde jumped at the sound and his cheeks flamed. This lout could never understand his connection to this place or its importance, but he had to try. He led Warge deeper into the complex by way of a series of security doors, each leading to another cavernous room like the first. All contained row after row of stasis pods.

As they walked, Warge grew increasingly more uncomfortable. "I had no idea this place was so huge. How many people are in stasis here?"

"Several thousand."

"That...that's unbelievable. How could that many people be that ill?"

"I imagine you've already been to the public areas of the center while you were conducting your research. So you already know that at any given time there are about a thousand or so people in the short-term stasis units. They generally stay anywhere from a few days to a few months, healing from injuries ranging from minor head traumas to second degree burns."

"Yes. I've read all the literature," Warge retorted. "What about the others?"

"More serious injuries require longer periods of time in stasis to allow for proper healing. Advances in health care over the years now allow us to heal major burns, mend severely fractured bones, and regrow damaged organs, but the price we pay is time. Some procedures take a year or two, others longer. And there are still a great many injuries and diseases we cannot cure. Those people are kept in stasis indefinitely until we can find a cure for them. Since the center has been operating for almost twenty years now, the number of those patients has increased at a steady rate each year."

"It's mind boggling. But what does any of this have to do with a holocast about a bunch of aliens exploring the galaxy?"

"Patience, Vander," Alde said as they stopped in front of a door. Bright red letters blinked AUTHORIZED PERSONNEL ONLY in a steady pattern.

Warge could hear his heart racing in his chest as Goord entered a complicated code on the security panel, then offered his eye for a retina scan. This was the story that was going to make his career. No more being ridiculed as a no-talent hack. Everything they had ever been told about *Intrepid* was a lie, and he intended to expose the truth.

The door slid open and they entered the room. Warge was surprised to find it was another stasis chamber. "What is this, Alde? Some kind of con? You promised me the truth. I know you're hiding some kind of studio here. There's no way that show is computer-generated. The makeup and sets are amazing but there's no way it's computer-generated."

Alde remained near the access door. "I am giving you the truth, Vander. If you're willing to accept it." He allowed himself the indulgence of a theatrical wave toward the three dozen stasis units radiating in three concentric circles from the center of the room. "Meet the crew of the *Intrepid*."

Still sputtering in anger, Warge stepped up to the closest pod, looked at the identification plate that read CAPTAIN MARK FORRESTER and lost the ability to breathe for several seconds.

"But, I...I don't understand. It's all a lie. I know you're hiding a studio here. As soon as I saw the blueprints I knew it. There's no way you need that much space for a stasis center. I just couldn't figure out how you've managed to hide the actors all this time. Is this how you keep them out of the public eye... and from aging? You keep them in stasis when they're not working?"

Alde couldn't help chuckling at the thought. "Nothing quite so sordid, I'm afraid."

"Then what?" Warge asked as he moved restlessly around the room, studying the nameplate on each pod.

"Almost 15 cycles ago, there were numerous reports of a strange light in the sky. Not long after, something crashed in the forest outside Digeri, about 20 miles from here. The military quickly sealed the area and reported that one of their craft had crashed."

"I remember that. All the conspiracy theorists went crazy. I did a couple of shows about it, but there was nothing to it."

Alde smiled. "The military will be very happy to hear that. I had only been here a few years, working on potential treatments for my sister and others like her. It was one of the most trying periods of my life. I don't know if you understand how difficult and expensive it is to keep a patient in stasis, Vander. The equipment must run continuously, without fail, or they could die. The chemical mixture used to maintain stasis is very expensive. Occasionally, some patients are taken out temporarily for surgery or other treatment, then returned to continue healing; that process costs a great deal as well. Only a small percentage of the patients being treated here actually have the resources to cover the full cost, especially if they have to stay for extended periods. Despite our best efforts, in the early years, some people had to be turned away because we didn't have either enough machines or the funds to turn on those we did have.

"So when the Authority came calling with thirty severely injured people and orders that we were to take care of them no matter what, and that we were to do so in total secrecy, it brought the situation to crisis level. They provided some funding but not nearly enough for the care that was needed.

"It was clear from their injuries that the *Intrepid* crew was going to require long-term stasis, with periodic removal for surgical procedures. But one of the most serious difficulties we've encountered with such stasis is that it can cause mental instability. Even in the most severely damaged brain, some mental activity continues, although stasis slows it significantly along with the rest of the bodily functions. As long as the mind functions, it attempts to derive and process input from the world around it. Stasis cuts the mind off from its usual sources of input, and without an alternate source, many patients suffer from stimulus withdrawal so severe, it drives them mad, like a prisoner kept in solitary confinement.

"I had been doing some experiments with shared dreaming as a tool to enable those in comas or in stasis to continue interacting with the world. We built an interface that allowed us to look at the dreams and record them for future study."

"I remember reading about that," Warge cut in. "But those experiments weren't very successful."

"Not at first. Initially we were working with a group of people who didn't know each other and had very little in common. The images we got from them were very disjointed and unfocused, and they had difficulty accepting input from each other. But something very interesting happened when we connected the crew of the *Intrepid* to each other. They had so many shared memories and experiences, every image was crisp and clear. Before long, they were reliving complete missions and other experiences from their lives. It kept their brains active and engaged while they healed, and provided us great insights into their civilization and culture, as well as nuances of their anatomy and physiology that were extremely helpful in establishing treatment protocols.

"Word of our progress made its way around the complex and before long, groups of employees were gathering to watch the playback. One employee was related to a holocast executive and told her what we were doing. She threatened to go public if we didn't show her the vids, and when she saw them, she came up with the idea of building a show around them. From the moment the show first aired, it was a hit, and the credits just cascaded in. As long as we maintained the pretext that the show was computer-generated so no one started asking questions that would lead to the real *Intrepid* crew, the government was more than happy to have the funding issue resolved.

"At first, the production company gave us only enough to keep the *Intrepid* crew alive, but eventually I convinced them that giving us a bigger piece of the pie would be in everyone's best interest. We finally had enough money to not only help every patient here, but we no longer had to turn away those who couldn't pay."

"That's quite enterprising, Alde. But what do these people get out of it?" Warge's casual wave encompassed the three dozen pods.

Alde looked at him in surprise. "They get healed, of course."

"Of course. And what is so terribly wrong with them that they had to stay in stasis for 15 cycles?"

Alde was quiet long enough for Warge's heart to start beating rapidly again.

"Everyone except Brianne is fully recovered, and she should be well enough to be released from stasis by next week."

"Just in time for the finale."

"I don't like your tone, Vander. The finale was timed for her exit from stasis, not the other way around."

"Really? So if the others are fully recovered, why are they still in stasis?"

"They are assisting in Brianne's recovery. They could probably be woken a few days before her without any ill effects, but the holocast producers wanted to wake them all up at the same time as part of the special."

"What? You are keeping completely healthy people in stasis unnecessarily to assist in a publicity stunt!"

"Of course not. You don't understand!"

"What's to understand? You're a doctor! What happened to doing no harm?"

"I assure you no harm is coming to them. The extra time in stasis will not affect them, and remaining connected to them is important to Brianne's full recovery."

"Oh, really. From what I read, people in stasis age slower, but they still age. How many years of their lives have they lost?"

Alde was silent again.

"Our deal is you give me answers and I keep your secrets. You're not holding up your end of the deal, Alde. How long have they been in stasis unnecessarily?"

"They all had extensive burns and damage to internal organs from the crash," Alde finally responded. "Captain Forrester was the first to fully recover. Approximately seven years ago."

"Seven years ago! Why didn't you wake him up then, tell him what was going on?"

"It's not that simple. The others needed more time to heal. He was their captain. We knew if we woke him he would have agreed to go back under to help them. Especially Brianne. There was no reason to wake him just to ask."

"And what about the others? Why didn't they get a vote?"

"There were technical problems. The quality of the images we were getting depended on how many people directly involved in the scene were giving us feeds. The more perspectives we had, the clearer the images and the less rendering work we had to do to prepare the episodes to air. Losing any of the main crew from the feeds would have been catastrophic."

"So you kept them in stasis for years just to keep the show going. Is that what you're telling me?"

"What do you think would have happened to the rest of them, to the rest of the people here if the show had gone under? Without the profits from the show, this place couldn't have survived and most of those people out there would have died."

"Including your sister."

Alde's breath caught. "Possibly."

"So what happened that you're no longer afraid of losing the money?"

"We've all known for years that time was running out for *Intrepid*. When we were ten cycles in, we were already running out of material. There were only so many stories in the crew's collective memories. So we started doing flashbacks to their younger selves. The image quality suffered, and it required a great deal more work from the production team, but it bought us some time while I started a new series of experiments based on my earlier work on shared memory. I started implanting images, story ideas as it were, into the memory matrix. At first the crew's minds rejected the alien ideas, but as we adapted and made the ideas less complex, their minds picked up on the familiar qualities and ran with them. They began building new stories on their own, anticipating their own actions and the actions of the other crewmembers. It was almost as if they actually believed they were living those adventures and not dreaming them. It was an exciting breakthrough."

"Are you telling me that none of the stories from the last five years actually happened? You were able to make up new memories for them?"

"Yes, that's right."

"Will they remember those stories when they wake up? Like they actually happened?"

Alde was clearly startled by the idea. "I don't know. The thought never occurred to me. It's possible, I suppose."

"How can you not know? You're treating these people like lab animals, poking and prodding at their brains, without any regard for what it's going to do to them when they actually wake up."

"I'm trying to help them, Warge," Alde responded icily. "Without the treatment they received here, every single member of that crew would have died within days or weeks of the crash, or would have been horribly disfigured if they had lived."

"I suppose thinking that lets you sleep at night, Doctor, but you haven't explained how this breakthrough changes things enough to allow you to wake the crew."

"Because we don't need them anymore. This technique works with any group of people who have some kind of shared history—family members, close friends. You may have noticed the seating areas around each of the pods. There are built-in connections to the pod that allow visitors to communicate with the sleeper. For example, one of the stasis chambers in the next room holds Councilor Kardo's daughter. You may recall she was seriously injured in a transport accident last month. Her family comes in for a few hours every day and her friends come in a few times a week. We are able to link them through this new technique. They are able to transmit their daily activities to her as though she were actively involved and living her life instead of healing in a stasis pod."

"The next best thing to actually being alive," Warge said coldly.

"Exactly!" Alde smiled, not noticing the anger blazing from the other man's eyes. "And with the new technique we'll be able to plant story ideas into these groups so they can produce fresh material for the holocasts, and that will pay for the person's continuing treatment. It's a win-win for everyone."

"Gods, Alde. You really have absolutely no idea of the implications of this, do you?"

Alde looked at him, bewildered. "What do you mean?"

"Dreams so detailed they seem like real life. How could you ever know whether you were awake or in stasis?"

"What a ridiculous question."

"Why is it ridiculous?"

"The injured person is better off believing it is real. It assists in their healing process to feel engaged in life. And the friends and family helping them—they are aware of being connected and of being brought out again. The time periods are specifically stated and controlled. The process we developed is flawless."

"And what if someday the Authority decides they need someone put in stasis, but believing they are still awake and living their lives?"

"We would never do such a thing!" Alde shouted.

"What if you had no choice? What if it's them or you—or one of your family members?"

"Ridiculous, absolutely ridiculous. They couldn't do any of this without me. No one else has the depth of knowledge I do. And I would never allow such a thing to happen. Never! I believe it's time for you to leave, Mr. Warge. This interview is over."

"Very well, Dr. Goord, but let me leave you with one last thought. What if your most knowledgeable and dedicated scientist on an important project collapsed one day and it was discovered he had developed a terminal disease and only had a few months left to live? What if he were the only one with the knowledge to keep that important project going? What would you do, Doctor? Might you place him in stasis and plug him into a network of colleagues, family and friends who allow him to believe his life is continuing quite normally so he can work away, transmitting his research results through this neural network to those now in charge of the facility he so painstakingly built to help people?"

"You're crazy, Warge. Now get out of my facility! Get out now! I never want to see you again."

Warge's smile was thin and strained. "I'm quite sure that won't be a problem, Doctor. Once the powers that be realize I made it through and had this conversation with you, well, I'm quite sure there will be an unfortunate malfunction resulting in my death."

At that moment, the security door slammed open and a phalanx of heavily armored security officers poured in, quickly surrounding Warge.

"What is the meaning of this?" Goord shrieked. "You're not allowed in this room. No one's allowed in this room. Get out! Get out right now!"

"Please calm yourself, Doctor," the officer in charge said. "This man managed to sneak through security. He is not authorized to be here."

"What do you mean? We had a deal. Whichever journalist found me first got the interview."

"He never agreed to the deal, Doctor. He was going to leave here and release the story. You understand that can't be allowed. If this story isn't controlled, isn't told in exactly the right way, people might not understand. It could endanger this facility and the *Intrepid* crew. That cannot be allowed."

"No. No, of course not. But how did he get in here? It's impossible. How..."

Alde muttered to himself as he followed the officers and their prisoner out of the chamber and back through the vast complex until he was outside his office. As the others continued on to the exterior door and disappeared into the night, he stopped and looked around the room, at this place he had constructed. The place where he spent most of his waking hours alone with his work, the soft mechanical sounds of the stasis chambers the only counterpoint to the silence. Warge's words ricocheted around his brain, slicing through the thin strands of certainty that anchored him to reality. Of course this world was real. Of course it was. Warge was insane.

An insistent buzzing from his console broke him from his reverie and he slowly moved toward it, tentatively reaching out his fingers to press the appropriate keys. His wife's beatific smile filled the screen and his world righted itself.

"Alde, I thought you said you were leaving an hour ago. Dinner is going to be cold by the time you get here," she scolded.

"I'm sorry, darling, something unexpected came up and I had to stay. I just this minute got free, so I couldn't call and let you know. I'm leaving right now, I promise."

"That should leave us just enough time for dessert," she said with a wink and a sultry smile. "Hurry home."

Alde quickly gathered the materials he needed to work on the final edits at home and slid them into his pack. A frown crossed his face as he took one last look at the rows of stasis chambers that stretched across the room. Their steady hiss and thrum had taken on a sinister quality that unnerved him. He hurried to the front door, stepped out into the cool night air and pulled it closed behind him. His hand shook as he activated the exterior locks and alarm system. Despite the heavy door, the steady hiss and thrum of the stasis chambers filled his ears.

His wife was right, he had been working too hard. Once the finale was over, he would take her on that often-postponed vacation. And when he got back, perhaps it was time to move his offices elsewhere.

DON'T GO FUSSIN' OVER ME
by Phil Giunta

At ninety-three and all of five feet two inches, Mona Bretton could still swing a mean rolling pin—which is precisely what she intended to do if her younger sister took one step closer.

"Mona, I only want to help," Cassie said.

She'd put on weight since Mona had last seen her, and she had orange hair. Orange! Good Lord, you'd think women would stop coloring their hair after eighty. Hell, after seventy. There was enough white showing in those roots to make her head look like a damn orange Creamsicle.

"Why?" Mona asked. "You haven't been around for seven years. See? I still have all my marbles. Don't need your help."

"I'm just concerned about you, Mona." Cassie stepped back and took a seat at the far end of the sofa, staring at Mona with those big brown cow eyes.

"Concerned about what you're gonna get from my will. That's all you care about."

"Mona! That's a miserable thing to say. I don't want anything from you. The truth is, I came here to make sure you were still able to take care of yourself."

Mona sneered at her. "To see if I was dying, you mean."

Cassie folded her arms across her chest and tilted her head to one side. "And if that were the case, I would do everything I could to make

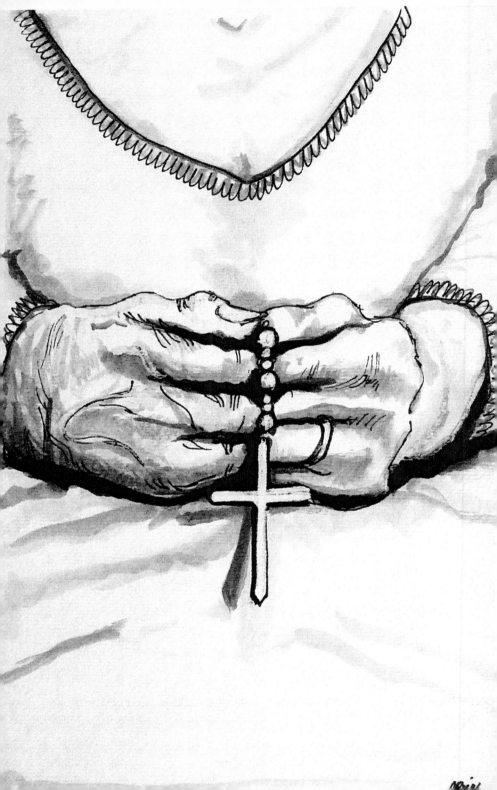

you comfortable, to ease your passage. Remember, I was a hospice nurse for—"

"Sorry to disappoint ya, Cass. Ain't gonna be no passage anytime soon." Mona pointed to herself with the rolling pin. "Still got lots to do."

"Mona, whether you like it or not, it's time to stop. I can feel it and so can you. As sisters, we've always had a bond. You've done all you need to."

"How would you know? Bond, my rear! You haven't been around for seven years. See? My mind's still sharp."

"You already said that."

"What?"

"Mona, why won't you let me help?"

"Because... when you slow down, you die. I'll go when I damn well please. Now, you know I don't like people fussin' over me. The only person I ever let make a fuss over me was Talbot. God bless his soul forever, but I ain't ready to join him just yet.

"Now it's getting late and I'm tired. You're welcome to spend the night here or see yourself out. Just so long's I don't have to put up with any more crap from you."

"Clement!"

Mona hobbled into the kitchen the following morning. She made her way past the table to the window and pushed the curtain aside. He was in the yard, trimming the barberries. Clement was a good man, who had been in high school when Mona's husband hired him to cut the lawn once a week. Twenty years later, Talbot was long gone but Clement still came every week to tend to the grounds and work on the house when needed. He was the only one who still cared.

"Clement! Would you come in here, please?"

After a moment, he towered over her in the kitchen. His red baseball cap was drenched. It was already seventy-five degrees out and Clement was a husky fellow these days, with a brown goatee. He barely resembled the kid that Mona remembered.

"Good morning, Mrs. Bretton. What can I do for ya?"

"Actually, I want to do something for you, Clement. You've been kinder to me than anyone in my own worthless family. You've taken care of me and fixed just about everything in this house. So, if you wouldn't mind driving me to my lawyer's office this afternoon, I'm having my will changed. When I'm gone, this house is all yours."

Clement's mouth opened slightly then closed again. It did that a few times before he finally spoke. "Uh, are you sure, ma'am?"

"My time on God's green Earth is just about over, Clement. I can feel it. Your son is getting married next month? Well, his life is just starting and this place could use some fresh air."

"Thank you, Mrs. Bretton."

"You've earned it, Clement. By the way, did you see my sister this morning?"

"Uh, no, ma'am, but then I just got here about an hour ago. Didn't see anyone."

"Good! Maybe I got rid of her. They always show up when you're near the end, Clement. Like vultures circling overhead, waiting to swoop down and pick you clean. Well, that's family for you, but they can't have something I'm not ready to give up." Mona tapped her chest. "I'm still using it!"

"You only have one sister, Cassie, right?"

"One's enough."

"You said she was here?"

"That's right. Are you feeling OK?"

Clement's eyes went wide and he gave her a slow, exaggerated nod. "I'm just fine, ma'am." He whipped his arm up and glanced at his watch. "I need to finish the shrubs and then fix the gutter along the back before I take you to the lawyer."

Mona watched Clement rush off and wondered just what the hell got into him all of the sudden.

———————

"How ya feelin', Mona?"

Talbot slid a muscular arm around her shoulders as they sat together on the porch swing. He placed another hand gently on her distended belly. They had been married for two years now, and despite the pressure from both sides of the family, had decided to wait until they owned their own home before starting a family.

"It must be a boy. He sure kicks hard now and again." Mona leaned back, letting her head rest on Talbot's forearm. She thought of her mother. Of her five pregnancies, only two of the infants survived—Mona, the oldest, then Cassie. God bless her parents, though, they never stopped trying. "I just hope everything will be OK."

"Of course it will, our baby's going to be fine and healthy."

"How do you know?"

Talbot reached beneath the collar of his undershirt and pulled out the sterling silver cross he'd worn ever since high school. "I have it on the highest authority."

He lifted the chain over his head and placed it over Mona's.

"Always remember the two of us who love you the most—me and God."

Mona fingered the cross now lying against her chest. "Will you love me as long as He will?"

"Longer."

"Mrs. Bretton?"

Mona opened her eyes. Everything was blurry. She glanced up at the man standing over her. "Talbot?"

"Uh, no, ma'am. It's me, Clement. Are you okay?"

Clement? Who is—oh, right. "I'm fine, just a tired old biddy. Are you finished with those gutters, Clement?"

"Oh...yes, ma'am."

"You ready to take me to the lawyer?"

Clement held out his hand to help her up from the swing. "Car's right over here."

"I know where it is, it's my driveway after all. At least for now. Wait'll my kids find out they ain't gettin' the house. They're flying in tomorrow, you know. Better make yourself scarce the next few days, Clement. I'll call you if I need you."

Wayne Bretton couldn't hope to be one-tenth the man his father had been. Still, Mona was proud of her boy. He made good money as a university professor in California. She only wished he had a damn spine. Maybe that's why Mona still thought of him as a boy, never mind that he was sixty-two with a bald spot bordered by thick white hair.

Truth be told, it was Wayne's second wife that rankled her and if anyone was apt to tell the truth, it would be Mona.

"You haven't called in four months."

Here and now, mother and son walked into the kitchen, arm in arm. She looked up at him as she spoke. His height came from Talbot's side, but he seemed to tower over her now more than ever.

It's because you shrunk, Mona. You shriveled old prune.

"I'm sorry," Wayne said. "The semester was busy."

"Well, I'm just glad you came by yourself and left her at home."

"I know you never cared much for Francine."

"I think the feeling's mutual. Every time she shows up here, she barely talks to me and when she does, it's with that haughty attitude. Makes me want to slap her. You could've done better."

Wayne sighed. Mona knew that he'd heard it all before. "We have a good marriage."

"I liked Tanya better. We all did."

Her son clenched his jaw and dropped his gaze to the table. Mona knew her comment stung and immediately regretted it, but it was the truth. The whole family loved that girl. She got along with everyone no matter where she went. In all her years, Mona had never seen such a large turnout at a funeral. She knew Wayne still missed her. *God, we sure had a lot of loss in this family.*

"I was going to make some coffee, or tea, if you'd like some."

Wayne nodded. "That would be nice. Where's Clement? Does he still work for you once in awhile?"

"Yes, but he's off today. Speaking of Clement, I have something to tell you. I went to my lawyer yesterday and changed the will. I'm leaving the house to him when I kick off."

Wayne looked at her for a moment, his expression impenetrable.

"Now before you go off the deep end, here me out. You and Francine have it made, although you never gave me any grandkids, but that's OK. Sonia took care of that. I suspect she'll get her bra in a bunch when she finds out, but she and that snob writer she married don't give a damn about me or this house. You know how she is, Little Miss Status Symbol all concerned about money and keeping up appearances. The plain truth is, I embarrass her. Clement is poor. He's been out of work for three years. His son just got married and they need a place to live. Maybe Clement, too, and he's here almost every day bustin' his hump."

Wayne tapped his chin thoughtfully as she spoke. Then he raised his eyebrows and shrugged. "Sounds good to me."

"I thought you'd raise Cain about it."

"I certainly don't need the place."

"Hmm. So what prompted this little family reunion?" Mona said as she put a full kettle on the stove.

"I suppose it would be useless to say that we just wanted to surprise you."

"Clement called you, didn't he?"

"I can honestly say he did not."

"Cassie, then?"

Wayne frowned. "Your sister?"

"She showed up yesterday out of the blue. Said she wanted to make me comfortable until I kick. Told me I should stop avoiding the inevitable and just lay down and die."

"She said that?"

Behind Mona, the kettle whistled softly.

"Not in so many words, but I got her meaning! I picked up that rolling pin on the counter there and threatened to whack her if she didn't get lost. She was gone the next day. Left before Clement showed up. I don't like people fussin' over me, 'cept for your Daddy. Cassie ain't been around for seven years. Why show up now?"

Wayne sat back in his chair. His expression was the same as Clement's when Mona had told him about Cassie's visit. "Did she say she'd be back?"

As if in response, the kettle began to screech.

———

In the hallway outside her bedroom, Mona could hear the hushed tones of an argument. The voices drifted in and out, or maybe that was just Mona. She was tired after all.

Sonia had only just arrived and was already irate. Wayne must have had told her about Mona's decision regarding the house, inspiring Sonia to march upstairs to confront her. Wayne had stopped her before she could wake Mona from her afternoon nap.

"Can you blame her?" Wayne whispered. "It's not like we're around for her. Clement's been taking care of the place for almost twenty years."

"I know that, Wayne. I was just hoping she would leave something for her grandchildren. My son's publisher cancelled his book series and his wife was laid off a month later. With three kids, they could've used the money from the sale of the house."

"Mom left something for all of us in her will, especially her grandchildren. I think she made the right decision with the house. It's less work for us. Look around, the town's fallen into depression. No one's buying here. This property would be a thorn in our side for God knows how long. Of course, you're more than welcome to talk her out of it once she wakes up."

"What's the point?" Sonia muttered. "You know we can never get through to her."

"Well, perhaps things could've turned out better if we'd been closer to her over the years. Before it was too late."

"This is no time for guilt trips."

"I'm just saying that we should have done better when we had the time, instead of being embarrassed by—"

"Don't start with me, Wayne. I have enough regrets right now. I wasn't embarrassed by Mom and Dad. I was just different from them. We both were. We're a different generation. Speaking of which, Mom said Cassie showed up?"

"So she claimed."

"She's been dead for what, seven years? The two of them were never close to begin with, why would Cassie show up now?"

"Apparently, Cassie was aware that Mom is dying and just wanted to make her comfortable in her final days. Of course, Mom told her to get lost in typical Mona Bretton fashion."

"Skillet or meat tenderizer?"

"Rolling pin."

"She's getting soft in her old age."

Wayne paused. "I just want to stick around to see if Cassie comes back."

"If she does, you can deal with her. The thought of that just gives me the creeps."

"Mona?"

She heard her name, barely louder than a whisper, and felt a gentle squeeze on her forearm. "Talbot?"

"No, it's Cassie."

Mona opened her eyes. It was a momentous effort. She wanted to lift her head from the pillow, but settled for turning it to one side. It was the most she could muster.

Cassie sat beside the bed, smiling warmly. "Didn't think you'd get rid of me for too long, did ya?"

Mona's throat was dry. Attempts to speak launched a brief coughing fit that caused both body and bed to shudder. "Did Wayne let you up here?"

Her sister hesitated. "Well, he didn't try to stop me."

"I heard them out there talkin'. I knew Sonia would be…upset about the house."

"She'll get over it. Sonia's always been high strung. Everyone's going to be fine. Don't you worry about a thing."

"I feel weak, shaky. I can't move. My arms and legs…so heavy."

Cassie squeezed her arm. "I know."

"Yeah, you always do." Mona let her eyes close. "Where's Talbot?"

Again, Cassie paused. "Downstairs."

"With Wayne?"

"Yes, with Wayne."

"And Sonia?"

"Yes, Mona. The family's all here."

"Clement…"

"Here, ma'am." His voice came from…somewhere, but she couldn't see him. She couldn't see anything as gray faded to black.

"Cassie, I don't have the energy…"

"I know."

"I can't stay awake. I can't..."

"You don't have to," Cassie whispered.

———————

Mona rested her head on his forearm, staring up at the violet impatiens in the hanging basket swaying in the spring breeze. She turned to look at her husband as the porch swing glided back and forth. A gust ruffled his thick black hair. Talbot smiled at her, young as the day they were married. On the table beside them, four glasses surrounded a pitcher of lemonade. Four?

"The kids?"

"Over here, Mom."

Mona lifted her head to see Wayne and Sonia, neither of them older than thirty, seated in the wicker chairs on the other side of the front door. Wayne's better half, Tanya, sat on his lap sipping from her glass. All was as it should be.

"How are you feeling?" Talbot asked.

Mona lifted a hand to her chest and ran a finger down the length of the silver cross. "Like I don't want to do anything."

"You don't have to. Not anymore. It's time to rest."

"Are you sure?"

"I have it on the highest authority."

———————

Clement gently lowered Mona's arm to her side and slipped his fingers from her wrist. He hurried from the room and approached the head nurse, Bonnie.

"Mrs. Bretton's passed."

Bonnie held up a finger while her eyes scanned the computer screen at the nurse's station. Finally, she looked up at him. "Mrs. Bretton, right." She turned her attention back to the computer. After another moment of typing and clicking, she nodded. "OK, why don't you gather her belongings into a box while I page Doctor Rapali."

Clement sighed. "Thanks."

"You all right?"

He hesitated, wondering whether his thoughts would be wasted on Bonnie. Death had become just another standard operating procedure here. Still, she stared at him expectantly.

"Just yesterday she asked me to drive her to her lawyer to have her will changed. She wanted to leave me her house when she died. She thought I was still taking care of the place like I did when I was a kid. Didn't even remember I was her nurse. I drove her around the block a few times until she forgot why she was in the van."

"Well, I know what she meant to you. You've known her for decades. It was sweet of you to indulge her since she's been here. You're a good friend for taking care of her funeral arrangements, too."

"She doesn't have anybody else. Her daughter died of leukemia five years ago and her son was killed in a plane crash four months ago. If it weren't for all that, she'd probably still be going."

"I hope he's fussin' over you now." Clement drew the sheet up over Mona's body. He stopped as his eyes came to rest on the silver cross between her thumb and forefinger. "You deserve it. I have it on the highest authority."

ABOUT THE AUTHORS

DANIEL PATRICK CORCORAN
"Apartment Hunting"

Daniel Patrick Corcoran, known as Renfield to his friends and family—yes, really—lives in Baltimore, Maryland with his wife and a small herd of house rabbits. When not busy turning beloved genres on their ears, he can usually be found wandering the countryside subsisting on nuts and berries brought to him by passing wildlife. Renfield performs on local stages with an amateur comedy troupe, much to the confusion of audiences expecting the advertised opera.

MICHAEL CRITZER
"Evelyn" and "Thorn"

Michael Critzer is the founder of NexGen Pulp and served as the editor for its five-year run. He holds a M.A. in English and is working on his M.F.A. in fiction while he teaches college writing in central Virginia. He is a co-founder of Manorwood Books LLC, and his pulpy tales of weirdness are popping up in various anthologies, while he puts the finishing touches on his first novel. You can find Michael's short stories in such anthologies as *Quixotic: Not Everyday Love Stories* and online at horrornovelrevies.com, hogglepot.com, and thestoryshack.com. You can stalk him and read more at facebook.com/authormichaelcritzer.

PHIL GIUNTA
"Water to Share", "Photos from the Attic",
"Don't Go Fussin' Over Me"

A Pennsylvania resident, Phil Giunta graduated from Saint Joseph's University in Philadelphia with a Bachelor of Science in Information Systems and he continues to work in the IT industry. His first novel, a paranormal mystery called *Testing the Prisoner*, debuted in March 2010 from Firebringer Press. His second novel in the same genre, *By Your Side*, was released in March 2013.

In August 2012, Phil was among an exclusive group of authors selected to participate in Crazy 8 Press's new venture, *ReDeus*, a collection of anthologies and novels depicting the return of all the world's mythological gods. This series was created by veteran authors Bob Greenberger, Aaron Rosenberg, Paul Kupperberg, and Steven Savile. Phil's short story about the Celtic gods, "There Be In Dreams No War", was featured in the premiere anthology, *ReDeus: Divine Tales*. His second tale, "Root for the Undergods" can be read in *ReDeus: Beyond Borders*.

Phil is also the narrator of an audio version of Testing the Prisoner, which can be heard for free at Podiobooks.com. The audio version of By Your Side is available on the Prometheus Radio Theatre feed at prometheus.libsynpro.com.

Visit Phil's website at www.philgiunta.com.

AMANDA HEADLEE
"Parallax"

Amanda Headlee always had a fascination with the macabre. So it is not surprising that most of her written material stems from waking nightmares. It was not until she attended Kutztown University, to major in Professional Writing, that she realized she could share her terrors with the world by writing them all down. When she is not validating clinical trial software or cycling through the rural hills of Pennsylvania, she can be found penning tales full of monsters, demons, and mayhem.

Amanda currently has a novel in progress that delves into Native American lore and Lovecraftian horror.

You can follow her on the collaborative blog The Sarcastic Muse (www.thesarcasticmuse.wordpress.com) or on Twitter @amandaheadlee

SUSANNA REILLY
"Form and Substance" and "Perchance to Dream"

Susanna Reilly has been enthusiastic about writing since she was named first runner-up in a story-writing contest at the age of 11. For many years, writing took a back seat to school, work and motherhood, but the fire stayed alive. It was stoked in the late 1990s and early 2000's when she joined a science fiction fan club that published an annual fanzine. Although the fanzine sold less than 30 copies per year (mostly to friends and family of the authors), the joy of writing stories in the Star Trek, Highlander and Stargate universes kept her going (some of those stories can still be found on www.fanfiction.net, author name SMR723). Susanna's first professional publication came in 2013 when her short story, "To Protect and To Serve," was included in the anthology, *Unclaimed Baggage: Voices of The Main Line Writers*.

STUART ROTH
"The Obligation of Kitsune" and "Deluge"

Stuart is a pragmatic optimist with a pessimistic streak living in the Northeastern United States. Happily married and settled, he now cranks out periodic short stories and is finalizing a novel for publication.

Having been a lifelong amateur writer, Stuart currently toils in the real-world occupation of finance and accounting. This career unwittingly gave a jump-start to his creative avocation by allowing him to travel the world as an auditor. Over a two-year period he visited 14 countries and got to experience a much larger world. Some Indiana Jones-like exploits included: concussing himself on a beam moments before introducing himself to the local management team; conducting an IT Audit in Morocco without speaking Arabic—to a staff who didn't speak English!—and presiding over an assignment in Vietnam while suffering from dehydration and the effects of malaria pills. To this day he cannot watch *Apocalypse Now* without having flashbacks to 'Nam: "The heat, the humidity... the horrible accounting."

Look for additional short stories and a novel currently in development. If you purchased this anthology and liked my work (or even if you didn't) drop me a line at stuartroth@hotmail.com

STEVEN H. WILSON
"Don't Go In The Barn, Johnny!"

Steven has written for Starlog, DC Comics' *Star Trek* and *Warlord,* and, most recently, served as principal writer and director for Prometheus

Radio Theatre and publisher of Firebringer Press. His original science fiction series, *The Arbiter Chronicles,* currently boasting nineteen full-cast audio dramas and the novel *Taken Liberty,* has won the Mark Time Silver Award and the Parsec Award for Best Audio Drama (long form). His third novel, *Unfriendly Persuasion,* was released in 2012, and four *Arbiter Logs* eBooks were released in the Summer of 2013. He is also a contributor to the *ReDeus* series from Crazy 8 Press, and, as of this writing, has contributed three tales of the mythological gods' return to earth.

As a podcaster, besides hosting the Prometheus Radio Theatre podcast, he has recorded Lester Del Rey's *Badge of Infamy* for podiobooks.com, performed multiple roles in J. Daniel Sawyer's production of *Antithesis,* and contributed narration to the audio novel *Geek Love.* Active in science fiction fandom since 1984, he has written, drawn, edited and published fanzines, acted and directed with a comedy troupe, and served as a gopher, a con chair or a guest at roughly a hundred conventions. Wilson, who works as CIO for Howard County (MD) Fire & Rescue, holds degrees from the University of Maryland College of Journalism and the Johns Hopkins University Whiting School of Engineering. He lives in Elkridge, MD with his wife Renee and sons Ethan and Christian. His weekly blog of ramblings on various topics, plus all kinds of information about his work, past, present and future, is available at www.stevenhwilson.com.

LANCE WOODS
"Dead Air"

Lance Woods loves Alfred Hitchcock movies and radio drama, so the fact that he wrote "Dead Air" – his first short story in many years, and his first sojourn ever into supernatural fiction – shouldn't surprise anyone. Normally, though, his writing veers toward the superhuman rather than the supernatural, as he's the author of Firebringer Press' *Heroic Park: A SuperHuman Times Novel* and the creator/writer of Prometheus Radio Theatre's *SuperHuman Times* radio anthology. He has also had two full-length comedy-thrillers produced by the Baltimore Playwrights Festival, *Murder Case* and *Breeding Will Tell.* He lives in a situation comedy format outside of Baltimore with his long-suffering family.

ABOUT THE ARTIST

MICHAEL RIEHL

Known in many circles as "The Ornament Guy", Mike Riehl has earned a following for his amazing and much sought-after hand-painted holiday ornaments featuring characters and vehicles from film and television. Mike has become a staple at many SF and horror conventions such as Shore Leave, Monster Mania, and Chiller Theatre, where some of his most famous customers have included LeVar Burton, Brent Spiner, Richard Herd, and others. As the cover and pages of this book prove, Mike is also a phenomenal painter and an incredible illustrator.

CPSIA information can be obtained at www.ICGtesting.com
Printed in the USA
BVOW07s0425150914

366713BV00001B/1/P